SHIPS

OF MY

FATHERS

DAN THOMPSON

QUANTUM FORGE PRESS

SHIPS OF MY FATHERS

ISBN: 978-0-9854146-1-0

Blog: www.MakingItUpAsIGo.com

www.QuantumForgePress.com

For my father...

SHIPS

OF MY

FATHERS

Chapter 1

"You know those times when everything works out exactly how you planned? Yeah, me neither." — Malcolm Fletcher

MICHAEL FLETCHER LOST BOTH of his fathers before he ever found out there had been two of them. He was present for both deaths, but he could only remember the second one. Discovering what had happened to his first father was neither simple nor painless.

On the day he lost his second father, however, he and Malcolm were loading cargo into *Sophie's Grace*. If they had been at a regular port, they would have been watching from the sidelines as the local cargo handlers did it, but the Shorthorn transfer station was far from a regular port. Instead, they were floating outside the ship, maneuvering the cargo through the vacuum of space.

"Skipper, down zero two, starboard one three," came the call from Isaac. He was officially the ship's first mate and was monitoring the bulky load's zero-gee maneuver from within the cargo bay. Michael liked to think of himself as the first mate, but at seventeen, he was not yet old enough to qualify for the rating.

"Got it," Malcolm replied, firing a few jets on the loader. "Down zero two, starboard one three." Malcolm Fletcher was the captain and owner of *Sophie's Grace*, but he often got his

1

hands dirty on these runs. "If you want the job done right," he had told Michael again and again, "don't hire it out."

Michael was floating about fifty meters aft watching his father drive the loader. He had already prepositioned the final array behind him with the backup loader, but he was at loose ends now while his father loaded this one. The work was trickier than usual, since these cargoes were loose pallets bundled together by cables instead of the standard ten-meter shipping containers.

This kind of load was not uncommon out beyond the borders of the Hudson Confederacy, and the Shorthorn transfer station was typical as well. It was less of an outpost than a collection of floating boxes in orbit around an empty moon. Someone had tried to terraform the moon a century before, reportedly drawn to the impressive view of the ringed gas giant above them, but the effort fell apart back in the 3350's. Since then, the orbital staging area had become a useful transfer point for some of the less orthodox shippers working in the border region. They were not technically smuggling anything illegal. They were simply dodging a number of tariffs and port fees.

"Overshot starboard, Skipper, port zero four."

"Adjusting."

Michael watched with a wry smile. Dad had ragged on him their last time through for his own sloppy handling of the loader. Today he had hit the mark straight on four times in a row while Dad had missed on two of them so far. "Careful, Skip," he chided, "or you're going to have to back it out." He could rag back on him a little, but he always called him Skip or Skipper in front of the rest of the crew, never Dad. It was a casual little ship, but it was still a ship.

"Fat chance, boy," Malcolm replied. "I've got this one."

"Skipper, you're still drifting starboard, and you're getting out of alignment. Another half-meter and you'll miss the rail guides."

Michael used his suit jets to move off to starboard so he could get a better look himself, but as he did, he caught a glance of what his father could not see. The loader was not much more than an open-framed cage around the driver, with grapplers and thrusters all around, but it did keep the driver facing forward. One of those thrusters behind Malcolm was firing, a little cloud jetting out at random intervals. "I see your problem, Skip. Your port thruster is still firing."

Malcolm twisted in the loader's harness to see the thrusters arrayed behind him. "Dammit, I thought we got this fixed back on Taschin."

"We did," Michael protested. "They told me it was solid."

"Skipper," Isaac called again, "you're out of the lane now."

"I know," he replied, his voice tense over the radio. "I'm shutting it down. Isaac, can you get the lift arm in there to brace me?"

There was a hesitation. "Yeah, but it's going to be close."

Michael watched the cargo array continue drifting to starboard, rotating as it went. Inside, Isaac would be moving their internal lifter out to the end of the bay to stop the pallet array from crashing into the side of the bay doors. "Hurry, Isaac," Michael called. "That thruster is still going."

"I see it," his father answered. "I'm trying to reach the shut-off valve." Michael could see him straining against the harness, stretching out his left arm towards the loader's frame and that sputtering thruster.

"I can get to it," Michael called, already firing his suit jets to come up behind the loader's frame.

"No, stay clear."

"No, really Skip, I can come in clear of the thruster and still reach that valve."

"Stay clear, son," his father repeated. "That's an order."

Arguments with Dad took three forms. Arguments over chores earned him scut work. Arguments over his studies cost him access to the entertainment library. Then came arguments over orders. The one time he had disobeyed a direct order had cost him port liberty for eight months.

Michael adjusted his trajectory to swing up above the ship, well clear of Malcolm and the loader. "Aye, sir."

"Gotcha!" Isaac cheered. The cargo lift arm grabbed onto the end of the pallet array.

"Good work, Isaac," Malcolm replied, but the crisis was not over. The misfiring loader continued to push at one end of the pallet array, only adding to the momentum of the free end. With one end locked down, the bundle started to bend, crushing some of the individual crates on one side while pulling hard on the cables on the other side.

All but one of them held.

The one that snapped swung out from the left side, wrapped around the port side of the loader's frame, and the final two meters of it whipped through the loader's open frame and slashed against Malcolm's leg.

"Oh, Christ fuck me!" he cried out.

"Dad!" Michael shouted into his microphone.

"What happened?" was all Isaac could say.

Orders or no orders, Michael started jetting in. He could see a mist of blood and air escaping from his father's left leg. The end of the cable was still embedded into the suit. "He's venting... Dad, you're venting!"

"Ugh, yeah..." he replied, his voice ragged. "We've got to... I'm releasing harness."

Michael jetted in from the right, well clear of the errant thruster, and he finally got a good look at Malcolm's injury. "The cable's still in your leg. Should I pull it out?"

"Gah... no. Not here. Get the cutter."

Michael climbed around the loader's frame to the toolbox. A small laser cutter was clipped on at the bottom. "Got it!"

"I'm coming out." It was Isaac's voice over the radio.

Michael climbed back through to the left side, still wary of the thruster, and started in on the cable.

"No," Malcolm replied, panting. "You'll never get through the cargo bay." He paused, breathing hard as he cranked up his oxygen. "We'll go in... dorsal."

4

The cable was not very thick, no more than a centimeter, but it was strong. "Just a few more seconds, Dad." He glanced back to his father, seeing him slowly disentangle himself from the loader's harness.

The cable snapped free and swung back around to the outside of the loader again, missing Michael's helmet by a hand's width. He moved back to his father who was floating free within the loader's frame.

"Dad?"

Inside the helmet, Malcolm nodded silently.

"What's going on out there?"

Michael grabbed at his father and kicked free of the loader's frame. "I've got... the skipper. He's venting and bleeding from his leg. We're headed to the dorsal airlock. Open it for us and stand by the other side with the med pack."

"Aye!"

Michael jetted back above *Sophie,* careening side to side as his father's weight threw off his center of gravity. "We're almost there, Dad."

"Too late," he said.

"Keep your air up, Dad. You're going to make it."

"Fuck... not the air."

The airlock was close ahead, gaping open, a two-meter-wide target. Michael pushed his feet out and hit the boot thrusters again, skewing them down into it. "We're in!" he called out.

"Bleeding..."

The door closed above them, first the iris and then the sliding hatch.

"Cycle it!"

"Bleeding out..."

"Dad, we're in, just hang on."

"I'm sorry, Michael."

"Cycle the damn lock!"

"I am!" It was Henry Bartz, the systems engineer. "Valves wide open."

Michael looked down at his father's face once more, separated by their two visors. "Dad, hang on!"

"I always meant to tell you... I'm so sorry, son. Forgive me."

"Cycle the God damned lock!"

But Malcolm was already gone.

Michael sat in the med bay next to his father's body. The mad rush from the airlock had been a futile formality. By the time they cut the suit away from his leg, it was clear what had killed him. The cable's tip had sliced into his hamstring, wrapped around the bone, and severed the deep femoral artery. Nothing short of a trauma surgeon could have saved him, even if they could have gotten him there in mere moments. But the *Sophie's Grace* was an independent freighter, crewed by seven. The closest trauma surgeon was light years away.

Michael had cleaned the wound, but Isaac had insisted he leave the cable inside. There might be an autopsy at some point, so it was best to disturb as little as possible. The body remained uncovered, and Michael sat there, still staring at the wound, replaying the accident in his mind over and over.

He could have come in and turned off the thruster.

He should have, orders or not.

Port liberty be damned, he should have come in and turned off that thruster.

A hand came to rest on his shoulder. It was Isaac.

"We're secure now. Henry and I got the rest of the load in, and we're sealed up."

Michael nodded.

"I'm sorry about your father. He was a good skipper."

"I should have—"

"No," Isaac cut him off. "No should haves. Not today. You'll have years of them down the road, but not today."

"What then?"

"Today we say goodbye to your father, and then we head back in to Taschin."

Michael finally turned from the body to look at Isaac. "Taschin? We just left there. Nasar is the next stop."

Isaac pulled his hand back and faced Michael squarely. "I'm afraid not, Michael. Taschin is the closest Confederate port, and we have to report your father's death."

Michael stood. "We're going to put him in storage, right?"

"Yes. Henry has a cold bay waiting for us."

"Then Dad can wait. He promised this cargo to someone on Nasar, and we're going to follow the skipper's orders."

Isaac shook his head. "He's not the skipper anymore, Michael."

Michael set his jaw. "Ok, then I say so. My father made a promise."

"It's not up to you," Isaac told him. "Look, you and the skipper ran a good ship, and between you and me, you made a good first officer, the best he could have hoped for. But on paper, you're not the first officer."

"That's only because I'm too young to take the licensing exam."

"I know, and I know you're going to ace it next year, but seventeen is not eighteen, and I'm on the books as the first officer. You know that."

Michael turned back to face the body again. "Yeah, I know."

"And you know the regulations, too. We may work out here on the border, but we're a Confederate flagged ship, and that means Confederate regs."

Michael nodded. Dad had drilled him on the regulations every week.

"I know you want to do the right thing here, but if we don't go back into Taschin, especially if something else were to happen between now and then, I'd lose my license, maybe even face charges."

His shoulders sagged as he leaned in against the table. His father's skin was pale and still. "You're right, I know."

"Then Taschin it is?" Isaac asked.

Michael nodded. "Taschin it is."

"You got any family there? I know your mom's been gone a while."

"Since I was a baby," he replied, only then taking it in. He was an orphan.

"Anyone else? Maybe back on Arvin?"

"I don't know."

"Well, we'll see when we get there." He put his hand on the boy's shoulder again. "Do you want me and Henry to take care of the body?"

He shook his head. "No, I'll do it. He was my father, after all."

Chapter 2

"Some goodbyes are really good riddance. It's the others that are hard." — Malcolm Fletcher

MICHAEL SAT NEXT TO Isaac as the Taschin port magistrate read over the files in his office. They had brought video of the accident from the rear cargo monitors, but he had not bothered to look at it. The rest of the crew was still back at the ship seeing to the offload of cargo and waiting to hand over the body to the authorities.

"Very regrettable," the magistrate said. He was graying and peered down at his reader through half-rim spectacles. "Though I find no fault in any of the crew or officers, you might have a case to make against the loader repair company... Wall-to-Sky, oh, that's here isn't it? Ah yes..."

"So you find no irregularities, sir?" Isaac asked.

He looked up to face them again. "No, everything looks by the book. I admit I've never particularly cared for the use of these border transfer points, but this kind of accident could have happened in any orbital facility, and I don't know if we'd have any better results. Barring any push back from the coroner, I'll mark this closed tomorrow morning."

"Thank you, sir," Isaac replied, "but there's also the issue of the ship ownership."

"Oh? Was Captain Fletcher also the owner?"

"Yes," Michael spoke up. "Well, actually, he always said it belonged to the two of us, him and me."

He looked back down at the file. "Ah, you must be the son, Michael."

"Yes, sir, I am."

"I'm sorry about your father."

"Thank you, sir."

The magistrate paged through a few files and followed a link. "It looks as though you're probably correct. *Sophie's Grace*'s owner is listed as the Fletcher Trust, an owner-share cooperative with Malcolm Fletcher as the executive agent. You'd have to look up the bylaws and structure to see how the ownership flows in the event of his death, but that's getting outside of my jurisdiction. My mandate is strictly to enforce the Confederacy's shipping regulations, and this is getting more into property law. Do you have a local lawyer to look into this?"

Michael hesitated. "I don't know."

"I'm sorry, what?"

"I mean Dad may have had one, but I don't know who that would be."

The magistrate took off his spectacles and looked back and forth between Isaac and Michael before focusing on the boy. "How old are you, Mr. Fletcher?"

"Why do you ask?"

He sighed. "It's a matter of public record, I'm sure. Are you going to make me look it up?"

"No, sir. I'll be eighteen next year."

"Next year, eh?"

"Yes, sir."

He frowned. "Well, I'm sorry to say that the law does not care how old you are next year. It only matters how old you are now, and at seventeen you're still not considered a legal adult. I gather from the fact that it's the Fletcher Trust rather than the Fletcher joint property that your mother is no longer in the picture. Is that correct?"

Michael shook his head.

"I believe, sir," Isaac offered, "that she died quite some time ago, before Captain Fletcher purchased the *Sophie*. He told me he named the ship after her."

"Sophie, eh?"

"Sophia," Michael corrected. "Sophia Grace Fletcher." If they were going to talk about her that way, they could at least get her name right. "She died during the Caspian rebellion, killed in a pirate attack before I was one, and now I've lost my dad at seventeen." He tried to fake a smile but failed. "So what, are you planning to lock me up in some orphanage for the next nine months?"

"It won't be me, Michael," the magistrate replied, "but I do feel I have to make a few calls on your behalf. I'm sure someone from the local child services or perhaps even the Captains' Guild can appoint a lawyer for you. They won't be able to take over your guardianship, but—"

"My guardianship?" Michael asked with a firm shake of his head. "No offense, sir, but I'm not some little kid who wandered into port. I've been on freighters my whole life, working as crew since I was a kid. I know how to take care of myself."

The magistrate leaned back. "Look, Mr. Fletcher, I am sorry for your loss, and I'm sure you could go on to be a fine owner and captain yourself, but if you are as old a hand as you say you are, then you know the regulations as well as I do. You're not going to captain that ship until you pass your exams, and the Guild will never offer them to someone your age."

"I could hire a captain," Michael insisted.

"Not on your own you can't," the magistrate replied. "You're too young to enter into a legally binding contract, and no captain is going to hire on without it."

Michael looked to Isaac for support, but Isaac merely shook his head. "He's right, Michael."

"It's not so bad, boy," the magistrate went on. "It's only nine months. It'll take a while to sort out the ownership transfer

SHIPS OF MY FATHERS

anyway. Take some time, grieve for your father, and figure out what you want to do with your life. From the sounds of it, you've been working since you got out of diapers. I think you've earned a little time off."

Michael set his duffel down on the bed as Isaac rolled the trunk into the corner.

"That should do it," Isaac said. "I've got my stuff in the other room."

"Thanks."

They had moved *Sophie's Grace* into a long-term storage bay on the outskirts of the port. The Port Authority team had then sealed it with a double-keyed lock. No one was getting back in without Michael's authorization, but he could not get back in either, not without an order from the Port Authority.

Packing had been hard, but he kept telling himself it was not forever. He brought the bulk of his civilian clothes along with a couple of uniforms, both functional and official. He copied all his files and most of the entertainment library from the ship's computer but had left quite a few personal belongings behind. This was temporary, after all.

His father's quarters had remained untouched with two exceptions. Michael had taken his father's utility knife and an old portrait of his mother. Sophia was in a blue-gray ship uniform, curled up against a circular viewport. A nebula dominated the star field beyond her in the view, and she was looking out into the void with a hint of a playful smile on her face. Father had always told him that the picture was taken shortly after she found out she was pregnant with him. It was the only picture his father had kept of her.

On ship, the picture had been mounted to the wall. After all, everything on ship was glued down, screwed in, or locked into a groove. There was no easy way to do that in the hotel room, so he settled on putting it on top of the dresser, leaned against the wall. It threatened to slip a bit, so he braced the bottom of the frame with a rolled up towel. It was not the most picturesque arrangement, but it would do.

Isaac stuck his head back through the door. "I'm all set, and the rest of the crew is waiting for us down at the Lucky Black. You ready?"

"I guess, though I've never been to a wake before."

"It's easy enough. Drink until you can only remember the good, and then drink some more."

The Lucky Black was better than the average spacer bar in that the bathrooms were as clean as most engine rooms, which as any engineer will tell you does not say much. It lay in the central crossroads section of the port, between the actual docks, the warehouses, and the administrative district. Even then, it was hard to find, tucked back off the main roads and behind the more touristy restaurants.

The rest of the crew was there, all four of them, but that was not so surprising. Where else would they be? What was surprising to Michael was how many familiar faces there were beyond the crew. Captain Wallace and most the crew of the *Johnny Rose* were there, already toasting to his father before he arrived.

Crews from seven other freighters trickled in over the next hour, though the captain of the *Quincy Quack* sent only his first officer and his regards. "It's some snafu over livestock quarantine," the officer had explained. "You know how it goes."

Michael nodded knowingly but only guessed at the details. Dad had never transported livestock, but he still appreciated being told of the problem with candor. Everyone there was treating him like a fellow spacer, not like a kid who had just lost his father.

The drinks kept flowing as various crewmembers took turns buying a round. Michael did his best to pace himself, but he was getting fairly wobbly. Dad had started teaching him to drink two years before, telling him that if he was going to be a spacer, he had to learn to handle his liquor. He tried to keep up the routine he had learned, buffering each drink with a handful of whatever the local snack was, along with the occasional drink of water. It worked for a while, but before long he had fallen behind and started losing track of how many it had been.

At one point, he found himself leaning against the bar, listening to Isaac and Captain Wallace swap stories about his father's love for local chili recipes, when a uniformed officer plopped down on the seat next to him. It was the uniform of the Confederate Navy, and the various tags identified him as Lt. Commander Montgomery Wheaton of the CFS *Alvarez*.

"Monty," he said, extending his hand.

"Michael," he replied, trying to take it, but then realized he had to switch his glass over to his left hand.

"Sorry to hear about your skipper. Your dad, right?"

Michael nodded. Monty was the first person to bring it up so far.

"Good man. Saved my ass once, back in the war."

Michael shook his head. "Dad was never in the service."

Monty nodded and downed his own shot. "Yeah, I know."

"Then how...?"

Monty put his hand on Michael's shoulder and gave it a good squeeze. "Don't believe all the stories, boy. He was as solid as they come."

"Stories?" Michael did not know what stories he was talking about, but he did know that the alcohol was making it hard to remember.

"But I guess I owe you one now, so if you ever need a favor, look me up."

But the very next moment Isaac turned around and grabbed at Michael. "Hey, what was that um, that spice Skip picked up back on Ringway? You know, the blue one with the bubbles?"

14

Michael tried to switch gears but only managed to mumble, "No idea."

When he turned back around, Monty was gone.

Hours later, people slipped out in twos and threes, always shaking his hand on the way out. The number of "if you ever need anything" offers piled up into one long blur of favors never to be collected. By midnight, it was down to just the *Sophie* crew. Isaac funneled them into a booth while Wendy Sheers and Liam Campbell brought over the final round.

They all gathered around and looked to him to make the last toast. It had been his father, but to them Malcolm Fletcher had been their captain, and Michael knew enough to know he had been a good one. "To Skipper," he said and raised his glass. Several clinks later, he downed it in one gulp.

"So what now?" Wendy asked. She was their senior drive engineer and a damn good one. She had come on seven months earlier and had managed a portside refit without putting *Sophie* into an orbital dry dock.

Isaac gave Michael a moment but then answered for him. "Well, I think we've definitely got something of a wait on our hands."

Michael shook his head. After seeing so many other spacers from other ships at the wake, he knew the score. "It's a wait, but it's probably too long for any of you to be beached. I haven't talked to the lawyers yet, but the *Sophie* and I are stuck here for a while, maybe as long as nine months."

Henry Bartz shrugged. "Nine months isn't so bad. I bet you can upgrade the scrubbers while you're here." Henry had been the systems engineer for the last year and a half and had complained about the environmental systems the entire time. They were far too fragile for his taste.

"But for the rest of us, yeah, nine months is a long time," Wendy replied.

James Nellis raised a finger. He was the steward and had only been on board for five months. "Well, I heard the *Johnny*

Rose has room for a cook, and with all due respect to Skipper, I'm thinking about it."

"You should take it," Isaac said. "Captain Wallace runs a good ship."

Captain Wallace indeed, Michael thought. Coming to his father's wake and hiring off his crew members. But it was true. From everything his father had said, Wallace ran a good ship. "Yeah," Michael heard himself saying. "The *Johnny Rose* is a fine berth. You should get it if you can."

The nods around the circle came one by one, so Michael prompted them. "Anyone else? I know you've got to work, and there's no point in hanging around playing nursemaid to me."

Wendy spoke up. "Takasumi Lines has a posting for an engineer. I'd have to play catch-up with whatever ship they post me to, but it's available today."

"You'd go corporate?" Liam asked. He had been their prime shift navigator for two years and never had a kind word for the larger shipping lines. Malcolm had hinted at some bad blood between Liam and one of the larger shipping lines, but he had never given the details.

She shrugged. "Hey, they're offering five-year contracts. Good money, too. You should check it out."

"No thanks," Liam replied. "Besides, with all my time logged past the border, I'll have no trouble finding a berth from here."

"Maybe for you," Henry said, "but I think Wendy's onto a good thing. Did you see anything for systems?"

She nodded. "Two of them, one general and one mechanical specialist."

Isaac gave him a nudge in the ribs. "Sounds like that mechanic spot might be your ticket out of the sludge tanks."

Henry nodded. "Yeah, it would."

"What about you, Isaac?" Michael asked. Isaac had been there longer than any of the others, a full four years, but even that was a little short compared to other family ships he knew.

Malcolm had been a good skipper, but he had also been a hard skipper.

The older man looked at him with a hint of sadness. "I don't think I'm ready to ship off quite yet. I'm no nursemaid, but I figure I should keep my eye on Skipper's boy at least a little longer."

They wrapped it up with a heartfelt round of handshakes, though Wendy had given him a hug that lasted a lot longer than Michael was expecting. They said their goodbyes at the door, and Michael and Isaac staggered to an auto-pod for the ride back to their hotel.

The message light was blinking when they got to the room, so Isaac hit it.

"Mr. Fletcher, this is Charles Hollings from Walters and Merrimack. The local court has appointed me as your representative for the dissolution of your father's estate as well as the advocate for your minority status. I have set up a meeting for ten tomorrow morning at my office," he said and rattled off the address. "Please be there."

Isaac turned back to face Michael. "Well, that was quick."

The room began to turn, and Michael stumbled towards the toilet to throw up. He did not make it in time.

Chapter 3

"It's not so much that I lied. It's more that I simply hadn't gotten around to telling her the truth yet." — Malcolm Fletcher

Michael sat in the reception lounge of Walters and Merrimack. It was high in one of the super towers downtown, well west of the port, but he could almost make out the control tower through the low morning haze. At the very least, he could see the occasional glint of a ship punching up through the fog, but he tried not to look too much. Even through the shaded glass of the office building, the glare of the sun made his head throb.

He had worn his dress uniform for the meeting. It was as close to a suit as he had, and he always thought he looked older in uniform than in his civvies. He knew his clothes were not going to fool the lawyer about his age, but he hoped it would at least impart some sense of maturity. Short of a Captain's star, these non-military uniforms rarely showed any rank, but it did show him as a working member of the crew rather than some ship-schooled passenger.

Isaac had offered to come along, but Michael had insisted he go alone. "I'm hoping to convince this guy I don't need much supervision," he had said. "Showing up with a chaperone

18

doesn't exactly help." Isaac had protested, but in the end he had stayed back at the hotel suite.

At five after ten, Charles Hollings emerged from the back offices. "Ah, Mr. Fletcher, come this way." He wore a formal suit with the double-breasted vest that was becoming fashionable on colder worlds. It had the effect of making Hollings look broader than he actually was. Michael had tried one once, but its bagginess only accented how thin he was.

He followed Hollings into his office and sat opposite the desk while Hollings opened the files on his desk screen. "First of all," he said, "let me offer my condolences for your loss. I never met Captain Fletcher, but from what I have read, he was a fine man."

Michael sighed. He still was not used to hearing about his father in the past tense, but at least he had stifled the urge to correct people. "Thank you."

"I see you came alone. Are you staying with anyone?"

He tried to sit a little straighter without making it look like he was puffing out his chest. "I asked my first officer to stay in port while we sort out the details on the ship ownership." It was sort of true, but phrasing it that way made Michael sound far more like the responsible party.

"I see, well, we can get to the guardianship in a moment. The ship ownership should be fairly simple." He swept his hands across the desk screen and the virtual papers shuffled around. "I see that *Sophie's Grace* is held by the Fletcher Trust. I read through the formation and bylaw documents yesterday afternoon, and if we wait until next year, the transfer should be a straightforward matter. We could proceed now if you wish, but the complexity would still add significant delay."

Michael tried to follow the language, but much of it turned to mush in his aching head. "What's the delay?"

"Well, as I said, if we wait until your eighteenth birthday, the transfer is not much more than a simple filing with the port registry. The bylaws of the trust are clear that on the death of Malcolm Fletcher, Michael Fletcher becomes the executive

19

trustee, and in that role, you can become the primary signatory for all the ship's business. However, there is a clause for taking care of things if the death occurred before your majority, which it has. If you want the ship to continue to operate, you and I will have to select an executive trustee to act for you, but I don't recommend it."

"Why not?

"Well, it's the short timeframe. For ship trusts, the executive trustee is typically someone with a captain's license and a background in law. We would have to select one, convince him to hire on, and then there are a few hearings and a filing to be sent to the sector registry offices. When it's all said and done, we're probably looking at three to six months before you would be operational. But the question is for how long? While you could keep the hired captain on, his role of executive trustee would evaporate after a few short months. I think we'd be very challenged to find someone willing to take it on for such a limited duration."

Michael thought it about for a moment. It would go much more smoothly if only Isaac could pass the Captain's exam, but he always insisted he did not have the engineering skills to pass. In truth, he was more of a glorified navigator than a true first officer, but then navigation had always been a mathematical mystery to Michael. "I'm not so sure," he said finally. "I do have a lot of friends in the shipping business. I might be able to convince one of them."

"To give up their own vessel or posting to take yours on for a few months? I can't speak to the quality of the friendship, but I would be truly surprised to hear of someone with the necessary background who would make that kind of decision."

Michael shrugged it off. "Well, I may ask around, but for now let's assume that I'll be clear in nine months."

"That may be the best attitude. Your luck may surprise me after all, but I wanted you to know what you were up against."

"So *Sophie* will sit there collecting dust in that sealed dock in the meantime. Who pays for that?"

The lawyer sighed. "Well, regrettably the storage fees accrue against you and the trust, but they aren't as much as you might think. I imagine Captain Fletcher's accounts would be sufficient, but failing that, I understand there is a possible litigation against one Wall-to-Sky repair facility here on Taschin?"

Michael shook his head at the thought of the accident, watching that errant thruster again in his head. At a trial there would be the video, cross-examinations, and questions of why he had not gone into help his father. Help his father like he should have. Damn.

"You'd rather avoid the trial?"

Michael looked up. "How did you know?"

"It's not uncommon. I'm not going to push it on you, and I imagine they would be eager to settle out of court. It wouldn't be enough to retire on, certainly, but it would easily cover your living expenses for the upcoming year along with any port fees that accrue. I could start the process if you'd like."

He nodded and looked out the window beyond Hollings. This one did not face the port, but north to the snow-capped mountains instead. It was not nearly as bright, so his head did not throb as much. "I guess the question is, what will I be doing for the next nine months?"

"Then let's move on to the matter of your guardianship."

Michael shook his head to clear it and focused on Hollings. "Yeah, I had a thought on that. I get along pretty well with my first officer, Isaac Rubin. He agreed to stick around for at least a while. I imagine I could hire him on to fulfill whatever guardian requirements there are for the next few months."

Hollings shifted the virtual pages around again. "With due respect, Mr. Fletcher, I don't think the court would be satisfied with that kind of arrangement. Traditionally the guardian holds authority over the child. He is not an employee of the child."

Michael waved his hands to cut him short. "Semantics aside, he's a good guy, and he's looked out for me before at other ports."

Hollings frowned briefly before masking it. "Certainly, the court is likely to look favorably upon his present assistance and will not press for foster placement, but I did perform a next-of-kin search, and without overriding factors, the living family takes precedence. In fact, I already took the liberty of sending notice to your uncle Hans, but with transit time and not knowing where he is on his own shipping route —"

"Wait, Uncle Hans? I don't have any Uncle Hans." He blinked twice and tried to focus on the virtual pages before Hollings. "For that matter, I don't have any uncles. Mom was an only child, and Dad's little sister died when she was my age."

Hollings referred back to the pages on the desk screen. "Oh, sorry, I meant Hans Schneider, the older brother of your birth father Peter."

"My what?"

"Your birth father," he replied, still reading the pages, "Peter Frederick Schneider."

"Birth father? What are you talking about? My father was Malcolm Fletcher."

Hollings looked up and paused. "Oh, dear Lord, I am so sorry. I thought you knew."

The room was threatening to spin. "Knew what?"

"Uh, perhaps we should take a moment. Can I get you something to drink?" He reached for the intercom. "Jenny, could you fetch Sarah for me?"

Michael leaned forward and grabbed hold of the edge of the desk. "Fuck the drink. You thought I knew what?"

Hollings licked his lips and swallowed. "I'm so sorry you have to find out this way, Michael, but you were adopted. Your parents, Sophia and Peter Schneider, died in 3381 on board the *Kaiser's Folly*. Malcolm Fletcher filed for adoption two weeks later. I have the paperwork right here."

Virtual pages fluttered across the desk screen towards Michael. He tried to read them, but his vision blurred. "No," he said. "There must be some mistake. Mom and Dad were married. She died on our old ship, the *Hammerhead*."

22

His memory of it was vivid, the day Dad showed him where it happened. It was the day after his seventh birthday when he had asked. They had gone back to the starboard cargo access, and Dad had pointed to the welds where the hull had blown out. "Fucking pirates," he had told him. "Never forget that, Mikey, and never let them get away with it."

He looked back up at Hollings. "The papers aren't true. They can't be."

Hollings sat there a moment with his jaw hanging. "I'm, uh, look Michael, I wasn't there. I don't have any firsthand knowledge of what happened or who did what. I only have the records, and that's all I have to work with."

Michael staggered to his feet. "Well, the records are wrong, and anyone who tells you different... well, they're lying. Malcolm Fletcher was my father, and Sophia Fletcher was his wife. You understand?"

"Perhaps another one of my associates could explain..."

"No, there's no explanation. I know what I know," he said, waving his hand across the virtual pages, "and all of this is bullshit."

The door opened behind him. "Charles? Jenny said you needed me."

Michael did not bother to look at her, keeping his gaze locked on Hollings instead. "Yeah, he needs help getting his facts straight."

"Michael, I don't know..."

Michael stood straight. "Yeah, you don't know shit." He stormed to the door, the startled Sarah stepping back and clenching a pad to her chest. He paused in the doorway and looked back at Hollings. "You ask around, and you'll hear the truth. Call me when you get your records squared away, and we can talk about my real father, Malcolm Fletcher."

Michael did not bother getting an autopod back to the port. He just ran. He ran for almost three kilometers before he even started to pay attention to his direction. He ran until he was winded, then he walked, and then as the confusion and anger built up, he ran some more. He arrived back at the hotel suite in mid-afternoon, hungry and dehydrated, but too exhausted to realize either.

"Michael!" Isaac called as soon as he came in. "Where have you been?"

"That bastard... bastard, ha, that's rich. That stupid lawyer Hollings doesn't even know who my parents are." He walked around in a circle before collapsing onto the sofa. "We've gotta get that magistrate to pick someone else."

Isaac pulled up a chair on the other side of the coffee table. "Yeah, he called me, said something about you being adopted."

Michael waved a hand in dismissal. "Yeah, can you believe the guy? His paperwork is totally fucked."

Isaac shrugged. "Well, I have to say, it makes a lot of sense."

Michael paused and scrutinized Isaac for a moment. "What are you talking about?"

"Well, I've known for a while Malcolm wasn't your dad. I mean, not biologically."

Michael sat up again. "What the hell? Did Dad tell you something?"

"No, of course not. I didn't think it was my place to ask either."

"Then you don't know what you're talking about either, Isaac."

Isaac stared at him a moment and looked away. "It was the eyes, Michael. That's what tipped me off at first." He looked back to face him. "Yours are as blue as the Lateran oceans, but Malcolm's were brown so dark, almost black."

Michael shook his head. "Dad always said I got Mom's eyes, and that's one of those recessive traits, so that doesn't mean shit."

24

"I know," he replied, nodding. "But it got me to thinking, so I pulled up the med files and checked your blood types."

Michael fidgeted. "So?"

"So what's your blood type?"

"I'm type O."

"Yeah, type O-positive. And Malcolm?"

Michael looked away, trying to remember. "He's A... no, AB."

"That's right, AB-negative."

"So, that's another one of those recessive things. You're still full of it."

Isaac shook his head. "You're right. It is one of those recessive things, but not like that. An AB parent can't have an O child. It just doesn't work that way."

Michael started fidgeting in his seat, trying to escape further back through the sofa. "No, Isaac. You've got that wrong. It's gotta be the other way. An O can't have an AB, something like that."

Isaac frowned. "I'm sorry, Michael. I wasn't sure at the time, but I looked it up in the medical texts — even asked a doctor at my physical last spring."

Michael got up and paced across the room to the kitchenette. He started the water running. He ran a wet hand across his face and through his short hair.

"Hey, the adoption is actually a good thing," Isaac continued. "I never really thought about it that way before. I had always thought maybe your mom... well, you know."

Michael turned off the water. "My mom what?"

"Sorry man, I know it's not my business."

"What?" Michael insisted.

"I've seen the picture, Michael. A fine looking woman like that? I figured maybe she'd had something on the side."

"Fuck you, Isaac! That's my mother you're talking about, not one of Dad's portside girls."

Isaac put up his hands and backed up a step. "No, Michael, that's not what I'm saying. I'm saying that it must not have been that, you know, with the adoption and all. I'm sure she was a good woman… a good mother."

Michael headed back out the door. "Fuck you, Isaac, and fuck Hollings too. You're both full of shit!"

Michael wanted to keep running, but he was exhausted. Instead, he wandered the port on foot, fuming and kicking at whatever loose debris he came across. He started getting sleepy around sunset. He knew he must be hungry since he had not had anything to eat since a light breakfast long ago, but he no longer cared.

He found himself in front of *Sophie's* locked hanger bay. He tried to twist the locking clip, but it held fast. He sat down on the ground, leaned into the corner of the door frame, and fell asleep.

Around midnight he was woken by a security guard. She had stayed in her little pod and was shining a small spotlight at him. "Hey!" came the amplified voice. "You can't sleep here. Move along."

Michael nodded and got up. His legs were stiff, his stomach rumbling and his head pounding. The sun-baked pavement had long ago given up its warmth and had been sucking the heat back out of him. He buttoned up his uniform jacket, and gave a perfunctory salute towards the spotlight and started walking back towards the center of the port. The guard trailed him for a minute but eventually peeled off onto another cross street.

At night, this part of the port was virtually deserted. He could hear the shifting whine of an electric motor echoing off the hangar walls, but he saw no one. The truth was the security guard might have saved his life. Taschin was not the most dangerous port by far, but he would have been easy prey for any manner of portside predators.

He needed to eat, drink, and get some rest, but he refused to go back to the hotel suite, not after what Isaac had said. Fucking disrespectful.

A different hotel would be his best option, but if Isaac or Hollings had notified the authorities, then they could track him by his bank card. Michael fished out his wallet as he walked. A fifty and two tens. That was not going to last long. His stomach rumbled again. First he would eat. Then he would worry about the money.

The late night district was in full swing, but he steered clear of the nicer places. They would use up too much of his money, and they might look at him a little too closely, so he headed further back on some of the side streets. He thought about the Lucky Black but knew better. That would be one of the first places Isaac would have looked, so the bartender was no doubt keeping an eye out for him.

Then he remembered a late night with Dad and a little twenty-six-hour diner behind the Far Meridian. Only one booth was occupied, with two more people eating at the counter. The dinner crowd was long since gone and the bar-closing throngs would not descend for another two or three hours. More than anything, he wanted another shot at breakfast, so he sat at the counter and ordered a large platter of eggs and sausage. The local flavor was a spicy mix with a lot of cheese. When he finished, he found he was still hungry, so he ordered another. After that, he finished off with a couple of sides and got the bill: twenty-six.

He broke the fifty and looked at the meager leftovers in his wallet. "Do you have any bank access here?"

"Around the side," the waitress told him, "next to the Meridian entrance."

He wandered outside, his full belly urging him towards sleep, but he found the bank machine. Dad had kept accounts at all his regular ports, and Michael was used to drawing his portside allowance this way.

He waved his chit over the reader, pressed his thumb, and then traced out his pass code shape, an asymmetric five-pointed star with four of the outlying points connected by separate downward strokes. Dad had helped him design it. "Never use a pass code with only one finger trace," he had always said. "Always add some touches."

He requested six hundred. It was the maximum he could pull in a single day. That had been another thing from Dad. He had figured that six hundred should be enough to get him out of any emergency long enough for him to report back to the ship. Now with no ship to report back to, six hundred would not last him long. The machine spat out the bills, and Michael stuffed them into his wallet. He could always try for more in the morning.

"Mikey? Is that you?"

He turned to see three women coming out the door of the Far Meridian, music blaring after them as the door swung closed. They were all dressed stylishly, with the oldest in an off-the-shoulder blue dress that left little to the imagination. He blinked a few times before he recognized her. "Annie?"

"Oh my dear Mikey," she said coming towards him with arms open. "I heard about Malcolm. I'm so sorry."

She put her arms around him, and he leaned against her. There had been a time when he could lean into her belly, but now even in heels, she was not quite as tall as he was. "I... oh, Annie."

She waved her friends off, and they made their own way down the alley. "Mikey, I'm sorry I couldn't be there at the wake. I didn't hear until this morning."

He did what he could to bury his face in her shoulder, but all he got was a face full of her hair. "It's ok. It was crew stuff, and I... oh God, Annie. Isaac said the most awful..."

She pulled back. "Hey, what's wrong? I mean, you're out awfully late. Where are you staying? Let me walk you back."

He shook his head. "I'm not going back there. They said that Mom and Dad... even Isaac. They say Dad's not my real father."

She reached up and tussled his hair. "Oh that's crazy talk. Let's go get you back to your bed."

"No, Annie. You know the truth, right? Dad said he's known you forever." Annie was Dad's most regular portside girl. Michael had figured out a few years back that there was some kind of money involved, but Annie had always been there for them: trips to the park when Dad had business, shopping for new clothes, even something approaching family dinners. Dad had other girls in other ports, but Annie was the closest thing Michael had ever had to a surrogate mother.

She nodded. "Yeah, I've known Malcolm since before the war. I was about your age when I first met him."

"Then you must remember him and Mom, you know, Sophia. They're telling me I'm adopted, that Mom was married to some Schruber... Schneider guy. But you know different, right?"

"Oh, Mikey..." she replied, but the look in her eyes told him all he needed to know.

"No," he pleaded, "don't..."

"I see how much you're hurting, Mikey. Do you really want the answer, or do you just want me to make it all better?"

He collapsed to his knees and buried his face in her belly once more. He had not yet cried over his father's death, and now that he finally was, he did not even know who he was weeping for.

Chapter 4

*"A friendly woman is a nice thing to have around. A wife...
well, that's something different."* — Malcolm Fletcher

ANNIE SAT OUT IN the front room with her crochet work. The repetitive nature always helped soothe her nerves when she was upset. After an hour of weeping, walking back to her place, and more weeping, the boy was finally asleep on her bed in the back room. Dawn was still a few hours away, but she knew she would not be able to sleep.

The front door opened, and Josie stumbled in. She was still in her party clothes, but her hair was all disheveled. She dropped her bag on the table by the door and only then looked up to see Annie sitting there.

"Oh shit!" she cried.

"What?" Annie asked, keeping her voice low.

The younger woman shook her head. "You startled me. What are you doing up so late? You said you weren't going to work tonight."

She shrugged. "Something came up. Can we talk a minute?"

"Sure, but I gotta hit the crapper first."

"Ok, but keep your voice down. I've got company back there."

"But you said you didn't—"

She shook her head. "Get yourself settled and come back."

Annie went back to her crochet. At the moment it looked like a shapeless lump of black yarn, but when she finished it was supposed to be a tease-worthy wrap she could wear over one of her red dresses on cooler evenings. She worked to the end of the row and tied it off just as Josie returned.

The younger woman was draped in a loose robe and sipping from a bottle of orange soda. Annie used to like the stuff too, but her tastes had refined with age. Josie's teen years were not so far behind her for her to have given up the sweet drinks. She plopped herself down in the papasan chair opposite Annie and sprawled one leg out onto the coffee table. "So, who's your company?"

"I've told you about Malcolm Fletcher, right?"

"Sure, I met him last year."

Annie was surprised. "Really?"

"Yeah, you and I did a double with him and that corporate guy from the clearing house."

Annie nodded, remembering. "Oh yeah, that was quite a party."

Josie took a sip from her soda. "Quite the party indeed, ka-ching! So, is that Malcolm you've got back there?"

"No. Malcolm died about a week ago."

"No shit?"

Annie nodded. "They had the wake last night, but I missed it."

"Oh, that's too bad." She took another sip. "Hey, didn't he have a kid?"

"Yeah, that's who I've got back in my room."

Josie sat up with a giant grin. "Damn girl, that's kind of freaky if you ask me."

Annie grabbed a throw pillow and threatened to toss it at her. "It's not like that, you little… anyway, he's in bad shape."

"Yeah, I guess. I don't see my folks much anymore, but I hate to think of what it's going to be like when they go."

Annie nodded. She was having a hard time believing it as well. She had been with Malcolm two short weeks before when he had passed through Taschin on his outward leg. They had taken in a movie with Michael, and then she and Malcolm had dressed up for dancing at the Far Meridian before settling in for the night at the top of the Spire. He had splurged on a room with a hot tub and a skylight.

She remembered changing back into her boring clothes and walking him back out to the *Sophie*'s dock. He had kissed her goodbye and gone over to talk to Michael who was overseeing the refueling team. She had waved to them, but they must not have seen her. That was the last time she had ever seen Malcolm, his hand on Michael's shoulder, talking to him about the business.

She looked back at Josie sipping on her soda. "It's pretty bad for Mikey... for Michael," she forced herself to say. "He and Malcolm were tight, but the truth of it is, Michael's adopted."

"Wow... the way you talked about them, I never would have figured."

She shrugged. "He played the part well, so I guess he deserved my support on it, but yeah, Michael's folks died when he was a baby."

"How?"

She shook her head. "Mal never wanted to talk about it, and now Michael is hearing about it from strangers who don't know anything either."

"So, Annie, what are you going to do with him?"

She smiled. "Actually Josie, it's what are you going to do with him?"

"Me?"

"Yeah, he's not taking the news well, and I think he ran out on whoever is supposed to be looking after him. I want to keep him distracted and out of trouble while I track down his crew and find out what's going on."

"How am I supposed to distract him? I'm not a babysitter."

She smiled at her younger protégé. "He's not that much of a kid anymore, and young men are still men where it counts."

"I suppose. Am I breaking him in, or what?"

She chuckled. "I honestly don't know, but he's pretty fragile right now. No hard press. Play it sweet and innocent, but do what you can to make him forget his sorrows."

Josie nodded. "I suppose, but for how long? I need the work."

"Consider him your rent payment this month, okay?"

She took another sip of her soda. "I do have other expenses, you know."

Annie sighed. "Look, do this for me, and the next time Captain Joe comes through with his high rollers, I'll take you with me."

Josie hopped up. "Deal. Let me get cleaned up, and I'll go in and crash with him. With luck, I'll have him in my bed by noon for the duration."

Annie picked up her crochet again as Josie headed down the hall, but before she could get far into the next row, Josie stuck her head back around the corner.

"Just how sweet and innocent do you want me to be?" she asked with a playful lilt to her voice. "I mean, do you want me to do the whole teddy bear and pig-tails thing or what?"

This time Annie did throw the pillow, but Josie ducked it easily and ran giggling down the hall.

Michael woke disoriented and numb. He did not know where he was. He did not what time it was. The only thing he was sure of was that there was a body pressed against him.

He opened his eyes to see light sneaking past the curtains to illuminate the room. It was a bedroom, cluttered with knick-knacks but otherwise tidy. That detail penetrated his brain enough to tell him he was on a planet. Which one? Where was Dad?

Then it all came rushing back: the accident, the adoption, Annie.

The blond hair spilling over his chest told him that it was not Annie. He could not quite make out her face, but her pale skin was another sure sign. She was not nude, but the pink t-shift clung to a shapely figure. Beneath the sheets, he could feel that he was still in his briefs, but otherwise, her bare legs wrapped around and between his.

The change in his breathing was enough to wake her, and she tilted her head back and opened her eyes. Deep blue, like his mother's.

"Hmmm, morning," she said.

He struggled to find his voice. "Good morning."

She smiled and snuggled her face into his chest. "Still too early."

"I'm Michael," he offered.

She lifted her head back up and swept the hair out of her face with a hand. She was beautiful: a clean sleepy face, a hint of pink in her cheeks, bright teeth, long lashes, and a cute nose. "Yeah," she replied. "Josie. I'm Annie's roommate."

"Is this your bed?"

She shook her head. "Annie said you could use some company, but you were sleeping. Simpler this way."

Simpler? Entangled as they were, Michael did not think so, but he liked her logic. "Where is Annie?"

"Out," she replied, rubbing at her right eye. She had lavender nails, with a white daisy painted on the thumb. "Stuff to do."

She shifted again, her thigh running up the inside of his. He suddenly became aware of his own erection and the pressure in his bladder. "I... um, can I..."

"Bathroom's through there," she replied with a head bob towards the far wall.

"Thanks." He extracted himself from her arms and legs as gingerly as he could, but she did nothing to make it easier for him. The bed was pressed against the wall on his side, so he ultimately had to climb over her to get out. She twisted with him and smiled up as she did so. He made his way across the room, almost tripping over his own pants on the floor.

"Cute butt," she said.

He closed the door behind him and splashed cold water on his face. He was pretty sure they had not had sex. He was certain he would have remembered that. His bladder urged him onward, so he went to the toilet and took a moment to focus. Just as he got started, he heard her calling.

"Hurry, Michael. It's cold out here by myself."

Shit. Focus.

He finished and washed up again. He checked his breath and found it atrocious. He glanced around and found some mouthwash. A few swishes later, he headed back out.

Josie had moved back over to his side of the bed and was facing him. She propped herself up on her elbow, and the v-neck of her t-shirt hung suggestively towards her breasts. She stared at him a moment and then looked aside with a blush. "Come on," she urged. "It really is cold."

He came back, doing his best not to get snagged by his pants again, and slipped under the covers with her. "So, Josie, right?"

"Yep," she replied, sliding her legs back towards his.

"Annie's roommate. Did she…"

"Say, Michael, do you like kolaches?"

He tried to remember them from his last time through Taschin. "Yeah, the little sausage things."

"Annie said she'd toss some in the warmer before she went."

"Okay."

She slid her arms around him, her nails grazing across his back. "Do you want to work up an appetite first?"

He was starving, but now food was the last thing on his mind.

Annie sipped coffee at one of the tables outside the café. She had been waiting half an hour, scanning the crowd for Isaac. She waved when she finally spotted him, and he changed course to head her way.

She motioned to a seat, but he remained standing. "I heard you were looking for me, but today's not a good day."

"I've got Michael," she said, and nodded to the seat again.

His shoulders sagged and he slumped into the offered chair. "Thank God. I've been all over the port looking for him since yesterday. Is he okay?"

"Well enough, but he's pretty upset."

"Yeah, he is. You know about Malcolm?"

"I heard it around port yesterday morning. I didn't believe it until I talked to Captain Wallace." She shook her head. "I spent most of the day in a haze and finally went out for drinks with a few friends. That's when I found Michael."

"You took him home?"

She nodded. "He cried for a while and then fell asleep. My roommate is keeping an eye on him for now."

"Good."

Annie reached for her coffee but stopped. She turned to Isaac instead. "Wallace said he'd been to the wake, but he couldn't tell me much about how it happened."

"It was a loading accident."

"That's all Wallace knew, but you were there. How did it... I mean, did he...?" she trailed off in a sigh.

Isaac looked away for a moment. "If you're asking me to tell you it was quick and painless... well, it wasn't."

She pulled her arms close and held in a sob. "He knew?"

"Yeah, but he still didn't have much time." He shook his head. "Too slow to be painless, too short to say goodbye."

"So he didn't get to tell Michael about the adoption at all?"

"No, but I think he... wait, you knew?"

She shrugged. "I knew Malcolm for almost twenty-five years, even before he met Sophia."

"Then what's the deal?"

36

"It's not my story to tell."

He gave a snort. "Well, there's not a hell of a lot of people left who actually know it."

"Not much to tell," she said. "She broke his heart, got hitched, and got killed in the war. Michael was all he had left of her."

A waitress passed near, and she signaled for another cup. Isaac held up two fingers to indicate his order as well.

"Too bad," he said. "But now Michael doesn't even have that much."

"I know. So what's the plan for him? He's still got Malcolm's ship, right?"

"It's complicated."

The waitress stopped by to fill Annie's cup and set one out for Isaac as well.

"Is it his age?"

Isaac took a sip and nodded. "It'll all sort out when he turns eighteen, but until then it's locked up tight, and then there's the guardianship thing. I talked to some lawyer about it yesterday, but I don't understand it. Hell, he's been working a ship all his life. In my book, that makes him an adult."

She chuckled. "It takes even less in my line of work. So, are you signing up to be his guardian?"

He sat up. "Oh, no, not for me. I like the kid and all, but he's never going to accept my authority. I may have been his superior on the books, but he's been giving me orders for two years now."

"Then who? I've known him most his life, but the courts wouldn't exactly consider my home to be appropriate."

Isaac took another few sips of coffee. "Probably not."

"So, what then?"

"The lawyer says he has an uncle, Hans Schneider."

She nodded. "That name sounds familiar."

"I'm not surprised. He's one of the senior partners in Schneider and Williams Shipping. They've got ships all over the sector."

She nodded. "So little Sophia married into money."

"I don't know, maybe. They've been around for a while. Hans is still in the Captains' Guild, and they list him as working the *Heavy Heinrich*."

Annie giggled. "The *Heavy Heinrich*?"

He shrugged. "I never know where folks get these names, but it makes a regular run through these parts. The lawyer put in a call to the local S&W office. Their next port is supposed to be Ballison. If they get word out on the next mail run, there's a chance they could divert to here."

"How long?"

"Hard to say. Maybe three weeks. Longer if they miss the connection, shorter if the uncle sends someone on a fast transport. I'll stick around until then at least." He drained his cup. "Shall we go get him?"

"Let's not," she said.

"What? I mean, I have to."

"But you're not his guardian."

"No, but the lawyer thinks I've got him, and I made promises to Malcolm."

She nodded. "And so did I. Look, let's just let this cool down for a while. His uncle will send someone soon enough. I can keep an eye on him for at least a week or two. I owe Malcolm that much."

"Okay," he said. "I suppose maybe he could use more of a woman's touch right now."

Annie repressed a grin. A woman's touch, indeed.

Michael relaxed in the shower. As bad as yesterday had been, today had been fantastic, from waking up, to breakfast, to after breakfast, and then back to Josie's room. He had lost count. He was no virgin. The McKenzie sisters had taken care of that last year, but he had been nothing more than a boy toy to them. With Josie it was different. She took their pleasure seriously.

He dried off with a towel, and held it to his face. He could still smell her on it. She had laid out a pair of boxers and some sweats for him. He needed to get his uniform hung up, but that could wait. For now, it was back to seeing what Josie was up to.

He walked out into the hall and checked her room. No Josie. He stepped out into the living room to look there, but instead of Josie's blond hair splayed out over the sofa, it was Annie's brunette hair tucked neatly into a bun.

"Come on out," she said.

He did, sitting on the sofa beside her. "Where's Josie?"

"I sent her on an errand. She'll be back soon."

"Oh." He looked around the room. He had not paid it much attention before, but it was nice. It was small for a common room, but it was only for a two-person apartment, not a seven-man ship.

"We need to talk, Michael."

He nodded. "I guess, but Josie said—"

"No," she cut him off with a chuckle. "Not about Josie. About your Dad."

He looked away. He should have known. "Yeah, my..." he trailed off. Dad was not truly his dad any more. He could not hide from it. "Malcolm. We should talk about Malcolm."

"Okay, let's talk. What do you want to know?"

Where to start? It seemed so unreal. "Did he even know my mother?"

"Yes, he did. He loved her very much."

"But he didn't marry her? What's the deal with that?"

She shrugged. "I'm sorry, Michael, but I never heard Sophia's side of it. You didn't know your fa—" she caught herself. "Malcolm was a different man back then. He grew gentler as you grew up."

Michael thought about his years under Malcolm's shipboard discipline. "Gentle?"

Annie smiled at him. "I know it's hard to see it that way, but he loved you more than he could say, and I think that softened him up a lot." She shook her head. "But back in the day, he was a brash man, hard, bold... exciting even. I think that's what first caught my eye."

Michael looked at Annie as she remembered with a far-off look. "So did you two...?"

She looked back to face him. "No, not until years later, after Sophia died. I didn't tear them apart, and I can't really blame Peter either."

"Peter." Michael did not want to think about him. Biological father. What did that even mean to him? "Then what did it? Didn't she love Malcolm?"

"Oh, I think she did. Like I said, he was a bold figure and ruggedly handsome, but I think in the end, she wanted more."

"What? Money, fame?"

Annie shrugged. "I don't know, maybe, but mostly I think what she wanted was you. She was an only child, and she always talked about wanting to have a big family. Malcolm... well, Malcolm didn't."

Michael had never thought about it, but he was hardly surprised. In all the lessons over the years, Malcolm had never talked about the joys of fatherhood. "Why not?"

"I think it was your aunt, Molly. You never knew her, of course."

"Yeah, but he told me about her. She died when she was a kid, right?"

"She was fourteen, four years behind Malcolm. I never knew her, but apparently he doted on her. Their dad had been gone for years, so he had played the man of the family. Then she got sick. I don't know if they ever found out what it was, but he watched her fade away over the summer. I think at some level, he didn't want to risk going through that again."

Michael nodded, absorbing it. "So he didn't want the responsibility." A hundred details of his shipboard childhood started to take on a different color. "He didn't want me."

"Never say that, Michael." Annie stood and walked over into the kitchen. "Never say that." She came back a minute later with two glasses of tea, setting one before him.

40

He did not take it. "So, I guess this Peter guy did want kids?"

"He was a little older, already established in his father's company. I only met him a few times, but he seemed like a nice man. I never heard the story of their courtship, but I know that he made the offer that Malcolm would not, a safe and stable life for Sophia and her children."

"Safe?" Michael scoffed. "They're dead, and... and Malcolm survived. If you ask me, she chose the wrong guy. This Peter Schubert—"

"Schneider," she corrected.

"Yeah, whatever, he couldn't keep her safe. He let her die."

"I doubt it was for lack of trying. He died too, remember."

"I guess..." he trailed off. "So how is it I'm even alive?"

"I don't know. Malcolm and I weren't in touch back then. He was off in his ship, and then those damn Caspians started their war." She gave a shudder. "It was a bad time for all of us. All I know is that when I saw him next, Malcolm had you in one arm and a diaper bag in the other."

Michael allowed himself a grin. "Diapers. I'm having a hard time picturing it."

Annie reached down with her tea glass and clinked it against Michael's, still sitting on the table. "He was versatile. You've got to give him that."

"Versatile," he said, nodding, "but not truthful. Why didn't he tell me? For that matter, why did he even keep me?"

She shrugged. "He never told me, and after a while, I stopped asking. Maybe it was just that you were his last link to Sophia, and he didn't want to give that up. Maybe he thought if you knew..." she trailed off, shaking her head. "I don't think he ever really wanted to be a father, even after all those years, but he wanted you to have one. He was always very clear on that. I guess he thought that if you knew he wasn't your biological father..."

"Then I'd feel like the orphan I am. Is that it?"

She nodded. "Something like that."

41

Michael shook his head, remembering all those stories about Malcolm and Sophia: how they met, their tiny wedding, how she died. They had all been lies. "So what, was he never going to tell me?"

"I think he was always planning on it, someday. Maybe he was going to do it when you turned eighteen. Maybe it would have been when you got your captain's license. I don't know, but he would mention it every now and then, some vague event in the nebulous future."

"But he never did."

Annie shrugged. "He always meant to."

Malcolm's dying words flashed back to him. "Meaning to do it isn't enough."

She sipped at her tea. "I'm sorry."

He looked down at the glass and finally lifted it to his nose. It smelled of raspberry. He took a tentative taste and set it back down. "So, however much he meant to, it's never going to happen now."

"And what is going to happen now?"

He sighed. "I don't know. I imagine Isaac is tearing apart the port by now."

"Don't worry about it. I talked to him this morning."

"When's he coming?"

She shook her head. "Let's take it easy for now. There's no rush."

A series of beeps sounded from the door and Josie burst in with two bags of takeout. "They were out of egg drop, so I hope you like hot and sour."

Chapter 5

"Sure, taking a break can be nice, but remember that the rest of the world is still going." — Malcolm Fletcher

TWO MEN SAT AT a conference table as the others filed out. When the last one left, closing the door behind her, the older man spoke. "You said you had some news, but I gather it's not about this latest Shiantic intrusion."

The younger one shook his head. "Malcolm Fletcher died."

"Murder?"

"Accident, something about loading cargo. I haven't seen the official report yet, but an acquaintance of mine was at his wake."

"Damn."

"I know. He'll be hard to replace."

The older man nodded. "Indeed. He had one of our specials, didn't he?"

"Yes, sir, *Sophie's Grace.*"

"Ha! Deceptively named. I like that. Are we going to pull it back?"

"We could, but I worry that the paper trail might expose the program."

"Well, we can't let it go to auction. We certainly don't want one of those ending up in Yoshido's hands."

The younger man picked up his pad. "I believe it's slated to go to his son, a Michael William Fletcher."

"Is he one of ours?"

"No. I believe he's still a minor... sixteen or seventeen years old. Do you want me to contact him?"

The older man rubbed at the stubble on his chin. "No, not yet. Let's see what the boy does. If he's got any of his father in him, he'll contact us. If not, then we'll deal with the special before he gets into any trouble with it."

"Are you sure about that, Admiral?"

He chuckled. "As sure as I can be about anything in this business. It'll do for now."

"Aye, sir."

Michael stared up at the sky, watching the clouds take on strange shapes. Josie lay beside him, having tugged the blanket back over them to guard against the chilly breeze. Sex on the mountain, he mused. That was one for the scrapbook.

Josie took another drag on the hand-rolled cigarette and passed it to him. He sucked it in, held it for a moment, and watched the clouds alter as he let it back out. "What's this called again?"

She set it aside and ran her hands over his bare chest. "Tonja root. It grows naturally on the slopes, but it's hard to spot."

"Wow. It's umm, different."

She started kissing him around the neck. "It definitely adds to the experience." Her voice had an echoed quality.

At some level, Michael recognized it as the effects of the drug coursing through his system. He reached over and ran a hand across her breast, his fingers tingling at the contact until the buzz cascaded up his entire arm. "It does at that."

A small animal darted out and grabbed part of their discarded picnic lunch, but Michael did not care. Planet-side excursions had always been a little strange, but this climb up the mountain slopes had been one of the strangest. The tonja root only underlined the fact.

"Is it legal?" he asked.

"Depends. Why?" She reached down and started tracing circles on his stomach.

"Mmm, was thinking about shipping, exporting, that kind of thing."

She slid a leg over him. "You and your cargo again. I think it's time for more distraction."

He reached over and picked up the tonja again for another long drag. "Sorry, lifelong habit, me and… Malcolm."

She took the tonja back and sucked it in while mounting him. "Yeah, time to start making new habits. You ready?"

He smiled up at her, naked against the sky. "Always."

Hans Schneider read over the report again. Disbelief melted into cheer. "How long has this message been in port?"

Walter Brookstone checked the log. "Thirty-eight hours."

Hans rose from the command chair and waved over his first officer. "Ms. Corazon, get us into the docking queue and come to my ready room as soon as you can hand it off."

"Aye, sir," she responded and took his place in the center seat.

Hans strode to the back of the bridge and through the side door to his ready room. He sat behind the desk, but he could not contain his excitement. He stood back up and paced the five steps back and forth a few times, chuckling beneath his breath. By the time Felicia Corazon pressed the chime, he was almost giggling.

He moved back to his chair and called out, "Enter."

"You wanted to speak to me, sir?"

"This may not mean much to you, Felicia, but Fletcher is dead. I never thought I'd outlive the bastard, but I did. He's gone, at long last."

She remained in a stiff pose. "Malcolm Fletcher?"

"Yes, yes. Malcolm Fletcher." As if there could be any other! "It was some cargo accident, no doubt off on one of his smuggling runs."

She nodded. "As I recall, didn't he have a cousin of yours in his crew?"

"No cousin, my nephew. My little brother's only son, Michael." He fought the urge to get out of his chair again. "At long last, he'll be coming home to his family."

"Then it's good news, sir. Where is he? Will you be sending for him?"

Hans laughed, surprised at his giddiness. "Send for him? Hardly! I'm going to get him myself. In fact, we're all going. He's only over at Taschin. We can divert there easily enough. In fact, if I can get a fast transport, I could get there first, sort out the details, and he'll be all ready to join us by the time the *Heinrich* arrives."

"That seems quite efficient, sir, but Taschin is not on our regular route. We have through cargo bound for Cenita."

He sighed. "Yes, I suppose, but do we have a performance clause on any of those shipments?"

"I would have to check, sir."

Hans shook his head. "Damn the penalties. The boy is family. If it eats into the crew share, I'll pay the penalties myself."

"Understandable, sir. Your orders?"

"Let's see... I want you to expedite our offload here. See if there's anything we can pick up to haul out to Taschin, but don't wait for it. If it delays your departure more than a day, we'll go with empty slots. Then get yourself out to Taschin."

"And you?"

"Have Brookstone find me a transport. I'll double-bunk in a commercial courier if I have to, but find me something fast."

"Aye, sir," she replied and left.

He rose to pace again. Malcolm Fletcher was dead. He wanted to head to the galley and open some champagne.

Michael snuck out of Josie's bed, being careful not to wake her. He heard Annie in the kitchen, so he slipped on a robe for his trip across the hall to the bathroom. When he came back out, Annie was waiting for him with a tray of cinnamon rolls.

"I think it's time we got caught up," she said.

The smell of cinnamon was very intense. Either they were actually that delicious, or the tonja was having a new effect. Regardless of the source, it would be worth the experience. "Sure," he said, following her back to the kitchen table.

"You doing okay these days?"

He nodded, biting into the first roll. They truly were that delicious.

"Have you been giving much thought to your future?"

He nodded again, chewing on the roll. More than anything, he was thinking about whether Josie could hook him up with her tonja suppliers. His research told him that you could ship the tonja plant raw and stay within the law, but given the extra volume and weight, he was not sure the refined quantity at the other end would be worth it. The public databases did not list the street price for hallucinogens on any of the nearby worlds.

"And what have you been thinking?"

He froze mid-bite. Even in his current state, he was pretty sure Annie did not want to hear his idle thoughts on setting up an illicit tonja network. "Oh, you know, getting back to the *Sophie*, making my own runs."

"I see," she replied, selecting a roll of her own. She picked at it with her fingers, delicately unwinding the spiral bit by bit. "You have your license ready then?"

"Not yet. They won't let you take the exam until you're eighteen."

"Are there a lot of eighteen-year-old captains?"

47

"No, but I wouldn't be the first. I looked it up. Some girl did it last year, and two guys the year before that." He did not tell her, however, that it had been seven years before that without anyone under thirty even trying.

She nodded, taking another tear off her own roll. "And that's here on Taschin?"

"No, that's in the whole Guild."

"The Guild in the Confederacy?"

He frowned. The Guild was recognized across most of known space, not merely in the Confederacy, and when you put the Solarian Union together with the League of Catai, that added up to a lot of ships, each with a Guild captain. A hundred thousand? A million? He had never looked up the total. "What are you getting at?"

"Simply that getting your license next year seems like a long shot."

He shook his head. "No, I already have ratings in drive and systems engineering — cargo, too, and that's not even part of the license exam."

"And isn't there something about navigation in there? Or maybe piloting?"

"Not piloting, though I'm not half-bad. The computer does most of the work anyway."

"And navigation?"

He put the roll down. "Okay, so I haven't passed that one yet. What's your point?"

"You don't look like the studying type, especially not when you're on the root."

He laughed. "This is about Josie's tonja?"

"I'm not going to tell you not to use it. You've got no reason to listen to me, but you've had enough by now to feel how it dumbs you down, numbs out your mind. Right?"

"Yeah, but Josie said that was only a few hours."

"Or days. It's got a long tail."

He shrugged. "So, I've been through a lot. Maybe I need the break."

48

"Yeah," she replied, picking at her roll again. "That's kind of my point. Instead of jumping through the hoops for your license, maybe you should take a year or two and go a little slower."

He picked up his roll again and crammed the rest of it into one bite. "Doing what? Get a job here?"

"Maybe. I don't think the local dockworkers' union will take you at your age, but I'm sure you could find something around port."

He shook his head. "No, I want to get... I mean, don't take this wrong. You've been really good to me, and Josie..." he trailed off. He had no idea what he wanted to do about Josie. With his captain's license, maybe even a first officer slot, he could take her with him, but she never wanted to talk about the future.

"You want to get out there, don't you? Back into the deep."

He sighed and picked up a second roll.

"It's okay," she told him. "I recognize the look. Malcolm had it bad."

"Yeah, I guess that's it. Genes or not, he passed it on."

"Have you thought about looking up your family? They were spacers too."

"You mean Mom's husband, that Peter guy?"

She finished unspooling the last of her own roll. "Didn't you say something that first night about an uncle?"

"Yeah, Han, something like that."

"Hans Schneider," she replied. "I looked him up. He's a spacer too."

"What's he do?"

"I think he's in the Captains' Guild, so I presume he runs a ship."

"Captain, huh?"

"Maybe he could help you with your navigation."

He looked down at the rolls again and back up to Annie. This had been an ambush. "He's already on his way, isn't he?"

"I don't know, but I know he's been sent for."

He leaned back from the table. "I guess I don't have a choice in this."

She shook her head. "But that doesn't mean it's going to be a bad one." She motioned to the uneaten roll in his hand. "Go ahead, eat it. I know the cinnamon is that much better on the tonja, so enjoy it while you can."

Chapter 6

"Life is going to smack you down, son. You've just got to get up and smack it back." — *Malcolm Fletcher*

HANS SCHNEIDER FIDGETED IN the chair opposite Charles Hollings' desk. Hollings was still sorting through the files on his desk screen. "I do apologize, sir. If I had known you were coming so soon, I'd have had this more organized."

Hans sighed. There was no point in getting angry with this man. "Since I arrived on the mail courier, I don't think my message would have reached you any sooner than I did."

"Well, I'm sure the court will take your eagerness as a good sign."

He waved it off. "I was too late sixteen years ago. I did not want to spare a second this time."

"Ah, here it is," Hollings announced, sending the virtual page across to Schneider's side. "This guardianship document meets the requirements of both the local Taschin laws along with the stricter Confederacy guidelines. You should have no problems travelling between worlds with him."

"Good. After all these years, I don't think I want to let him out of my sight." He pressed his thumb into the appropriate box on the page. It flashed and sounded a chime.

"And the addendum for the Solarian Union should sort out any border issues…"

Hans flipped to the next document and thumbed it as well. "Now, what about this ship?"

"Yes, the *Sophie's Grace*."

"The what? Did you say it was called *Sophie Grace*?"

Hollings checked the file again. "No, *Sophie's Grace*, the possessive. I gather it was named for his mother."

Hans took a calming breath. The nerve of that man, to use her name after she had rejected him. "I suppose it was. Do you have its specifications?"

"Not in any detail. It's listed as a light transport, twenty-one thousand tons."

"Is that cargo?"

"Sorry, no, that's the total displacement. The cargo displacement is listed as thirty-two hundred tons."

Hans dismissed it with a shake of his head. The ship was useless to him. It was too small to work any of the main routes with any efficiency. Still, its sale price would go far towards advancing the boy's position in the company. "Have you had it appraised for auction yet?"

"No, I haven't even looked into it."

"Why not? You've had almost three weeks."

"To tell you the truth, sir, I had not expected it to be sold. Mr. Fletcher seemed—"

"His name is Schneider," Hans interrupted. "I don't care what the record says. I won't have you call him by that other name."

Hollings nodded. "Certainly. I understand, but Michael seemed quite set on taking the ship over for himself next year."

"At his age? They'll laugh him out of the Guild hall. Childish nonsense."

"Quite possibly. I'm sure you would know that better than me, but the ownership trust is clear. The ship cannot be sold without his authorization."

Hans patted the desk twice as if that settled it. "Whatever. Send me the documents. I'll have our lawyers go over them, and I'll talk some sense into our young adventurer."

Hollings' assistant opened the door. "Mr. Rubin to see you."

Hans stood and straightened his uniform's vest. At long last, he was going to meet his nephew. Isaac Rubin stepped through the door, nodded to the two of them, and then the assistant closed the door behind him.

"Where's the boy?" Hans asked.

"I wasn't sure I should bring him yet."

Hans bit down on his immediate response. He was not sure? "I suppose I had not made myself clear then. I have come to collect my nephew. The *Heinrich* should dock with your orbital in two days. I have little to no other business to conduct in this system, so I plan to leave with it and the boy in no more than three days."

"I understand that, Mr. Schneider. I only thought that we should talk first."

Hans looked at the man. He was hardly a youngster, but he still had a rough ungroomed appearance. His uniform was a bland and generic one, clearly not issued by one of the elite ship service companies of the major worlds. In fact, the only thing custom about it was the stitched ship patch of the *Sophie's Grace*. So this was one of the malcontents Fletcher had employed.

"Talk then," he replied, taking his seat again. "By all means, talk. And for your information, it's not Mr. Schneider. It's Captain Schneider."

"Certainly, Captain." Isaac took the seat beside him, and Hans forced himself to swivel around to at least look at him. "Michael is well and enjoying some portside liberty, but I think he will be eager to get back into the deep. You understand that, of course."

Hans nodded. The man was at least a fellow spacer. He had to give him that. "I do, but please understand that I am eager to see him. We have a lot of catching up to do, he and I. I gather he did not know that his father and I even existed."

"No, I don't believe Captain Fletcher had told him."

Hans stiffened at the name. Captain, indeed. "Then he has a lot of family history to catch up on."

"That's what I wanted to talk to you about. You see, he and the skipper were very tight, a hell of a lot closer than me and my dad ever were. They loved each other, you know, and I think he's going to have a hard time making the adjustment."

"Boys love puppies, too, but they get over it," Hans snapped.

Isaac sat back with his eyebrows raised. "Puppies?"

Hans already regretted it. He was close to losing his temper, and he could not allow it, not when he was so close to his goal. "My apologies. This is difficult for me. I did not approve of your Captain Fletcher adopting my nephew, but in the midst of the Caspian rebellion I was not given the opportunity to make my case. For all these years, I've been waiting for a second chance."

Isaac nodded. "That's understandable."

"So," Hans resumed with a smile, "how do you suggest we help Michael make this adjustment?"

Isaac's posture relaxed. "Well, it's just that family is going to be a touchy subject."

Hans nodded. "I do realize that I am hardly a replacement for a loving father, adopted or otherwise, but I am not the only family he has. I have two daughters, one of them aboard the *Heinrich*, along with a number of cousins and such. It's not exactly a family ship, but Michael will have the love and support of more family than he has ever known."

Hollings cleared his throat. "Mr. Rubin and I had also discussed the possibility that you might bring him along. He's known Michael for four years, and he's currently looking for a posting."

Hans did his best to keep his reaction cool. "I would certainly consider it. What are your qualifications?"

Isaac seemed to sit a little straighter. "Twenty-three years in service, Captain, the last four as Captain Fletcher's first officer."

"Ratings and license?"

"I have a systems-1 and navigation-2, sir."

Hans took it in. It made for a decent personnel jacket, but hardly worthy of a twenty-three year veteran. "And your officer's license?"

"Still provisional, sir, but only because I haven't had the chance to take my drives exam. I do have the hours on it, though, from my last posting."

Hans smiled knowingly. Drive experience going stale for four years, and he still had not had a chance to take the exam? Far more likely he did not know the material and could not pass the practice exams. Still, he had Michael squirreled away somewhere, and the last thing Hans wanted to do was waste time getting the authorities involved.

"Well, unfortunately the *Heinrich*'s only open slot is on the engineering deck, and company policy requires a drives-1 rating. Still, if you get your jacket down to our offices here, I'll be sure to flag it for expedited consideration. There might be another posting on another of our ships, and I'm sure we could ferry you to that assignment."

Isaac gave a curt nod. "I understand, sir, and any help you can offer me would be most appreciated, but my main concern is Michael."

"But of course, and when might I see Michael?"

"Well, I'd like to let him know you're coming, first."

Hans smiled through gritted teeth. "You haven't told him yet? Is he not staying with you?"

"Well, I'm letting him visit with an old friend, actually an old girlfriend of Captain Fletcher's."

Hans did his best not to roll his eyes. Men like Malcolm Fletcher did not have girlfriends. They had whores. "I'm dying to meet her."

Michael draped his uniform jacket over Josie's shoulders and sat down next to her.

"Thanks," she said.

The breeze blowing in off the ocean was colder than he expected. They had gone down to the barrier island east of the port. In the cooler weather of the local autumn, it was empty of tourists, though they saw a few people fishing off the longer docks. Their meandering had wound down on an empty stretch of beach, and they sat to watch the tide roll in alone.

"Malcolm and I never came down here before," he said. He poked a finger into the sand and fished out a rounded stone.

"That's a shame. It's so much nicer in the summer. You can swim or surf or simply lay out in the sun. The nude section is past that ridge, but the waves are better here."

He thought about it while brushing the sand away from the stone. He had seen enough vids to know what that kind of life was supposed to look like, relaxing in the sun, swimming in the water, spending the day with no agenda. It was both appealing and terrifying. In space, solar radiation was dangerous, pools could become lethal hazards if the gravity went out, and the idea of not having a daily shipboard routine was almost alien. "Do you come down here often?"

"In the afternoons. I sleep pretty late in the summer. The best parties don't start until twenty-four or twenty-five."

He picked a target down by the waterline, a lump of sand that looked out of place. With an overhand toss, he dropped the stone down onto it from above. "You go to a lot of parties?"

She shrugged and then pulled the jacket tight again. "It's fun."

He nodded and dug out another stone. "But you and I haven't been going."

The wind caught her hair and she swept it back out her face with her hand. The lavender polish had been replaced by a deep cobalt blue. "You didn't seem the type."

He nodded. He doubted he would have been in the mood had she asked. He had been enjoying the time in his little

56

cocoon with her, but he had come to suspect it was as artificial as it was temporary. "Maybe when I'm older."

"Maybe," she replied. "You'd be surprised."

"Surprised, yeah. Like you being twenty-six?"

She looked back at him through briefly slitted eyes. "So you know?"

He aimed for the same lump of sand and hit it with a low-angle sidearm throw. "I looked at your I.D. a few days back."

"Yeah, well, it's not like twenty-six is all that old."

He chuckled and dug for another stone. "Is that what you thought at seventeen?"

She smiled at him. "Fair enough. Does it matter that much?"

"I guess not."

They watched the waves roll in for a few moments of silence. The lump of sand seemed to be moving, eventually revealing a small armored crab. It sidestepped across the beach faster than Michael would have expected and started digging a new hole further down the waterline.

He turned to face her. "You and Annie are professionals, right?"

She did not look back at him. "Of a sort. I don't know how things were with Annie and your dad, but she said you could use a friend."

"A friend… yeah. And you?"

This time she did look back at him. The wind whipped her hair, but it did nothing to hide her beauty. "Sometimes I need a friend, too."

He nodded. "Thanks."

She looked back out at the ocean and giggled. "Besides, you're actually becoming a halfway decent lay."

He laughed. "Halfway decent? Is that all?"

"What? You want another chance to prove yourself?"

He sighed, thinking about it. "Yeah, but my uncle comes for me tomorrow."

"Then you'd better make this one count."

He reached for her but she wiggled away. "Ick! Not here in the sand, Michael," she said, skipping away. "Let's go home and do it right."

He chased her down the beach. One last night with a friend was all he had, but he was going to savor it.

They met at the same coffee shop Annie and Isaac had used weeks earlier. It was cool but sunny. Annie had run Michael's uniform out to an overnight cleaner, so it looked and felt quite fresh. "You'll want to make a good impression on your uncle," she had said.

Josie had agreed. "You look sharp, Michael. Quite the dashing officer."

The three of them waited at the café and talked about inconsequential matters. Michael even tried some of the coffee. It was much smoother than what he had tried on ship, not nearly so bitter.

Isaac and Hans Schneider arrived two minutes before ten. Michael had been hoping they would be late instead, but the moment was inevitable.

They all stood, and Isaac did the introduction. "Michael, this is your uncle, Hans Schneider. Captain, this is your nephew."

They bowed their heads briefly to each other, and Michael extended his hand. The older man reached for it, but he seemed lost in thought. "You have Peter's chin," he said at last.

"And my mother's eyes."

"You remember her?"

He shook his head. "I have a picture."

"You do?" Hans seemed surprised.

"Yeah." Why would he not have a picture of his own mother?

Hans gave a quick nod and shrugged it off. "Of course you would. Sorry. And your friends?"

Michael turned to Annie. "This is Annie Fowler, a friend of my... adopted father."

Annie came forward to shake Hans' hand. "A pleasure to meet you."

"And this is my friend Josephine Coron." He took great care to get the accent right.

She stepped forward and took the offered hand. "An honor," she said.

"A shared one to be sure," Hans replied. "I understand the two of you have been keeping an eye on my nephew for the last three weeks. Thank you for your attentive care. If there has been any expense or — "

"No," Annie cut him off. "No, it was the least I could do for Malcolm. He was a good man, and a good father."

Hans gave a brief, tight-lipped smile. "I'm sure he was." He turned to Michael. "Are you packed? The *Heinrich* leaves today, and we still have to get a shuttle up to the station."

Michael pointed to his case and duffel. "It's all there."

Hans gave an approving nod. "You travel light. Good."

"Well, I did leave a few things on board the *Sophie*, but I won't need any of them until next year." He expected to get some resistance on this, but he wanted to put it out there at the beginning. This family reunion was temporary at best. "It's under seal, so there's no point in worrying about it now."

Hans gave him another measured look. "Well, you're right, no point in it now. I don't know what our schedule will be at that point, but I'm sure we can work something out when the time comes."

"So Isaac, are you coming with us?"

Isaac shook his head. "Maybe someday, but not right now." He turned to Hans. "I did apply at your local office, but they said it would be two weeks before they got a current list of postings."

Hans frowned. "Ah, I should have realized. Taschin isn't on our main line, so they don't get all the updates that our central offices get. If you can get out to Ballison or perhaps Arvin, they'll be a lot better prepared for you. In the meantime, I'll make sure to forward your jacket to the rest of the fleet." Hans turned back to Michael. "Shall we?"

Annie gave him a hug and a kiss on the cheek. "Write to me, ok? I want to know how you're doing."

Isaac shook his hand and finally pulled him close for a back-pounding hug. "Give 'em hell, sir," he said.

Josie was waiting for him by his bags. He slid into her embrace and kissed her softly on the lips. She held him close and whispered in his ear. "You study hard and pass that exam. I've never had a captain before, and I want you to be my first."

She gave him one last, long kiss and turned away.

With final nods to Isaac and Annie, Michael gathered his bags and started after his uncle. He was leaving behind everything he knew.

But he would be back.

Chapter 7

"Yeah, it's a big ship, but that doesn't mean they know shit from sherbet." — Malcolm Fletcher

THE SHUTTLE RIDE UP to the orbital was nothing spectacular. Hans had insisted on giving Michael the window seat, apparently hoping to impress him with the excitement. The truth of the matter was that he had seen more lift-offs than he could remember, and most of those had offered an even better view from the *Sophie*'s bridge. He had even piloted four such lift-offs in the last year, but that was strictly off the books.

His uncle sat next to him, listing off the various family members who were waiting for him aboard the *Heavy Heinrich*. His own daughter, Gabrielle, was on board. There were also three more second cousins, four first cousins once-removed, a third cousin, and Harriet who was simply family. "I honestly can't remember her connection," Hans explained, "but it goes back a ways."

"Is the crew all family?"

Hans laughed. "Oh, far from it. *Heinrich*'s full complement is sixty-four. We were down one, but you'll bring us back to full."

Sixty-four? Michael tried to imagine it. *Sophie*'s life support topped out at twelve. The only way they could carry that many would be as cargo, but it would not be live cargo. "Exactly how big is the *Heinrich*?"

Hans pointed out the window at the station coming into view. "There she is on the upper right quadrant."

Michael looked and saw it sticking out, even at this distance. The *Heinrich* was one of the giant container ships, with section after section of radial-loading container racks. It was the largest ship docked at the station by far.

"Four hundred thousand tons," Hans said. "Impressive?"

"Is that displacement?"

"No, that's cargo. *Heinrich* displaces almost six hundred thousand."

Michael pressed his face against the porthole to get a better angle to view it. He realized now that this was why his uncle has insisted he take the window seat. Michael had seen ships of this size only three times before, but never this close. These container ships were strictly station-to-station carriers and incapable of atmospheric maneuvers or even landing on a gravitational mass. *Sophie* almost always went down to the planet. "It's more direct that way," Malcolm had always explained.

"How often do you make it to Taschin?" Michael asked.

"First time, probably the last, too. Taschin doesn't have enough trade to warrant something like the *Heinrich*. S&W normally serves Taschin with some smaller vessels. No, I diverted the *Heinrich* here specifically to get you."

"Seems like a bit of a waste."

"You're family, Michael. Family is worth it."

Docking took longer than it should have, but it always does. His luggage was checked through to the *Heinrich*, so Michael did not have anything to carry as they left the shuttle. They were not all that far from the *Heinrich*, so it was a short walk. This was due less to luck and more to the small size of Taschin station. All the docking was on a single ring, so the average walk from ship to ship was only a quarter turn.

From inside the station, the *Heinrich* looked no different than any other ship. It was simply a personnel airlock and an array of cargo locks. They walked up to the airlock, and a man in his thirties snapped to attention.

"Welcome back, sir."

"Good to be back, Karl. Ship status?"

"Load-in should be done within the hour. Pushback scheduled for fourteen hundred local, fifteen forty-two by ship clock."

"Excellent," Hans replied. "Karl, this is your third cousin, Michael."

The man stepped forward and extended his hand. "Karl Roth, good to meet you, Michael. Station comm said your bags will be here shortly, so I'll see to them."

Michael took the hand. Karl had a firm grip. "Third cousin, right."

"Don't worry. You've got a week before they test you on it."

Michael chuckled and followed his uncle inside.

The docking tube ran about thirty meters, and the gravity inside was variable, heavier towards each end but almost gone in the middle. Michael had run into this kind of thing before and took his cue from Hans in front of him as to when he should be gripping the handrails and when he could trust his own feet.

The airlock at the other end was pristine. It was one of the ones that pulled in before hinging over. It was a better failsafe design, but it made the airlocks bigger, something smaller ships like the *Sophie* could not afford. The inner door had the same design, but it looked like it also had a second sliding hatch that could be closed more quickly. Everywhere he looked, the metal gleamed and the white fittings were spotless.

Inside, two crew were waiting, both standing, one behind a desk and another in the hallway. "Good afternoon, sir," said the closer one.

"Billy, this is my nephew, Michael."

They shook hands, and the other one stepped forward from the hallway. "And I'm Charlie Feldman, systems lead on the first watch. If I did the math right, I think we're second cousins."

Michael shook his hand as well. "Charlie, OK."

"Don't worry—"

"I know. I've got a week before they test me."

Charlie looked back to Hans. "He's going to fit right in, sir."

"All right, Charlie, get him down to Harry for some uniforms, let him grab a bite, show him to quarters, and give him the tour."

"The full tour?"

"No, keep to the fore. We'll save the drive for another time."

"Aye, sir. Come on, Michael, follow me."

They went down the hall, passed through two open pressure doors, took a left, and then went down two sets of steep stair-ladders, and another set of turns. Michael had known the *Sophie* well enough to navigate it blind, upside down, and in zero gravity, but here he was already lost.

Their destination seemed to be the laundry, but the sign above the hatch said "Quartermaster."

"Harry, you in here?" Charlie called out.

She came out from behind racks of uniforms and undershirts. "Hey, Charlie. Is this our new guy?"

Michael stepped forward and extended his hand, but she pulled him in for a quick hug. "Welcome to the family," she said. "I'm Harriet, but most folks call me Harry."

"Ok, why Harry?"

She chuckled and pointed to the stitched name patch on her shirt. It read "HARRIET THROCKMORTON", the letters pressed together so close he could barely make them out. "It wasn't until I got this post that I was finally able to tweak one of the machines into fitting it all in there. At my first posting, all I got was Harry Throckmo. Thankfully only the Harry stuck."

"He's going to need the usual," Charlie said, "uniforms, personals, environmental, and I'm pretty sure Captain will want him to have a dress uniform."

"No problem. Department?"

Charlie shrugged. "I don't know yet."

Harry pulled a measuring tape out of her pocket and started stretching it across him in several places, rattling off numbers as she did it. "You've got big feet, Michael. Was your dad tall?"

"No," he replied. Malcolm had come in well short of two meters. Then he caught himself. "Actually, I guess I don't know."

"Oh that's right. You're Peter's kid." She went on to measure the girth of his knees. "He was a tall one. Damn, but your e-suit is going to take a few days to size right."

"You knew him?"

Harry stood up again and started jotting notes on a pad. "Not really. I met him once, long time back."

Michael turned to Charlie. "And you?"

Charlie nodded. "Your mom, too. I was at the wedding."

Gravity seemed to shift a bit, but nothing was wrong with the ship. It was only Michael. The idea of the wedding was a little too surreal, his mother in a gown exchanging vows with someone other than Malcolm.

"You okay?" Charlie asked.

"It's a lot to take in."

Harry had returned with a small crate filled with clothing, boots, toothpaste, and so on. "You didn't know?"

Michael shook his head. "So these are my uniforms?"

"Nah, just a rough fit from stores. I have to make some adjustments, so it'll be a shift or two before I can get you your real uniforms, but this ought to get you through today."

He took the crate from her. "Thanks. It was good to meet you, Harry."

She patted him on the shoulder. "See you around, Michael, and don't worry."

He nodded, already starting to worry. "Yeah, a week, right?"

"You'll be fine."

Charlie led him back, past the stairs, down another turn, and pressed a button on the wall. "Ladders are a bitch if you've got something to carry, so it's ok to use the lift."

"Say, Charlie, is everyone in on this whole 'week until they test you' joke?"

"Oh, it's no joke," he replied as the lift chimed and slid open.

Michael followed him in. "You're serious?"

"Deadly serious," he answered. The lift showed five decks. Charlie selected deck four. "The crew is a team, a family in a very real sense. Say we have some emergency and we're all running around in our environment suits, we can't have people guessing at who's who."

Michael bit back his panic. "But that's over sixty people."

"Sixty-four, actually, and you're one of them. Trust me, you'll do fine."

Michael nodded and took a deep breath. "If you say so."

Hans strolled into his first officer's ready room and signaled the door to close behind him. "He's aboard," he announced with satisfaction.

"No trouble with the locals then?" Felicia Corazon asked. She had been reviewing a systems report, but she set it aside.

"Nothing significant. I got a little brush back from one of his old crew, but I dangled the possibility of employment in front of him, and he knuckled under."

Felicia raised an eyebrow. "Are you posting him here?"

"Oh heavens no," Hans replied. "One of Fletcher's thugs? No, I flagged him through the entire company network, but I suppose I should arrange something for him. Maybe we can foist him off on Takasumi Lines with some kind of doctored-up recommendation. We still owe them for that fiasco last year. Berkshire was it?"

She nodded. "Benny Berkshire. If only he had been as competent as his forged ratings. Do you need me to take care of it?"

He waved it off. "I'll file something myself when we reach Cenita. No, for now I want you to focus on Michael. Have you had a chance to review his personnel jacket yet?"

"I downloaded his public file from the standards registry before we left Ballison. If it's accurate, he's got an impressive set of ratings for someone so young."

"It might be. He's got Peter's ambition, I'll grant you that, but I don't know if it has translated into as much skill as his jacket would imply. Fletcher is the signatory on most of those ratings, so I don't put much faith in them."

Felecia shrugged. "I'll see to it he's put through his paces. The department heads should be able to sniff out any fishy ratings."

"Good enough, but for now let's try to treat him with some respect. He may still have the stink of Fletcher on him, but he's a Schneider. I want him to know that means something."

"Understood, sir. Will you be killing the fatted calf for dinner tonight? Prodigal son and all that?"

Hans chuckled. "Excellent idea, Ms. Corazon. He is indeed our prodigal son, once lost, but now he is found."

Michael finished unpacking in his quarters. He actually had his own stateroom. It was small, probably no more than six or seven square meters, but he had figured that coming in on a ship with this many crew he would have been in a bunk or at least had roommates. His room back on *Sophie* had been a little bigger, but this one was laid out better.

The bed was against the side wall, snugged up between the far wall and the side of his desk. The bed had a padded slope by the wall, letting it double as a sofa. His desk chair was on a forked groove, letting him reposition it several ways. It also reclined, which was an unexpected bonus. The room even had a fold-down bench seat across from the bed for a visitor. He had a sink by the door, and plenty of storage in the closet and the cabinets above and below his bed. He started to wish he had brought more of his things from *Sophie*, but he imagined he could fill up the space with other things soon enough.

The only amenity he missed from his old room on *Sophie* was his own toilet and shower. Those were at the end of this hall, and he had to share the banks of them with the other twelve crewmembers on this wing. Still, given the spread of shifts and the number of stalls, it seemed unlikely to cause a bottleneck. Plus, he mused, at least he would not have a toilet in his room if the gravity went out. He had had to clean up that mess too many times back on *Sophie*.

The rest of the tour had gone well, but he still had no firm feel for his way around the ship. At best, he could remember the decks. The bridge and control systems were up on deck one. Crew quarters, mostly the officers, were up on deck two. Deck three was the largest with the galley, the gym, the theater, and access to the long shaft running down the cargo section to the drives. It also had the main airlock and a ring of escape pods.

Michael's quarters were down on deck four with the bulk of the rest of the crew. It turned out no one was in bunks. Two crewmembers were paired up as roommates, but it was voluntary. "Mark and Sylvia Carruthers got married last year," Charlie had explained, "so we reconfigured a couple of staterooms to give them a double."

Deck five had laundry and a couple of other support systems, but mostly it was dominated by the forward environmental systems. "CO_2 has a tendency to sink, so there's a slight efficiency to be gained putting the scrubbers down here at the bottom of the gravity gradient. Plus, the water treatment stinks," Charlie had said with a grin, "and this puts it as far from officer country as practical."

They had paused at the galley long enough to get Michael a sandwich, and they had ridden out the pushback from the station and the initial maneuvers while he ate it. It all felt very smooth. He could not explain it, but he had always assumed that the larger ships would be full of creaks and shudders when they moved. Apparently not. The transition to tach drive had been so seamless that had it not been for the announcement, he would never have noticed it during his unpacking.

Reluctantly, he hung up his old uniform in the closet with the *Sophie's Grace* arm patch facing out. His new *Heavy Heinrich* uniform was nice but largely unadorned. The blue and gray were vaguely reminiscent of the one in his mother's portrait, but the only symbols were the "S&W" logo for Schneider and Williams and the *Heavy Heinrich* arm patch featuring an overly muscular arm holding a hammer against a starscape. Still, he put it on. Charlie had passed along word that the captain and first officer were hosting a dinner in honor of his joining the crew. The least he could do was wear their uniform.

Chapter 8

"You'll meet a lot of new folk as the years go by, son, but don't think all of them are gonna be your friends." — *Malcolm Fletcher*

THE WOMAN WALKED INTO the Solid Rock on Ballison station and scanned her eyes across the various patrons, the dancers on the stage, and the tattooed bouncer. Her gaze settled on one man sitting at the far end of the bar where he could watch the entrance. He raised his glass to her and took a sip.

She crossed the room, winding her way through the tables. She waved off a waitress trying to help and settled herself on the seat next to him. "What do you have for me, Jimmy?"

He slid a data card across the bar to her. "Wreckage of the *Argus Twin*. I already salvaged the cargo, but her drives and one reactor are still intact."

She took the card and tucked it into the inside pocket of her jacket. "And the computer core?"

He shook his head. "The whole forward section was slagged, so I doubt it, but you can always have your boys try for it."

The bartender approached, but she waved him off. "All right. Standard fifteen percent finder's fee, and if we manage to pull any data, I'll try to get you a copy. It's what... four years old?"

"Something like that, but you never know what you'll find in those records. You should know that better than any, Elsa."

She stiffened. She hated when anyone used that name. "Anything else?" She had places to be.

"A bit of good news. You remember Malcolm Fletcher?"

"Wish I didn't," she replied. "I only wish he could forget about me."

"Then your wish is granted. He's dead."

She turned to face him. "You're serious?"

He downed the rest of his whiskey. "Got squished last month loading cargo out at Shorthorn." He made a pinching motion with his fingers.

A smile crept across her face. "That is good news, good enough to drink to." She waved the bartender to come back. "Two of whatever he's having."

He nodded and turned back to get the bottle back down from the shelf.

"Pity it didn't happen sooner," she said.

Jimmy shrugged. "I suppose. He was a decent fence, you know, for salvaged goods. Discreet."

"I'm sure you can find someone new. What about his old crew, his ship? Maybe one of them."

"Maybe," he replied. "I think the ship might be going to his boy."

"I don't need to tell you that that's a computer core I'd like to get my hands on."

Jimmy gave a little grin. "It had crossed my mind. I may head on down to Taschin and check it out."

The bartender returned with their drinks, and Elsa threw a couple of bills on the bar.

She raised her glass. "To Malcolm Fletcher, not just a mother-fucking bastard, but a dead mother-fucking bastard."

Jimmy clinked her glass and slammed his back. "Ahh! I'll be sure to take a piss on his grave if I get the chance."

She poured her whiskey back more slowly, savoring it. "Send me the location. I know a lot of people who would want to have their turn as well."

The dinner was served in the officers' wardroom on deck two. There did not seem to be a kitchen, only warming trays, so Michael gathered that the stewards brought the food up from the galley on deck three. The table was set for twelve, but it looked a little cramped.

Charlie was there again, as was Karl Roth from the docks. An attractive young woman stepped forward and introduced herself. "Gabrielle Schneider," she said with a smile. "I'm your cousin, first cousin actually. Peter was my uncle."

He shook her hand. "So you're the captain's daughter?"

She nodded. "Yeah, but don't think that's how I got the alpha navigation slot. I earned that rating one year out of the academy, but Dad made me qualify again under his own test."

He smiled in amusement. Malcolm's tests always seemed unnaturally more difficult than the official exams in the book. "I completely understand."

The introductions continued. It seemed like most of the watch leads were present, including two of his second cousins, one of the first cousins once removed, and a woman named Terri Schwartz. "I married in," she explained, "so technically I'm an in-law."

A few others introduced themselves as being no relation, and he kept looking back and forth between faces and name tags. The assurances that he still had a week to learn them all kept up until they were all saying it in unison. One of them, a man in his early thirties, arrived in his dress uniform, complete with the shoulder braids and the gold-embossed name pin reading Walter Brookstone.

Gabrielle knocked his hat off when she saw him. "Wally, the XO said no dress uniforms. Michael doesn't have his yet."

72

ANTHROPIC

Wally shrugged. "Sorry, Gabby, I didn't get the memo." He glanced around and spotted Michael. "Even then, I had to show young Mr. Schneider how fabulous he's going to look when his is ready."

"Then you should have gotten a prettier face to demo it with," Terri shot back at him. "Right, Michael?"

Michael managed a weak smile at them. "Actually, it's not Schneider. It's Fletcher."

The door opened and his uncle Hans walked in followed by a red-headed woman. A round of "sir" and "ma'am" swept through the room as they came in. Hans went right to the head of the table, while the woman took up position on his left. She looked around the room and settled in on Wally.

"I like your utilities, Mr. Brookstone," she said. "Remind me to assign you some special duties in them."

Wally swallowed audibly in the silence. "Yes, ma'am."

Hans gave a chuckle. "I think we can dispense with the discipline tonight, Felicia. It's a night to celebrate. Michael," he motioned him over. "I'd like you to meet my first officer, Felicia Corazon. She keeps all the wheels turning for me so that I can keep an eye on the larger picture."

She extended her hand across the table, and Michael took it. "It's a pleasure, Ms. Corazon."

She gave his hand a firm shake and released it. "I look forward to working with you, Mr. Schneider."

Michael set his jaw. This time he said it more clearly. "Actually, it's Fletcher, not Schneider."

Hans shot him a brief glare, his nostrils flaring in a quick breath. He cleared his throat and announced to the room. "Places everyone. Let's enjoy ourselves."

People began to shuffle, and Michael looked down at the table. Right before him was a formal name card with the *Heavy Heinrich* logo in a light gray background. The name on it read Michael W. Schneider. The rest of the diners started settling into their seats, and it became clear that swapping was not allowed.

He bit back his response and sat to the right of his uncle, directly across from the XO.

The stewards stepped forward from the corners and began to fill the wine glasses with an amber bubbling liquid. Michael sniffed at it. It was seemed light and sweet, not at all like Malcolm's celebratory drinks. He was about to take a sip when a foot poked at him under the table. Gabrielle glared at him from across the table next to the XO. He set it back down and she nodded with a smile.

When all the glasses were filled, Hans stood with his glass and faced Michael. "To Michael, in remembrance of lost family and in appreciation of joyful returns."

Everyone else stood and raised their glasses. "To Michael," they said.

He felt rather self-conscious from the attention, but he knew enough to stand and nod. "Thank you," was all he could think to say.

They drank, and he sat back down and took a discreet sip for himself. It bubbled across his tongue and down his throat, the scent wafting back up into his nose. It almost tickled. "What is this?" he asked.

"You've never had champagne before?" Gabrielle asked.

He shook his head.

Hans patted his arm. "I imagine there are a number of luxuries our young cousin has yet to sample."

"Of course, it's not technically champagne," Wally chimed in. "That only comes from a certain region on Earth." He took another sip. "I suspect this is from the vineyards on Latera, north of Stonefall."

Hans nodded. "That's a good nose, Wally. I actually have some true champagne back at the home office. I only wish I'd brought it with me."

The stewards came in with a soup course, and Michael fumbled through the spoons, keeping a keen eye on Corazon across from him, and the conversations began to flow. Eventually, the champagne was switched out with a red wine for the main course, a mouth-watering rib-eye with crisp green beans still steaming.

The talk at his end of the table predictably turned to his own past, and he did his best to glamorize his own spacer life. He recounted many of those trips deep into the frontier, his first space walk at seven, the near-fatal accident when old *Hammerhead*'s tach drive blew out, his first time piloting *Sophie*, and of course, the time he and Malcolm had been arrested on Nestor.

"It was all a case of mistaken identity," he assured them. "The man they actually wanted was some local, a gambler's thug."

"And you?" Charlie asked from down the table.

"Well, I was only nine, but it turned out the thug had a midget for a partner, so there you are."

Hans smiled at him blandly. "It's a shame you didn't have Peter looking out for you. You would have had a much less turbulent childhood."

Michael shrugged. "I don't know. I kind of liked all the excitement."

"Oh, I'm sure you enjoyed it. I was only saying that Peter would have focused you more on your school work and less on gamblers and midgets."

Michael set his fork down, the green bean dangling limply. "I think Malcolm Fletcher did a good job. He was a good captain and a good father to me."

Hans screwed up his face tightly and seethed for a moment, his breath hissing out through his nose. "Your father was Peter, my brother, and he was a good man."

Michael became aware that the rest of the conversations had stopped. "I'm sure he was, Uncle, but at least Malcolm Fletcher was there for me. Your brother wasn't."

Hans made a fist and pounded it once on the table. "My brother..." he trailed off and lifted his head up to the ceiling with closed eyes. He took two breaths and returned his glare to Michael. "Look, Michael, I don't know what that man told you about your mother and father, but you're back with your real family now. Peter loved you very much, and this is the life he wanted for you. You're a Schneider, and the sooner you accept that, the better."

Michael looked away, down the table at all the eyes looking at him, cousins of all stripes that he never knew, and finally his gaze landed on the name card before him. Michael W. Schneider. He picked it up and held it out in front of his uncle. "My name is Fletcher," he said, and tore the card in two. "And Malcolm Fletcher is not 'that man'. He was—"

"Your father?" Hans finished it for him. "Your father was Peter Schneider." He pushed back from the table. "He was a good man, and he loved your mother very much, and she loved him. This colorful father figure of yours had always been a no-good ruffian with no family and no breeding, tossed aside by your mother's good judgment. A better man would have accepted it and moved on."

"But—"

"No buts," Hans cut him off. He shook his head twice, struggling with his words before turning to stare him right in eye. "The unpleasant truth is that Malcolm Fletcher was nothing more than a pirate with friends in high places, and when he couldn't have your mother, he murdered her right along with my brother. That's right, Michael, murder. You can think of him what you will, but you are never to speak of him to me again."

Hans stood, pulled his napkin from his lap, and threw it onto his unfinished dinner. He walked from the room in silence.

Chapter 9

"Don't like the new guy? Too bad, because he's the one who keeps you supplied with oxygen." — *Malcolm Fletcher*

MICHAEL BOLTED FROM THE room after a few more seconds of silence, but Hans was nowhere to be seen, already lost around one corner or another. He paced back and forth for a few moments, but decided he had had enough for one day. He went back down the corridor, past the lift, and started down the ladders.

Two decks down, he wandered down one hall, then another, and then backtracked to the correct turn. He found his quarters, now with a name plate slid into the bracket. Michael Schneider. Again.

"Dammit!" he shouted, and pried the name plate out with his fingers.

A head popped out from two doors down towards the bathrooms. "You ok?"

He shook his head. "Long day."

The head was followed by a body, a short muscular woman in a tank top and sweat pants. "You're the new guy. Michael, right?"

He sighed and punched the door's button. "Yeah, but I've had enough introductions for one day." He walked in before she could remind him that he had a full week before the test.

Inside, a double-wide crate blocked access to his bed. He flipped open the lid and found his new utilities. Harry worked quickly. He lifted up the top shirt and looked it over. It seemed a bit trimmer than the one he was wearing now, and this one had the name tag.

Michael Schneider.

"Fuck!"

Elsa Watkins relaxed in her cabin aboard the *Blue Jaguar*. The name on the door was Jana Lewis, and that was fine with her. After sixteen years, it fit fairly well. The title of Captain fit even better. The *Jaguar* was not her first command, but she had held it longer than any other before.

Her security chief was waiting outside the door. She did not have to look at the security monitor to know it. He was due for a meeting in another minute, and his punctuality was notorious. She could have opened the door to let him in early, but she was enjoying making him wait. As the seconds counted down, she started to refill her wineglass.

He entered after she signaled the door and stood before her, watching her empty the bottle. There was no second glass laid out for him.

"You said you had news, Bishop," she prompted.

"Nothing concrete," he replied, "but I heard through a well-informed source that the organization is about to complete a long-running operation at Arvin."

She raised an eyebrow. Normally she would have ignored such a vague report, but Robert Bishop had proven to be a prescient judge of information. "What kind of operation?"

"I believe it to be the acquisition of valuable property."

She thought it over. Arvin was one of the larger trading hubs in the sector, but it also had the largest naval base for thirty or forty light years in any direction. "Military property?"

"That is what my source led me to believe."

"Are we being tasked in this operation?"

Bishop shook his head. "My source would not have had that information. If we are going to transport the property, I would expect those orders to come through your channels."

She eyed his tentative stance. "But?"

"But the source implied that this operation might have originated with a very high patron within the Yoshido organization."

Father Chessman. Bishop was unlikely to say the name out loud even in the security of her cabin, but it was clear that was who he meant. She waved her hand for him to continue.

"If you wanted to be involved in the operation, particularly in the transport or use of that military property, it might be wise of us to stay within the Arvin operational area. The decision, of course, is yours."

She weighed it. Good performance on one of Chessman's missions was what earned her this command, as well as her elevated status within the Yoshido organization. Another critical success might vault her even further up the chain. On the other hand, she knew of a miserable few who had failed the mysterious Chessman. They simply were not around anymore.

"Anything else?" she asked.

He shook his head.

She started sipping at the wine. "It might work out to stay in this sector for a little while anyway. Have you ever heard of a man named Malcolm Fletcher?"

"I'm familiar with him, something of a fence and smuggler," he replied. "I believe he died recently."

She saluted him with her glass. "You are well informed."

Bishop gave a single nod.

"You may or may not know, however, that Fletcher has been an irritant for certain parts of the organization."

"I had heard rumors. I understand he was, shall we say, a collector of secrets."

"Among other things," she said. "I have an interest in his collection."

"You intend to acquire it?"

"Perhaps. Failing that, I would like to see it destroyed."

"I see. Is it nearby?"

"Taschin."

"Do you intend to go yourself?"

She shook her head. "There appear to be some complications, and Fletcher's son is involved. I encouraged Jimmy Anders to investigate it."

Bishop scowled.

"You disapprove?"

He tried to hide his frown. "Captain Anders has been useful in the past, to be sure, but if Fletcher's... collection... is as extensive as I have heard, I would prefer a more reliable agent to handle its extraction."

"All the more reason for us to stay in this sector, don't you think?"

Bishop nodded. "Is there anything else, my Lady?"

"One last thing," she replied, setting the wineglass down on the table, careful to align it precisely with the empty bottle. "Your source for the Arvin operation..."

"Yes?"

"I don't believe the organization appreciates the careless spread of information about its long-running operations, especially if those operations are being run by that particular patron."

"No, my Lady, I don't believe he would appreciate it at all."

"Did you make that clear to your source?"

Bishop allowed a brief smile. "Rest assured, my Lady. This source will not be spreading any more information. Ever."

She locked eyes with him and nodded. "Thank you, Mr. Bishop. Your initiative will be noted."

Karen Larkin spun around in her chair as her shift wound down. Air quality was fine. Clean water tanks were down to eighty-two percent, but that was typical as the first shift went through its morning routines. The new pump on tank four was working as advertised, keeping the pressure up on deck two portside. It was another perfectly boring third shift.

Charlie Feldman came in through the pressure hatch forty minutes before shift change. "Morning, Karen. Everything flowing that's supposed to be flowing?"

"Sure thing, boss."

"Tank four?"

She nodded and punched up the readout on the big display. "Five point five four K-P and holding."

"Good."

She nodded. "You're early."

"Yeah, I wanted to chat a moment before the rest of the shift comes on. Have you met the new guy?"

She sat up a bit more. "Briefly. I saw him in the hall last night. Looked like he was having a bad day."

"Yeah, well, let me tell you —"

"About the blowup with the captain? I already heard."

He frowned. "From who?"

She shrugged. "I've got my sources. You know how it goes. Brown water isn't the only thing that finds its way down here."

"Well, it was bad."

"Is he going to work out?"

"I don't know, but I think it's up to us to help him out, because it doesn't look like the captain is exactly smoothing the path. I was talking with the other shift leads, and unless we get orders otherwise, he gets full new-guy privileges, hand-holding, drilling, the whole thing."

She thought about it. The *Heavy Heinrich* was something of an elite crew. She had had to work two other posts at S&W before she could get it. Even then, it had been a bumpy transition, and she could remember some others who had had an even harder time. "I hear you. For how long?"

"As long as it takes. He'll either make it, or he'll wash out, but I think it's a point of *Heinrich* honor to see to it he makes it. The Old Man can shit family politics all day, but we're going to welcome this kid. Got it?"

She nodded.

"Good. You'll pass the word?"

Michael woke to the sound of a chime. The screen by his desk was flashing. He poked at it and the screen switched to a login prompt. A keyboard rose from the desk. He thumbed the scanner, and the screen read, "Michael W. Schneider recognized. Messages: 2"

He resisted the urge to scream again. His throat was pretty raw from the last night, not so much the screaming as the crying. He had not wept for Malcolm like that since his first night at Annie's.

He went to the sink for a drink and looked at himself in the mirror. He looked like shit, he realized. His hair was all askew, and he had slept in his unlabeled utility uniform, giving it all manner of wrinkles. He was desperate for the bathroom, but the screen started flashing at him again.

He went back and stabbed at the screen again. Red text flashed, "Appointment in five minutes."

He pulled up the interface and looked at the messages. The first was from Harry late last night. "Please come by for environmental fitting. You've got some funky shins."

The second was from the XO, Felicia Corazon. "Report to my ready room, 09:30."

He looked at the clock in the corner of the screen: 09:26.

Crap, and he desperately needed to use the bathroom. He thought it over for all of two seconds and dashed down the hall. He finished up as fast as he could and got back to his room. 09:28.

He washed his face and slicked back his hair. This uniform absolutely would not do. In addition to the wrinkles, he had sweated through it during the night. He looked back at his new utilities scattered across the floor from the night before, all with their damned name tags. No, it was time to make the point. He stripped off his dirty utilities and grabbed his old *Sophie* utility uniform out of the closet. He put it on with practiced ease and pulled on his boots. 09:32.

He headed out the door, back to the ladders and started climbing. He had to switch to a different ladder to get from deck two up to deck one, but at least now he knew he had been portside and knew the other ladder would be more central. He came up on deck one and bounded into Gabrielle.

She caught him and steadied him. "You okay?" she asked.

"I'm late. Where's the XO?"

She pointed forward. "Through there and right. Find me later."

He waved and kept going. He stepped through the pressure door into another short corridor that led forward and onto the bridge. The door to his right read "XO Corazon." The door to his left was "Captain Schneider."

He signaled the door on his right, and it opened.

"Come in," she said from behind her desk.

He stepped forward and stood at something like attention. "You asked to see me."

She came out from behind her desk and faced him. "You're late, Mr. Schneider."

"My name isn't Schneider."

She looked him up and down. "You're also out of uniform. Ms. Throckmorton's shift report indicated that she had delivered your new utilities last night."

He shook his head. "They weren't mine."

"Oh? Then whose were they?"

"I don't know. Some guy named Schneider."

She shook her head. "Do you think this is funny, Mr. Schneider?"

"No."

She stepped closer. "Then do you have some kind of attitude problem, Mr. Schneider?"

"No."

She got right in his face. "Or are you just too stupid to know the difference, Mis-ter Schnei-der?" she asked, drawing it out.

"My name's not fucking Schneider!"

She stepped back and looked him over again.

"So, is this the kind of discipline Captain Fletcher instilled in you?"

He fumed, but even the mention of Malcolm stiffened him into the kind of attention he held during the worst of his dressing downs. "No, it is not."

"You're angry with me, aren't you?"

"Yes."

"Of course you are. You're even making a fist."

Michael's eyes went wide when he realized she was right. He tried to relax his hands, but they would not.

"You'd like to take a swing at me, wouldn't you, Mr. Schneider?"

"Yes, sir, I would like that very much."

"But you're not going to hit a superior officer, are you?"

As soon as she had said it, he knew it was true. "No, I'm not."

"And do you know why?"

He took a deep breath and answered as calmly as he could. "Because that's not the kind of discipline Captain Fletcher instilled in me." He took another breath, proud that he had gotten it out without cracking his voice. He thought a moment and added a belated, "Sir."

"That's the proper response," she replied, leaning back to sit on the edge of her desk. "But for the record, I prefer ma'am."

He relaxed, his fists finally letting go. "Yes, ma'am."

"I have some sympathy for your situation, Michael, but have no doubt that I am under your uncle's orders. If you want us to believe that Malcolm Fletcher was the kind of captain you say he was, it's up to you to prove it through your actions. Do you understand?"

He nodded, feeling the rage fade. "Yes, ma'am, I understand."

"The way we do things here is that new crew get rotated through all the departments for the first week. We want you to get to know the ship and all her crew. There will be a test on this in six days. You will not be allowed to hold a post until you can pass that test, and Captain's nephew or not, I do not tolerate slackers under my orders. Is that clear?"

"Yes, ma'am."

"All right then. Take the rest of the day to familiarize yourself with the forward sections. Tomorrow you'll report to Mr. Feldman for a shift in Systems."

He blanked. "Mr. Feldman?"

She looked at him. "Yes, you know Mr. Feldman."

He racked his brain. "Charlie Feldman."

She nodded.

He looked down at himself. "But what about my uniforms?"

She gave a slight frown. "I prefer to stay out of family politics, but I think if you put your mind to it, you'll find a solution. Now, you're dismissed, and don't let me find you out of uniform again."

"Aye, ma'am."

He had to rummage through his stateroom and the small common room at the head of his section, but Michael eventually found what he needed. After a little work, he stood at his sink in front of his mirror and examined his handiwork. He was wearing one of his new utility uniforms, but the offending

Schneider on the name tag was covered by a piece of tape, and on that tape he had carefully written out "Fletcher." The lettering was not nearly as good as the stitched font, but it made the point.

He stepped out into the corridor just as the short woman from last night walked past.

"Hey, new guy," she said.

He winced, but he turned to look at her. "Hi."

"You look like you're doing a little better this morning."

He nodded. "A little."

She looked at the tape on his name tag. "Good solution for now, but you should get Harry to fix you up right."

"I plan on it."

"Good," she replied. "But while we're on the subject of names, have folks started drilling you yet? You've only got... what, six days now?"

"Six days, I guess, but what do you mean drilling?"

She smiled up at him. "Here's how it works, new guy." She pointed to her own name tag.

"Karen Larkin," he said.

"Right. Now look at this," she said, pointing the patch above her name. It showed a green diagram of letters connected by lines, like a molecular diagram. "Environmental. We're about half of the Systems department."

He nodded. "OK."

"So here's what you do, when you meet someone new, you look at their tags, read them out loud, and they'll tell you what shift they're on or which section, that kind of thing."

"All right," he replied. "Karen Larkin, environmental systems."

"That's right," she answered. "Now look at my face. Ok, third shift."

"Third shift?"

"I work midnight to oh eight hundred. First shift goes from eight to sixteen hundred, and then second shift takes it from there back to midnight. Always report a half-hour before your shift and plan on staying a half-hour after for any changeover duties."

He nodded. "Yeah, I'm supposed to report to Charlie for first shift tomorrow."

"Great," she said, giving him a playful punch to the shoulder. "I'll be finishing off then."

"And now?"

"Now I'm headed for a shower and bed."

"Thanks, Karen," he said.

She walked away with a wave. "See you around, Michael Fletcher."

His chest swelled, but he was glad she had not seen it. He was pretty sure he was blushing too.

Quartermaster was his next stop, so he found the ladder and went down one deck. He wandered around through the corridors, turning back from the smell of environmental, and eventually found the laundry. Harry was there, dumping towels into a folding machine.

"Hey, new guy, are you here for your fitting?" she asked, but as he approached, she looked at his name patch and raised an eyebrow. "Well that's different."

"Yeah, I was hoping you could help me out on that."

She bit at her lower lip for a moment. "I heard about dinner last night."

"You did? How?"

"Shit, Michael, if we could ship cargo by word of mouth, we would set speed records. I'm sure by now everyone has heard about it."

He sighed. "So, are you going to help me?"

"Well, that's where I have a little bit of a problem. The captain put you on the crew manifest as Michael Schnei... well, by that other name. He says I'm to make uniforms according to the crew manifest. No fake officer bars for portside liberty, that kind of thing, you see. I don't want to have to explain to him how I made you an irregular patch because you asked."

He shook his head. "Then tape it is."

She shrugged. "Or not. I don't think I have any standing orders about preventing someone else from making an irregular patch."

He started to smile. "Ok, how do I do that?"

"The machine's back here," she said, beckoning him back into the maze of shelves and crates.

Michael walked into the galley at noon, starving. He had not eaten since the half dinner the night before. It was crowded already with at least thirty crewmembers either sitting or in line at the counter, and the moment he came in, he felt every pair of eyes on him.

It was not as though the room fell silent, but he did notice a momentary drop in volume, as though many of the conversations had shifted to the whisper of "new guy." The older man in front of him turned and nodded to him. "Michael Fletcher," he said, reading his newly stitched name patch. He then pointed to his own patch.

Michael looked at it. "Zane Forrester," he read and then looked to the departmental patch above it. It was a purple swirl. "Tach drive?" he guessed, and looked up the man's face: thin, dark hair with a hint of gray at the temples.

"Yep, first shift." He glanced back to the moving line in front of him. "Meatloaf today. Everyone else loves it, but the gravy aggravates my heartburn, so I'm getting a sandwich. You ever do much tach work?"

He nodded. "I've sat more than a few shifts," he answered. He thought better of bragging about his rating in it.

"Good. We could use another good tach man. We're still one short. It makes a couple of the maintenance jobs a pain in the ass."

They got to the front of the line, and true to his word, Zane got a turkey sandwich. The woman behind the counter looked up at him. "Mr. Fletcher!" she exclaimed. "I heard you missed out on the dessert last night."

He faked a smile. "Yeah, I umm, I had to go."

She put some meatloaf on a plate for him. "No worries, dear. I saved it for you. Find a seat, and I'll send it out in a few minutes."

He got some corn to go with the meatloaf and picked up a cup of iced tea at the end of the line, and when he turned back to the array of tables and benches, he saw a hand waving to him. It was Gabrielle. He made his way over, nodding to several smiles and waves along the way, and sat down opposite her in the corner table.

She added a puffy white roll to his plate. "It looked like they were running out before, so I went back and saved one for you."

"Thanks," he said, dabbing it into the gravy and taking a bite. It was delicious, a far cry better than Malcolm's cooking had ever been.

"I'm sorry about last night," she said. "You know, with my dad."

He nodded, still feeling the sting. "It's not your fault."

"Still, it was a shitty way to welcome you to the family."

"You don't like him?"

She shrugged. "He's my dad, so I love him, but I don't always like him."

He chuckled. "That's a fine distinction."

She lowered her voice and leaned in. "Oh, he can definitely be a self-righteous prick sometimes, but that doesn't change the fact that he's been a good father to me. Plus, he makes a pretty good captain, too."

"Compared to?"

"I grew up on his ships, sure, but I had three other postings at the academy and one since. I only came back here last year when a navigator slot opened up."

"Oh, that's not what I meant. I guess... never mind."

Her eyes went wide. "Oh, you thought I was comparing him to Fletcher?"

He lowered his eyes. "Yeah."

"Oh, sorry. I honestly didn't mean to imply anything. I never met your... old skipper. I certainly never served under him, so I wouldn't know."

He met her eyes, looking so earnest. Either she was telling the truth, or she was a better actress than a navigator. "Do you believe what he said, about him murdering Peter and my mom?"

Gabrielle reached out and took his hand. "Oh God, Michael, I honestly don't know. I mean, I was just a kid when it happened. We were on a run into the League of Catai when we got the news. Peter's ship had been destroyed in some battle, all hands lost, and by then the news was already three months old."

"All hands?"

"Yeah, it turns out that four people got out. You and the chief steward in one pod, and two of the cargo handlers in another, but we didn't find out about them until six months later when they showed up at one of our offices."

"And me?"

She shook her head. "By then the adoption had already gone through, and we had no idea where to find you."

He nodded, recalling fragments. "I remember a few worlds we saw back in those years. Looking them up later, I can tell you that at least some of them were in the Solarian Union, but mostly I remember we were moving around a lot."

"A lot? Compared to what?"

He shrugged. "It's a good point. I guess that's the life. We're always moving around, but I don't think we had much of a regular schedule back then. About the only regularity I remember is Annie."

He saw the quizzical look on her face.

"A girlfriend of Malcolm's. She was always sweet to me."

She smiled at him. "Well, look, I've got to get back to the bridge. Jake is watching my station so that I could eat, but I have to spell him now. My advice to you is steer clear of Dad for a while. Give him time, and his temper will fade."

"Thanks," he said and bid her goodbye.

She had not taken more than five steps when another woman sat in her place. She was older, perhaps near fifty with a round face and vivid green eyes. "Hi, new guy," she said, pointing to her name patch.

"Roxanne Collier," he said, following her finger to the department patch. It was a red wrench. "I'm going to guess systems, mechanical."

"First shift. I'm the one to call if the door jams or the lift wobbles, that kind of thing. And most folks call me Roxy. So, I hear you've got a lifetime of small-ship experience."

A lifetime? "Sure," he replied, "seventeen years of it."

They chatted for a few minutes. She had done twelve years in Confederate survey and then bounced around cargo carriers ever since. She had two daughters, one who was now working for Takasumi Lines as a cargo handler, and one who had gone to dirt and decided to raise pigs with her husband. She got up after a bit, saying she had to investigate a grating noise in the long core shaft.

He started digging into his food again only to see another man sitting across from him. He slid a piece of cherry pie across the table towards him. "Compliments of Maggie," he said, pointing to his own name patch.

"Reginald Hawthorne," Michael said through a mouthful of meatloaf. The department patch looked like a crate. "Cargo?"

"Yep, Reggie."

Behind him, Michael saw four others looming, doing their best to look like they were not. Drilling indeed.

Chapter 10

"Don't be afraid to get your hands dirty, boy. The best results are covered in grime." — *Malcolm Fletcher*

MICHAEL WAS SURE TO arrive more than thirty minutes early to his first shift with Charlie. He had swept through the breakfast line, learning Gary, Susan, and Maggie along the way, and tucked a couple of extra biscuits in his pockets for later. He had also mapped it out on the console the night before, so he did not get lost in the turns of deck five this time. Charlie was already there talking to Karen, but no one else from first shift had arrived.

"...vibration on tank four," she was saying. "I wasn't sure at first, so I got out the scope and gave it a listen."

"Was it the whole night?"

She looked up and saw him come in. "Morning, Michael." She covered up her name patch.

"Karen Larkin, environmental, third watch," he said.

"Good boy," she replied with a smile.

Charlie nodded to Michael but turned back to Karen.

"My question?"

"Oh, sorry," she answered, sitting up a little straighter. "No, it started around oh five thirty and has been going off and on since."

"Morning showers," he suggested. "Did it correlate to the new pump?"

"No, it was more intermittent than that, more like every few minutes. It would start with a louder thump and then rattle around for a while. I can't seem to narrow it down to any of the fittings down here."

Charlie shook his head. "It's probably one of the air gaps."

Karen's face lit up. "Ah, so that would be the back shock from one of the spring valves. Gotcha."

Charlie turned to Michael. "Did you ever do much plumbing work?"

"A little, mostly scraping out the sludge tanks and the likes."

"Never did much with fittings?"

He smiled. "Not much. I had a toilet lock that kept breaking loose, but that was about it."

"Well, I think we're going to take you on a leak hunt today."

"A leak hunt? Not again!" cried out a new voice.

They all turned to see two crewmen walking in. Michael grinned as they approached. He had planned ahead the night before. "I believe that's Alfred Kessler and Edward Tennyson," he said, long before they got close enough to read their name patches.

The one on the right laughed and covered both his own and the other's name patch. "New guy's been studying, but which is which?"

Michael put on his best consternation face. "I believe you would be Edward, while your friend here is my second cousin, Alfred Kessler."

Alfred brushed Edward's hand away and extended his own to Michael. "Pretty good, cousin, but can you tell me the names of the relatives in between us?"

Michael froze as he took the offered hand. "I, um…"

Alfred busted out laughing. "Don't sweat it, Michael. I can't either. I know it's on my mom's side, but beyond that I have no idea."

A round of laughter and handshakes ensued, but eventually Charlie brought it back to the job. "Ok, so a leak hunt up on deck two. Anything else, Karen?"

"Air scrubber six is down to fifty-eight percent, and yes, that's a six percent drop since shift-change."

"Yeah, I figured it was due. Eddie and Al, looks like you two are reskinning the scrubber today."

They chatted a little longer, mostly Eddie saying how glad he was to be spared from the leak hunt, but then Karen pointed to the bulge in Michael's pocket. "Is that a biscuit?" she asked.

"Yeah," he admitted. "I thought I might get hungry later."

"Oh god," she said, "could I please have it? They're always out by the time I get to the galley, and I get stuck with toast. I hate toast."

He handed it over and then fished out the second one for her as well. "Oh, thank you, Michael. I was starving."

"You could have sent for some," Eddie chided.

Michael was surprised. "You get delivery?"

"Sure," Charlie replied. "If you're ever stuck on a station and can't get away, call in to the galley. They'll send something out to you."

"Yeah, but they'll take their sweet time about it," Karen said, devouring the rest of the first biscuit. "It's never as warm as this, so thank you."

"No problem," Michael replied.

She turned back to Charlie. "Mr. Feldman, do you have the watch?"

Charlie nodded stiffly. "Yes, Ms. Larkin, I have the watch. You are relieved."

She held up the second biscuit. "Thanks again," she said and skipped away down the corridor.

Charlie and the rest of his crew went through the diagnostic screens again and confirmed everything was as Karen had told them, but from the time they had first come down, scrubber six had dropped another percentage point. "At fifty, it signals an alarm on the screens. At thirty-five we get the klaxons. Trust me, you don't want to let it get to thirty-five."

"Well, what do you do when you're reskinning it?"

Al was already back at one of the controls working on something. "We reroute the ducts around the scrubbers. Number six can go to number four or number eight."

Eddie was at the main station monitor. "Go to four. It's still reading in the nineties."

"Switching to four."

Charlie tugged at Michael's sleeve. "Let's get you a kit and get started."

The kit was little more than a zero-g tool belt. It still had pockets for the tools, but they were also all held in with straps. This one was stocked with mostly wrenches, screwdrivers, and a few tubes of something gooey. He noticed that Charlie's also had a small torch and goggles. They both suited up and headed up to deck two, officer country.

Michael worried about running into his uncle. They had not crossed paths since the disastrous dinner, and he was in no hurry to see him again. As it was, deck two was almost deserted. He saw one man duck through a cross corridor. It was not anyone he knew yet, but he spotted the purple swirl of the tach engineering patch.

They came to a narrow floor-to-ceiling wall panel, no more than half a meter across. The only thing that marked it as being different was a small collection of letters and numbers along the bottom. "W/P/A 2-1 & 2-3". Charlie pulled out a power screwdriver and started detaching the panel from the wall.

"Here's how we're going to do this. We open all the panels, one at a time, and you go in and look for the leak while I go into the officer's baths and test the fixtures."

The panel came away to reveal a narrow gap between two walls, wide enough for Michael to slide into but also filled with pipes, cables, and ducts. "In there?"

"Yeah, your first warning," Charlie replied while sucking in his belly, "watch your weight when you work systems. You never know where you're going to need to crawl."

"Okay," he replied, squeezing in. "What am I looking for anyway?"

"First of all, look up, towards the back. Do you see a flex pipe going up to a T-junction in each of the two walls?"

He looked. Flex pipes were everywhere in different sizes and colors, some thick and blue, some thinner and clear, and a few near the floor that were thick and brown. This was in addition to a jungle of bundled cables and several air ducts. He had to maneuver around a couple of ducts before he could get far enough back to see. There they were, right up at the height of a typical shower nozzle. "Yeah, I see them."

"Do you see the pipe going up from that junction, should be hard pipe, not flex pipe."

He looked again. There it was, about twenty centimeters tall going up towards the solid ceiling. It was topped by a fat cap, screwed down onto threads. "Yeah, I see it."

"Ok, that pipe holds an air gap, and we want to make sure it's not leaking."

Michael looked back towards Charlie in confusion. "Why do you want air in your pipes?"

"Only in that one pipe. That's why it's sticking up. The water beneath it keeps it from going anywhere else."

"Ok, but why do you even want it there?" he asked.

"It acts as a shock absorber," he answered. "All the user valves on the plumbing are spring loaded. You noticed that, right?"

He had, in fact. *Sophie's* were like that, too. One of the luxuries in port, especially ground ports, was turning on a shower and leaving the water running to steam up the bathroom. On ship, he was used to holding down the water chain to rinse off. Letting go cut the water automatically. "Don't all ships have that? Go easy on the water system and all that?"

"Yep, and when that valve snaps shut, it sends a pressure wave back through the water in the pipes. If you're not careful, it'll rattle through every pipe in the system. The air gap in that top pipe absorbs the shock, letting the water slam up before dropping back down. From the rattling Karen was hearing this morning, my guess is that one of those pipes has leaked most of its air out."

Michael nodded. "No air, no shock absorber. Okay, so how do I tell if it has a leak? Am I looking for a puddle in here?"

"No, you're feeling for the vibration. I'm going to go play with the fixtures in two-one. There should be three air-gaps on that wall. Find them, and put your hands on them one at a time. When the valve closes, you should feel a slight thump, but only a slight one. If it's a big thump, start looking for any water near the pipe, even a single drop."

He scanned around and found the other two vertical gap pipes on the first wall. He figured they corresponded to the shower, the sink faucet, and the toilet. He heard movement on the other side of the wall, grabbed the one for the sink and called out, "Ready on the sink!"

He felt a slight ping, heard water moving through the pipes briefly, and then felt a firmer thump, but it was not much. "Negative, I think," he called through the wall. "Ready on the shower."

They progressed through the six fixtures accessible from that crawl space, but none of them felt particularly bad. Michael wiggled his way back out and helped Charlie reattach the panel. "So what now?"

Charlie smiled and turned across the hall. Another narrow panel was labeled "W/P/A 2-2 & 2-4". Michael's shoulders sagged. "How many of these are there?"

"Now do you see why Eddie and Al were so happy not to go on the leak hunt?"

Michael chuckled. He had pulled worse duties. When he was nine he had flushed the navigator's passport down the toilet. Guess who got to disassemble the sludge tank looking for it?

They opened the panel, and Michael crawled inside. Once he heard Charlie on the other side, he called out, "Ready on the sink!"

And so it went. They hit pay dirt on sink 2-7. Michael felt it jump in his hand, and he could hear it almost grunt, like Malcolm trying to hold in a sneeze in his environment suit. From the other side of the wall, Charlie said, "That sounded promising."

"Yeah," Michael replied. "Hit it again." He let go of it this time and watched. He could actually see the shock, almost like someone had hit it with a hammer, and then he saw what he was looking for. A single drop of water trickled down the side of the pipe. He followed its trail all the way back up to the threaded cap at the top. "I think we found our leak."

Charlie reappeared out in the corridor. "Okay, now we have to turn the water off. Look for a blue-handled valve near the floor on that side."

Michael had been expecting Charlie to come in and do the actual work, but no, he insisted that Michael learn it. He talked him through draining the water out of the pipes, unscrewing the cap, cleaning the threads, coating them with fresh sealant, and tightening it up again. The tightening was the hardest part in such a cramped space, but he got it done. Afterwards, they turned the water back on and tested it. The visible hammering had dropped down to a mild thump that he could only feel, not hear.

Michael climbed back out and helped Charlie seal up the panel. "Great, now what?"

Charlie tilted his head down the hall. "We've still got eight more panels to check."

"But we found our leak."

Charlie shook his head. "No, we found a leak. We still have to check the others to make sure it's the only leak."

Michael sagged back against the wall. "Yeah, you're right."

"But first, let's go get some lunch before the crowd shows up."

"Good idea."

They were the first to report for lunch, but not by much. By the time they were sitting, three more were in the line. Lunch was a spicy sausage and rice combination with a side of black beans. Over time, various crew stopped by to do the name-patch dance. He met two more cargo handlers, another drive engineer, and the pilot, Jake Norris.

"First shift," he said. "Actually the only shift, since I only get to do my thing during docking maneuvers."

"What do you do the rest of the time?"

"I have passable knowledge of most of the bridge systems, so I do a lot of shift covering. As soon as I'm done here, I'm heading back up to let Gabrielle get lunch."

They chatted a little longer since Michael was curious what it was like piloting such a behemoth, and Jake was more than happy to brag about his skill, but all too soon he had to go.

Charlie nudged Michael, "Time for us as well. Let's head down and cover for Eddie and Al, then back to our leak hunt."

Down on deck five, scrubber six was back up and running, and Al and Eddie were playing a word game the rules of which escaped Michael. He and Charlie took their places at the station and watched the various indicators update. Mostly though, they did not update, holding steady in their green state.

"Is it always this boring?" Michael asked.

"When you're lucky," Charlie replied.

Forty minutes later, they headed back up to deck two to resume their leak hunt, and when he was getting ready to test stateroom 2-11, his worst fears were realized. He heard his uncle's voice in the hallway. "Who is that back there?"

He panicked for a moment, but before he could respond, he heard Charlie's voice. "Good afternoon, Captain."

"Afternoon, Mr. Feldman. What's up here?"

"We're on a leak hunt, sir. Now that we finally have tank four up to full pressure, we're getting some vibration in the system, so we're checking all the air gaps."

"Found anything yet?"

"Yes, sir, in Mr. Brookstone's quarters, but we're checking the rest to be safe."

"Good job, Mr. Feldman. My compliments to you and your team."

"Thank you, sir. I'll be sure to pass that along."

A few minutes later, as they closed up the access panel, Charlie brought it up. "By the way, the Captain wants me to pass on his compliments to you."

Michael nodded, trying not to frown. "Yeah, I heard."

Charlie shrugged. "He's not all that bad," he said, heading down the corridor. "Come on, four more to go."

Much to Michael's surprise, their vigilance paid off. He was musing about Malcolm's past when the air gap for shower fifteen jumped in his hands. "We've got a live one," he called.

Charlie reappeared at the access panel. "Okay, this time you tell me how you're going to fix it."

It was worth it. He got all the way through without a single correction. They finished checking the final few pipes and headed back down with an hour left in the shift. He sat down in one of the seats and let himself go limp. He was exhausted.

Charlie checked in with the status boards again and got an update from Eddie and Al. Then he took a look at Michael. "You did good work today, especially for a first shift on a new ship. How about you knock off early? Get some rest before dinner. They're showing *Blue Fins of the Void* tonight. It should be fun." He made a suggestive gesture over his chest. "Paula Stone fun, if you know what I mean."

Michael smiled. Malcolm had been all over Paula Stone's movies for years, but Michael had never liked her as much. She was hot and all, but she was getting old, pushing into her forties even. "I'll try," he said, "but if it's all the same to you, I'd like to finish out my first shift. You know, just to keep me honest."

Charlie patted him on the shoulder. "Yep, name or not, you've got that Schneider work ethic. You'll do well here."

Michael fumed briefly but held it in check. Whatever was in his genes, his work ethic came from Malcolm Fletcher. Besides, most of his shifts on the *Sophie* had been twelve hours, not eight. The last thing he was going to do was wimp out in front of these slackers.

The rest of the shift went quickly as he listened to Eddie and Al play their word games. He finally discerned the rule for one of them, a back and forth pun contest where each subsequent pun had to start with the next letter in the alphabet. He was waiting to jump in at V with a virgin-vegan pun, but Doug Gould came in at S.

"Hey guys, how was the shift?"

"Scrubber skin," Eddie chimed in.

"That wasn't a pun," Al complained.

"Whatever," Eddie replied. "Plus, Charlie and new guy here got to do a leak hunt up on two."

"Pump four?" he asked.

"Yeah," Michael heard himself replying, surprised at himself. "We found two leaky air gaps."

Doug nodded. "You know, I thought I heard something last night, but I wasn't sure." He stepped over to Michael and pointed to his patch.

"Douglas Gould, environment systems," he read. Doug had blond hair and a scar on his forehead.

"Second shift," he replied holding out his hand. "Good work on the leak hunt. Those access gaps are a bitch."

Michael took the hand. "That they are."

Dinner was a blur of beef stew, six more new crew, and Eddie and Al trying to gross him out with increasingly noxious tales from sludge tanks gone bad. He caught a quick shower after dinner and put on a fresh set of utilities for the movie. About twenty of the crew were there, and he was hit with four new names, but soon enough he settled down in the back row.

He was asleep before the first appearance of Paula Stone's cleavage.

Chapter 11

"Watch what you're doing, Michael. You might actually learn something this time." — Malcolm Fletcher

IN THE MORNING, MICHAEL knew he was supposed to report to Terri Schwarz in engineering for the day, but he was not sure how to get there. None of his tours had taken him back to the drive section yet, but he did know where the access hatch was. In fact, he had passed right by it on the way back from the movie the night before, but it was closed and had large stenciled letters reading, "HATCH REMAINS CLOSED AT ALL TIMES".

Fortunately, he ran into Zane Forrester in the mess line at breakfast. He had turned to Michael and covered his name patch. "Good morning, new guy."

Michael nodded at the game. "Zane Forrester, tach engineer, first watch."

Zane dropped his hand and picked up his tray. "I hear we get you for today's shift."

"Yeah. Any chance I can tag along with you? I haven't been back there yet." Breakfast looked to be eggs or pancakes. Michael wanted both.

"Sure, meet me at the forward access hatch by seven fifteen."

Michael wolfed down his food and went back to the end of the serving line. There were five biscuits left. He grabbed one and stuffed it in his pocket. On his way out he got hit with two more "Hey, new guy" introductions, but he made it out with enough time to spare.

He was already dressed, so he had no need to get back to his quarters. Instead, he slid down the ladders to deck five, turned two corners and saw Karen sitting at her station watching the displays. "Think fast!" he called and tossed the biscuit over the intervening consoles.

She looked up just in time to clutch it to her chest. "Oh my!" she exclaimed.

"Gotta run," he said, and headed back the other way.

"Thank you, Michael!" she called out, and he caught one last look at her smile as he turned the corner.

Up two ladders on deck three, Zane was waiting for him at the access hatch. "Ready?"

Michael nodded, and Zane swung the hatch inwards. On the other side was a proper airlock. They went in, and Zane closed the hatch behind him. Zane grabbed a couple of looped belts and tossed one to Michael. He then stepped into the loop and pulled it snug around his waist. Michael did his best to mirror the older man's actions.

When Zane went to open the opposite hatch, Michael grabbed at his arm. "Wait, don't we need environment suits?"

Zane chuckled. "Ah, because of the lock? No, that's a design precaution in case we lose atmosphere in the spine." He pointed to a display next to the door. "See, all green. Even a millibar of pressure difference would get you a yellow. Much beyond that, and you'd never be able to pull it open." He then proceeded to open up the rear hatch.

The corridor beyond stretched to forever and back, and Michael had a brief sense of vertigo. It was about six meters across and ran the entire length of the long cargo section, all three hundred meters. Zane had already gone through, while

104

Michael paused in the hatchway. Behind him, he heard someone pounding against the other hatch.

"Hurry up, Michael," Zane urged him.

Once through, Zane closed the hatch. "We're not supposed to have both hatches open at once. It can slow down the shift change, but it's a safety issue."

"What happens if both are open?"

"If we have atmosphere on both sides, nothing, but it will signal an alarm on the bridge, and you don't want to have to explain yourself to the XO."

"Why?" He felt foolish asking. He remembered what it had been like the last time he has stood under her withering glare.

Zane smiled. "Because she'll make it viscerally clear to you what would happen if we had any kind of hull breach with those hatches open." He shuddered.

Michael let it go as he heard the next batch of crewman coming in through the forward hatch. Before him, Zane had stepped up to a pulley and cable system mounted in the center of the spine, supported by three columns radiating out. The pattern of supports continued down the length of the spine, visually breaking it up into three wedged paths. He followed Zane in but was surprised by some dizziness. "Is there gravity in here?"

"A little at each end, but zero for the length of it. I hope you didn't eat too much at breakfast."

Michael briefly regretted his double helping, but he did not worry much. He had been working in and out of zero gravity most of his life. He stepped forward and saw a handle come around the pulley and catch on the other side, the cable moving along without it.

Zane stepped towards it. "This is the spine express," he said, pointing to the wedges on the left and right. "You can always glide the length of it on your own, but if you do, use those," he said, pointing up towards a series of rungs along the ceiling. "Keep the express lanes clear."

Michael looked at the end of his belt loop. It had a carabineer that would slip right over the handle. Zane clipped his belt loop onto the waiting handle and grabbed it with his hand.

"Clip on and take hold," he said. "Then give it a little twist." When he did, Zane was pulled down the corridor by the handle moving along with the cable.

Michael waited for another handle to appear, and when it did, he clipped on. With a deep breath, he twisted the handle and immediately lost his grip on it as it accelerated down the cable. He had less than a second to worry as the belt pulled tight around him and yanked him off his feet. He braced his arms to catch himself, but he never fell to the deck. Gravity slipped away within a couple of meters, and he was flying down the corridor.

He caught back up with the handle and grabbed hold of it. Zane was ahead of him by about thirty meters. He looked back and waved. Michael nodded and started looking around the passing corridor. It was well lit but fairly boring. Its main features were the central cable system and the rungs along the ceiling. He did pass by some other hatches along those rungs. He could not make out all the lettering, but the biggest read "CARGO 3", followed by "CARGO 4" and so on.

He did not have much time to wonder about them, because after about thirty seconds, Zane began to slow down and before Michael could wonder how, he slowed as well. He unclipped his belt as Zane had, and when the handle finally reached the far pulley, he was already on his feet in the returning gravity of the drive section.

Another full airlock marked the end of the spine, and Michael and Zane passed through it quickly. Terri Schwartz was waiting for them at the other end. "Ah, good to see you made it," she said.

"It was an unexpected ride." More than anything, though, Michael was looking forward to making the trip again. Despite his uncertainty, it had been a lot of fun.

"So I understand you already have a rating in tach drives."

He nodded. The overnight shift was gathering together to depart, but one woman remained steadfast at the console. "Yes, I have a two-T rating."

"That's what the XO said." She looked him up and down. "Awfully young for such a rating."

"I've been on ships my whole life," he replied. In truth, most of these ratings were simply a matter of having picked up the skills necessary to stay alive on a ship for as long as he had. That, and math. Math was always the problem. His struggle with vector calculus was the main reason he had not gotten his navigation rating yet.

"Well, then, we'll see if we can put you to some use."

The rest of the drive crew arrived, and he went through the new guy routine with them. He had studied them on the computer before breakfast, so he was in good shape there. The outgoing shift was all new to him, so he went through the whole routine. Frankly, he was surprised the overnight shift had been so large.

"It's not like environmental," Zane explained. "Their first shift does all the maintenance, both fore and aft, while the other shifts mostly babysit the system. But back here in drives, once we're under tach, we're always monitoring and keeping it running smoothly all the way around the clock."

He was paired up with Zane for the morning, and they went aft to the massive tach sail generators. He had never seen any so big, and the *Heinrich* had not merely one generator like *Sophie*, but four. They sat at a station between the lower two, while Nathan Colton sat at a similar station on a catwalk twenty meters above them.

"Why four?" Michael asked after they had settled in. "Why not a single bigger one instead?"

"Off-axis polarization is a lot easier with more than one." When he saw Michael's confusion, he asked, "Most of your time has been on smaller ships, right?"

He nodded, though *Sophie* was not exactly tiny like the little yachts or touring ships. Still, compared to the *Heinrich*, everything short of the big navy carriers seemed small. "Why would you ever want to polarize the sail off-axis?"

"You're used to the eddies and shifts in the ambient tachyon winds, right?"

"Of course," he replied. Everyone who had ever been on a starship knew about that. The tachyon winds were leftovers from the universe's hyperinflation stage in the first fractional second after the Big Bang, and in an otherwise empty universe they would be uniform and omnidirectional. However, in a universe with planets, stars, and black holes, the winds were perturbed. Tachyons got funny in gravitational fields, and in a galaxy as crowded as the Milky Way, it led to a very chaotic system complete with prevailing winds, storms, and even shock fronts. The chaos was one of the reasons navigation required so much math. "But I still don't see why you'd go off-axis. Why not reorient the ship?"

"Well, if it's going to be significant or for more than an hour or so, yes, we can make course adjustments, but in a ship this size, it's better just to reorient the sails a little. Otherwise, the shearing forces along the spine can start to cause damage."

He thought about the kind of twists and slews the *Sophie* used to do in flight and tried to imagine the *Heinrich* attempting that. "I got it. So you're here to change the polarization?"

Zane nodded. "Kind of. The navigator can actually drive it from her station, but we're here to do any hands-on recalibration if the sails don't respond to her orders."

"Her orders?"

He nodded. "In fact, here comes one now," he said pointing to the monitor. "See that line dip there? That's the tachyon capture rate on the port ventral sail. If that doesn't come back up in another few seconds..."

Several more lights jumped to life on the display as Gabrielle's voice came on over the speaker. "Navigator ordering sail change, port-side ventral, two degrees clockwise, one degree starboard."

Michael sat upright. "What do we do?"

Zane eased him back down with his hand. "Hopefully nothing, but watch the panel. See the sail adjusting?"

He looked back down at the displays and heard the whine of shifting motors above him in the sail generator. The polarization angle was adjusting, first one degree, then one and a half, and eventually two degrees clockwise of its original position. Meanwhile, the sail had tilted itself starboard by a degree. The tachyon capture rate display began to trend back up and after another moment or two settled in on the center line where it had been before.

"See," Zane said. "We're here to make sure it responds according to her orders."

"And if it doesn't?"

"Then we've got a lot of work to do, and we have to do it fast. Usually, of course, there's no hitch, but on that run out to Taschin we hit a nasty patch of turbulence and had both the upper sails lock in the wrong position. We had to drop to about half-speed for two hours while we sorted it out."

Michael nodded. *Sophie*'s sail had jammed on him a few times, pushing them off course, but he knew how to smooth it out. There was a feel to it, he thought, where you could time the power fluctuations to dampen out the sail vibrations.

But looking up at the four massive generators around him, he knew that it would take him a while to learn the feel of these engines.

He caught up with Gabrielle after dinner. After that day in engineering, navigation was taking on a whole new dimension.

"Yeah, I heard you were down in engineering today," she said as they settled into the small common room at the end of his section of deck four.

"Was that typical? I mean, the four sail shifts?"

She considered it. "Pretty typical. Sometimes there are more, sometimes less. I almost never get through a shift without moving the sails at least once, but like today, they're almost always small shifts. Anything more than that and we would change course."

He nodded. "How often does that happen?"

She shrugged. "Depends, maybe every two or three weeks. We're almost always in the main shipping lanes, and we have good data on those, so there's rarely anything to skirt around that we didn't already plan for when setting out from port. But then last week we got surprised by a transient eddy moving across the lane."

"And can you order a course change on your own?"

"Technically no. Whoever has the bridge gives that order, usually the XO on my shift, but I've never had a course change overridden on the *Heinrich*." She smiled to herself. "On my last post I had a captain who was always second guessing, but Corazon has confidence in me."

He thought about it. He did not think the XO had much confidence in him. "What's she like, the XO? I've really only talked to her once," he said. He did not add that it had almost devolved into insubordination.

"She's good," Gabrielle answered, glancing around lowering her voice. "She's practically a captain on her own, licensed and everything."

Michael let his confusion show. "Then why is she here?"

"It's how S&W selects new captains. They pull a stint as XO for either Dad or old man Williams, but since he's been flying a desk back on Callista Prime, it's pretty much just Dad. If they pass muster, then the next captain slot that opens is theirs."

"And if they don't?"

"Usually they end up serving as first officer on another of our ships, but Dad bounced the last one right out of the company. I never heard the full story, but she had to cash out all her shares at a discount."

"Shares?"

"Yeah, ship shares as opposed to corporate shares. You know about ship shares, right?"

He shook his head still not understanding. Malcolm had simply been the owner, no questions asked. Sure, he gave out bonuses after particularly successful runs, but no one else had any claim of shares on the *Sophie*.

"Wow," Gabrielle said. "I guess when you grow up with it, it's all part of the background of life. Corporate shares are shares in the S&W company, and they give you certain voting rights along with a dividend from corporate profits. Ship shares are shares in your own ship. They don't have voting rights or anything — after all, the captain's word is law — but they give you a share of the ship's profit. Corporate always hangs onto at least thirty percent of the ship's shares, but it's common for the crew to hold the majority."

"Which kind is better?"

"Depends on the ship. For a good ship like the *Heinrich*, ship shares make you a lot more money, so I've been shifting as many of my corporate shares over as I can." She must have seen his confusion, so she went on. "You can move shares back and forth between ship and corporate at a rate based on the ship's past performance. The *Heinrich* buy-in is a steep price, but I think it's worth it."

Michael thought about it, trying to understand the shifting ownership structures between corporate and crew. "But wouldn't you be better off buying into a poorer ship and turning it around?"

She shrugged. "I'd have to be on that other ship, or course, but if I could bring in enough of the right crew, maybe. That's actually how a lot of our newer captains make their mark. Captain Kashari did that on the *Jack of Diamonds* two years ago. She got her posting, hand selected four officers to buy in with her, and they turned it from the laggard of the fleet into the third best earner, which given its smaller size is saying something."

Michael was not about to give up on *Sophie*, but he was curious about his own prospects. "What about me? Do I have any shares?"

Gabrielle shrugged. "Dad would know. Since you're family, you automatically earn a few ship shares, but not very fast. Still, you're bound to have some corporate shares from your folks. Uncle Pete died young, of course, but I think Grandfather staked him out pretty well."

Grandfather? That was a bit much to take in. "And how is Gramps?"

She shook her head. "Died two years ago. Dad took it hard. I think that's why he was so glad to find you."

Michael shuddered. "He's got a funny way of showing it."

She frowned. "I don't know what happened in the past, but I can tell you the future. Sooner or later, you're going to have to make peace with him."

"Why should I?" he scoffed.

She set her jaw. "He's family, just like I am, and we're the only family you have now."

He shook his head. "He's the one that walked away. He's the one who has to make peace with me."

Chapter 12

"I once thought I'd found my place in life, but then the place moved." — Malcolm Fletcher

THE REST OF THE week went by in a blur. He pulled shifts in mechanical, technical, aft environmental — little more than a watch-stander — and one on the bridge. He observed the pilot and got a few simulations from the communications officer, but mostly he sat next to Gabrielle and watched her at the navigation console.

He had seen displays like it before on *Sophie*, but he did not understand them any more now than he had then. Still, she was patient and tried to explain as it was happening. "See that inflection point on the crosswind third derivative," she said, pointing. "If that holds, we'll get an inflection on the second derivative and may have to shift sails to compensate."

"But... why do you care about the crosswind? I mean, the whole point of the polarization filters on the sails is to only capture the on-axis wind, right?"

"Yes, but you have to understand the shape of the tachyon winds in all four dimensions including spin. See there," she said, pointing again, "we're heading into a second derivative inflection on the crosswind. See how the on-axis capture is starting to slacken off?"

That much he knew how to read. It was almost an exact duplicate of the readout in engineering. "Yeah, but how could you tell it was coming?"

She shook her head in disappointment. "Because the inflection points on the crosswind derivative told me we were riding through the leading edge of an eddy curve."

He shook his own head. So much math. "And you knew it was an eddy curve and not shock front because...?"

She shrugged. "The coefficient curve looks different. I can show you the proof in the integrals later, but right now I have orders to give." She nodded to the XO and opened up the comm to the drive section. "Navigation ordering sail change, starboard side both, three degrees up, eight degrees counter-clockwise."

It went on from there. He never saw his uncle, but he felt him twice. It was something in the way the rest of the bridge crew stiffened when he came on deck. At one point, he would swear Hans had been standing right behind him, but he never turned to look, and his uncle never said a word.

Michael spent most of his evenings split between the gym and his quarters studying names and faces. With all the shifts he had pulled, he had already met everyone, and most were becoming familiar, but he did not want to take any chances. He kept flashing through the crew manifest on his monitor until he felt he could remember them all.

By the sixth day, the rest of the crew had taken on a new ritual in the corridors. Every time they approached, they would cover up their name patches, and call out, "Hey, new guy!" He would then call back with their name, department, and shift. It was a little maddening, but he was growing in confidence that he would pass whatever test they had in mind.

The sixth night, he got a message from Corazon. "Report to my office, 08:00. Not 08:01."

He set himself an alarm for six and ran through the faces one more time until he was confident. It occurred to him then, that in all the faces he had looked at, there was one he had never pulled up: Peter Schneider. He was not on the crew of course, but he figured there had to be some records of his biological father in the computer. He started to type the name into the search field but stopped himself.

"No," he said aloud. "The last thing I need right now is one more face."

He woke before his alarm, decided against running through the faces again, took a shower, and got dressed. He was the first in line at breakfast. They had not even finished setting out all the food, but he could see what he was in store for. All three of the galley crew had taped over their name and department patches.

He took it as best as he could. While waiting at the counter, he greeted each one in turn. Name, department, shift. He snagged three kolaches and some eggs.

He sat where he could watch the doors, and sure enough, each crewmember coming in had taped over their patches. They would wave and call out, "Hey, new guy!" and he would respond with name, department, and shift.

It seemed like everyone cycled through breakfast that morning, even those on the third shift. His neighbor Karen called out from the line, holding two steaming biscuits, "Hey, new guy!"

And so it went. Name, department, shift. Name, department, shift.

He had not kept count, but when the line stopped growing, he felt he had gotten them all but two, his uncle and the XO. It was still only 07:20.

He thought about going up then and seeing if the XO was in yet, but he did not want to look desperate. Instead, he wandered around deck three for a while, peeking in at the clock in the galley on every orbit. When it finally reached 7:45 he went up.

He pressed the signal on the XO's door, but he heard no response. A flip-down seat hung from the wall outside her office, so he took it. The shift change was well underway, but most of them ignored him as they filtered past. The one person who did pause to speak was the last one he would have expected.

It was his uncle.

He paused upon entering the hall at the rear of the bridge. He glanced down at him, but he did not try to make eye contact. "Michael," he said.

"Yes, sir?"

"Good luck," he said, and then walked into his own office.

The XO walked past at 7:55 and paused at the door. "I told you to report at oh-eight-hundred."

He hopped to his feet. "Yes, ma'am."

"It's five 'til."

He nodded. "Yes, ma'am. You also told me not to report at eight oh one. You did not give any orders about not arriving before that."

She took a sip of her coffee. "Very well then, I'll see you in five minutes."

He watched her go into her own office and leaned back against the bulkhead, banging his head against it softly.

At 7:59 he stepped to her door and looked forward at the clock on the center viewscreen of the bridge. With ten seconds left, he put his finger on the chime, and when the clock ticked over, he pressed it.

The door opened, and he walked in. The XO looked up from behind her desk. "Well, I see you've learned the lesson of punctuality."

"Yes, ma'am."

"And did you learn any other lessons this week?"

"Yes, ma'am. Several."

She took another sip of her coffee. It was already half gone. "And what would you say was the most important lesson to you, personally?"

116

His eyes went wide. The list of names and faces flashed by, of course, but that hardly counted as a lesson. He had definitely been impressed by the off-axis sail polarization, but then there had been that glimmer of insight when he finally saw that the navigation math truly could tell you about the shape of the tachyon winds. Of course, he also remembered matters of water pressure, multi-user computer management, measuring lubrication viscosity on the lift rails, and algae life cycles.

He had already known many of these skills. Most were a little different on *Heinrich* than they had been on *Sophie*, but Malcolm had taught him well. That, of course, reminded him of one of the very first lessons, with Harry taking him in hand and showing him how to run the patch-stitcher. Without that he would not have even had his own name.

He opened his mouth to tell the XO precisely that, but he caught himself. Harry could have told him he was out of luck. Charlie could have let his uncle find him on that first shift, deep in the plumbing, but he had not. And then Zane had guided him back along the spine to report to his first engineering shift, and Gabrielle had gone to great lengths to show not merely how the math worked but why it mattered. Yes, he was family, for whatever that mattered to the various cousins, but he was fundamentally the New Guy, dumb and useless.

He realized he was standing there with his mouth hanging open as Corazon looked up at him, so he closed it, blinked a couple of times and said the first thing that rolled out of his brain. "The crew looks out for each other."

She smiled. "That's a good answer. Not your first one though?"

He shrugged. "I thought about the name patch machine," he confessed.

She chuckled. "Fair enough. Let's get to the names." She pointed to the wall display at the end of the room. "I'm going to flash their pictures on that wall. I want to know the crewmember's name, their department, their shift, and anything else that comes to mind."

He nodded, bracing himself.

The first image came up. It was the upper third of an environmental suit, with a strong light shining against it, obscuring most of the faceplate in a shiny reflective white-out. He blinked twice and starting panting, his heart surging towards panic. How was he supposed to pick out the faces in this? He could barely even spot the chin, covered in a dark goatee. His mind raced. He could think of three men on board with goatees, but Richardson was a red-head. That left Majors and Brookstone.

And then he realized how stupid he really was. The environment suits all have the occupant's name painted onto the chest plate right along with their departmental symbol. He started laughing, and he kept laughing almost to the point of bending over. He was finally brought up short by a curt "Ahem!" from Corazon.

He looked back at her, completely unable to contain his grin. "Yes, ma'am?"

"Is there something funny about the test you'd like to share?"

He shook his head and did his best to regain his composure. "No, ma'am. That's Walter Brookstone, comm and computers, first shift." He remembered him clearly, including his uniform gaffe at that first disastrous dinner. "He looks good in his dress uniform, but I think the vest is too tight across his belly."

Corazon nodded, and the screen changed. It was another environment suit. "That's Roxy Collier, mechanical systems, first shift. She has a daughter who raises pigs."

"Pigs?"

"Yes, ma'am," he replied, all of it coming back. "Her son-in-law has a farm on Arvin."

Then came Billy Mason and his card tricks, Karen Larkin and her kickboxing, Maggie Nelson and her grandmother's sourdough recipe, and on through the rest of the crew. For his uncle, he merely said, "Hans Schneider, Captain." He could have said more, of course. At a minimum he probably should have mentioned that he was his uncle, but he was not ready to give ground on that yet.

The final picture was the XO. "Felicia Corazon, first officer." He turned back to face her. "The rumor is you'll get the next captaincy slot in Schneider and Williams."

She raised an eyebrow. "Is that so?"

"Yes, ma'am. That is the rumor."

She nodded to him. "All right. Now tell me, mister, who was missing?"

He blinked at her. "Missing?"

"That's right. One of the crew was missing from that sequence of photographs. Who was it?"

He started to panic again. He had not been keeping count. He started running through them, department by department, trying to remember whether or not he had seen them in the photos. He counted them up on his hands as he went, but it kept adding up to all of them. He could not think of a single crewman who had not been in the photos.

He shook his head grimly. "I'm sorry, ma'am. I can't think of anyone."

"Clearly you were thinking of quite a few. I saw you counting. How many were there?"

"Sixty-three," he replied.

She sighed. "I'm sorry, mister, but our crew complement is sixty-four, not sixty-three."

And then Charlie's words came back to him, from his first day on board. "Sixty-four," he had said, "and you're one of them."

Michael looked back to meet the XO's eyes. "It's me, ma'am. Michael Fletcher, currently unassigned."

She smiled at him. "Indeed it is, Mr. Fletcher. Welcome to the crew."

The relief hit him so hard, he almost fell over. "Thank you, ma'am."

She shook his hand. "You're to report to Ms. Schwartz in engineering, first shift. That's your best rating, and that's where we have an opening. It's almost nine, so get a move on."

He stepped out of her office to find the bridge and hallway packed with his fellow crewmates. There must have been thirty of forty crammed in, all clapping and chanting his name. "Michael! Michael! Michael!"

He was one of them now. New Guy no more.

But his uncle's door remained closed.

Chapter 13

"Your crewmates are your best friends out here. They'll get you out of at least as many jams as they'll get you into."
— *Malcolm Fletcher*

FELICIA CORAZON ATE DINNER with Hans Schneider that night, alone in the officers' wardroom. She had dispatched the steward after the main course, promising to finish off all the serving herself if need be. This was not a rare occurrence. This kind of dinner was one of the few times she and her ostensible captain could speak privately outside the formality of the captain's ready room.

"We're scheduled to reach Ballison in the morning, about an hour after shift change."

"That's good time, maybe half a day early."

"Which puts us only six days behind from the Taschin detour," she replied.

He shrugged. "It had to be done."

She poured herself another cup of coffee. "I'm not complaining, sir. Your nephew looks to be a solid crewman and seems likely to fill that engineer post quite well."

"Well, I'm sure the boy is fairly sharp. Peter was always at the head of his class, and Sophia seemed to have her wits about her. But what do you make of his ratings? Are they the result of lax testing?"

She considered it. From what she had heard so far, she was starting to suspect the opposite, but she wanted to tread lightly. "It's too early to say, and no one has given him a proper evaluation on any of them. However, from what Ms. Schwartz says, I think he definitely qualifies for a tach drive one rating. I'll give her a few weeks before I ask her to give an opinion on his supposed drive two rating."

Hans toyed with his dessert. "Fair enough."

"Nonetheless, sir, I would like to mark that position as filled for now and pull the posting from the corporate office on Ballison."

"You're that confident?"

"Yes, provided he stays."

Hans sighed. "Well, then I suppose we should vest his ship shares and start him on the proper family track."

"Obviously, I leave that decision to you, sir. Does he have any corporate shares?"

"Only a handful," he replied, taking a tentative bite of the custard. "Peter and Sophia had a reasonably large piece, but they had shifted most of it into ship shares of the *Kaiser's Folly*."

"And those are gone?"

"Indeed, perished with the ship. Normally we would use the insurance to repatriate the shares back to corporate, but..." he trailed off, pushing the dessert away.

"An act of war?"

He nodded. "Somewhere past Malcolm Fletcher on my revenge list is the adjuster from Eternity Trust. It's only money, but I've done what I can to him. I know four shipping lines that pulled their business from Eternity on my word alone."

"About Fletcher..." she trailed off.

"What of him? He's already dead. Very little I can do to him now."

This was what she had been dancing around. "I was actually speaking of your nephew Michael. He seems attached to Fletcher's name."

Hans set his jaw into a firm frown. "I believe I've already made my feelings known on this."

"I know you have, sir, and so has your nephew."

"I'm sure he has, but he's only a boy. He doesn't understand yet."

She shrugged. "Well, he seems quite adamant, sir. I understand he made his own uniform patches. I think he even repainted his environment suit, and I hear he got out the engraver set to rework the tag on his formal jacket."

He shook his head. "That's exactly my point. He's a doer, just like Peter. Sooner or later, he's going to realize how much he truly is his father's son."

She hesitated, looking for another angle. "Perhaps, but in the meantime, his ratings are in the name of Michael Fletcher. Even his Confederate passport is in that name. I know you listed him as Schneider on the crew manifest, but I must point out that we're going to run afoul at the docks if we're mismatched."

Hans brushed it aside with his hands. "None of that matters. When he was born, I made a promise to his father."

"I understand that, sir, but you also made a promise to me when I became your first officer, that you leave decisions about the crew to me, and I have a crewman who may very well jump ship if his captain will not bend on this."

Hans stared at her. "You would really... you would make a stand over this, for this boy you don't know?"

She sat as straight as she could. This is what it came down to. "Yes, sir. He is a member of my crew, and I will make a stand for him."

He gritted his teeth, but a sigh eventually stole the stiffness away from his shoulders. "Very well, Felicia. I will yield to your decision here. I disagree, but I will not override it."

"Thank you, sir."

He looked over the table. "You may go," he told her. "I'll send for the steward when I'm done."

She stood and walked to the door. "Good night, sir."

Michael was still settling into his station next to Zane the next morning when the order came. "Sail release, stage one, in sixty seconds... mark."

Michael looked up at the clock. He knew it was all handled by the computers, that he had nothing to do by hand, but it was still a habit.

Zane pointed at the displays. "You can see our capture rate is already down twelve percent from the star's interference. When we come up on the planet, it'll really drop."

The sixty second mark came, and the sails stepped down in size sharply. Their capture rate fell accordingly, but at least it smoothed out. The smaller sail configuration was less prone to gravitational interference. He knew the theory well, but again, it was the math that had scared him off of attempting the tach-three rating.

The capture rate settled down to a steady line, and Michael did what figuring he could do. "We're down to about fifty lights now, right?"

Zane nodded. "Thereabouts, should be forty-eight according to specs. The next release should bring us down to about five, then about one and a half before she sets the final transition vectors."

Gabrielle's voice sounded again. "Sail release, stage two, in thirty seconds... mark."

The sails pulled in even tighter, though Michael could see the bottom port sail flutter in the process, with its capture rate fluctuating chaotically through the spin direction. He was reaching to give it a polarization thump when Zane pulled his hand back. "No, let it go," he said.

Sure enough, it settled on its own. "What was that?" Michael asked.

Zane shook his head. "That generator has been stuttering on the down-tachs for three months. It always settles out, and it's otherwise operating to specs, but I don't like it."

Michael thought about it. There had been plenty of imperfections on *Sophie*, some they lived with, some they feared they might not live with. "What are we going to do about it?"

"Nothing for now. It's never on the final down-tach, so Gabrielle and the navigation computers can always make any final adjustments. Wait, here comes the next one."

"Stage three in fifteen… mark."

Michael watched it more closely this time, and the sails pulled in smoothly, snapping into their smallest configuration immediately.

"See," Zane said. "In six months we've got a three-week layover scheduled at Callista Prime. I suspect that will be a working holiday for us, but until then we're keeping our eyes on it."

"Transition set, drop sails in twenty… mark."

Michael took a deep breath. He always hated this part. Transition was the point of letting go of all the tachyon wind and keeping whatever sublight momentum you wanted to pull off them. When everything worked out, you put yourself on a nice vector into the orbital traffic patterns, but if the navigator did it wrong, you could easily end up on a high-speed course into a very large rock. It had not happened for over forty years, but that was only because navigation math had gotten that good.

Yeah, math.

He only kept his eyes open to be able to watch the displays. Back on *Sophie* he usually had them closed when he could.

But the clock ticked down, and the sails dropped precisely on schedule.

The speaker was silent for a moment, and then Jake Norris came on. "Secure sails, prepare low power deceleration thrust."

125

They flipped through the switches to take the sail generators offline and spun around in their seats to the consoles behind them. The sublight gravity pulse drives were not nearly so massive, but they would never take them far either. When they came online, Zane pointed him towards the status switch. "If you'll do the honors, you can report us ready."

Michael flipped it over to green and waited for the pilot's controls to start flowing into the engines. Within a minute they did, and the hum of the gravity pulses started up, much softer and lower pitched than the sail generators.

The next voice they heard was the XO's. "Estimate docking at eleven hundred. Cargo crew to load stations by twelve hundred. Crew liberty to begin at thirteen hundred. Check watch schedule for station duty rotation."

Zane's face took on a contented look. "Ah, liberty, sweet liberty."

Michael nodded. "What's station liberty usually like? I'm more used to groundside."

He shrugged. "Depends on the station. I've got a lady friend on Ballison, so that makes this one particularly sweet, but Ballison is ok. Arvin's a lot better, what with the navy base and all, but I don't know any of the locals."

A lady friend. He thought of Josie, and it stung. Even if they ever went back to Taschin for some reason, Josie would be down on the ground, not on the station. Not that it mattered. The *Heinrich* would likely never pass through Taschin again.

They all piled into the same hotel and rented out the bulk of one floor, only to find out that the crew of the *Windy Wilhelm* had bought out the floor below them. This brought about a raucous cheer from the rest of the crew.

"The *Windy Wilhelm*?" Michael asked.

Karen was the closest. "Our sister ship," she answered over the cheers. "We usually intersect with her every few months. Always a big party."

"To the Hopping Hole!" Gabrielle declared from the registration desk. "Leave your bags and pick up your keys later. It's time to teach those windy windbags how to drink!"

And off they went. Ballison station was significantly larger than Taschin station, with three full rings, but most of the cargo vessels were clustered on the bottom one, and the Hopping Hole bar was not far from the hotel.

The bar looked big from the outside, mostly in that it was the only door for thirty meters in either direction. The crew lined up in front of the entrance as the bouncer waved them in. Karen went in just before him and immediately jumped on the back of another man in the blue and gray of the S&W uniforms. He laughed and staggered over to one of the bars where he dropped her off on a stool.

Michael was about to follow when the bouncer put out his hand. "Excuse me, can I see some ID?"

He reached for his pocket and then realized he had left his passport in his bag back at the hotel. "I'm sorry, man. I don't have it."

Charlie stepped up behind him. "What's the problem?"

"Your friend doesn't have any ID."

"Well, I can vouch for him. He's *Heavy Heinrich* like the rest of us."

The bouncer shook his head. "He looks a little young."

Charlie looked past them and waved his hand. "Gabrielle!" He turned back to the bouncer. "Don't say I didn't give you a chance, buster."

The bouncer was opening his mouth to reply when Gabrielle came back, already with a mug of beer in her hand. "What's the problem, Charlie?"

He pointed to the bouncer. "This guy doesn't want to let Michael in."

Gabrielle turned her eyes towards the bouncer, and in that moment, Michael saw his friendly cousin disappear. It was like looking at the XO, or worse, his uncle. She cocked an eyebrow and asked, "Is that so?"

"Look, miss, I'm not trying to cause any trouble, but the station regs say he's got to be eighteen. If I'm not sure, I'm required to ask for ID."

"Well, I don't want to cause any trouble either," she replied, "but I'm telling you that he's with us, and he's fine to come in."

The bouncer looked back and forth between Gabrielle and Michael. Michael opened his mouth to say something, but Gabrielle silenced him with a glare. The bouncer summoned a passable smile. "Perhaps we can send someone for his ID, miss. I wouldn't think it would take long."

She shook her head and took a step closer. An older man with an officer's stripe stepped up behind her. His name patch read Williams, and he was from the *Windy Wilhelm*. "Hey, Gabby, is there a problem?"

"No," she replied. "I was simply explaining that either he lets my cousin in, or we all leave."

The bouncer stammered. "I, um, I don't think..."

She tapped at her name patch with one finger. "Do you know who my father is?"

He gulped. "I can guess."

"Then I think you should know that there are fifteen other clubs on this station that would love to hold the tab for Schneider & Williams shipping. It's up to you whether your bosses get to keep it."

The *Wilhelm* crewman leaned forward beside Gabrielle. "You know," he said with a little nod, "what she said."

The bartender turned back to Michael, apparently to escape Gabrielle's withering stare if nothing else. "I'm so sorry for the misunderstanding, sir. All Schneider and Williams crew are welcome here, of course. My mistake."

Michael stepped past, and Gabrielle guided him to the bar. "Michael, this is Quincy Williams of the *Windy Windbag*."

Quincy gave her a quick swat on the behind. "*Wilhelm*, you heavy heiny!"

Michael extended a hand, and Quincy took it. "So you're Gabrielle's cousin… on her mom's side, right?"

"No," Gabrielle answered. "Dad's."

Quincy's eyes went wide. "Holy shit, you're Pete's kid."

Michael nodded.

Quincy stepped forward and grabbed him by both shoulders. "My God, it's like a time machine. You look just like him!"

Gabrielle stepped between them with a couple of beer mugs. "Except for the mustache, remember?"

Quincy took the mug. "Oh, that's right. The Broom of Doom!"

Michael took his mug as well. "Broom?"

Gabrielle shook her head. "He had this incredibly bristly mustache, always tickled when he'd kiss me on the cheek."

Quincy raised his mug to them. "To long-lost Pete and the Broom of Doom!"

Michael raised his glass and joined in the chorus.

Quincy drank it all back and slammed the glass down on the counter. He seemed about to say something to Michael when someone else caught his eye. "Maggie Nelson, you get your fine ass over here!"

Michael looked to see Maggie, their head chef, running into Quincy's waiting arms. After a long kiss, Quincy threw one look back at them. "I'll catch up with you two later."

Gabrielle laughed and turned back to the bar, beckoning Michael to join her. "It's always a good time when we run into another ship in the fleet, but the *Wilhelm* is a special treat."

He nodded and took a sip of his beer. Further back in the club, he could see Karen sitting on a table talking to one of the men from the *Wilhelm*. "So, tell me, what are the rules?"

"What rules?"

He shrugged, trying to play it cool but failing. "You know, rules on fraterizing. Fratization. Dammit!"

"Fraternization?" she asked.

"Yes, that."

"I say knock yourself out. I can think of several pretty gals on the *Wilhelm*." She started scanning around. "I bet Suzie Milton would love to pounce you, but I haven't seen her yet."

"Oh, yeah, I guess."

She turned back to look at him. "Oh, you meant within the crew, didn't you?"

"Yeah. I'm curious."

She shook her head with a smile. "It's not disallowed, but don't do it within your own department. Try it and you'll both find yourselves on opposing twelve-hour shifts."

He nodded. "Not much pickings back in engineering anyway."

Gabrielle's eyes lit up. "You're already thinking about someone, aren't you?

He sat bolt upright. "No, honest, I was only curious."

She laughed at him and raised her empty mug for a refill. "You've got the hots for Karen Larkin, don't you?"

"What? Why would you say that?"

She leaned over and lowered her voice beneath the din of the club. "Word travels, biscuit boy. Word travels."

"Oh," he replied and took another sip of his beer.

"Look, let her have her fun in port, and see what happens on board. Just don't let it get too serious. Things can get messy. Understand?"

He nodded. "Thanks, and thanks for before."

"What? That flunky at the door?"

"Yeah."

"You're crew, Michael. It comes with the territory, and despite what you might think, the name does have certain advantages."

He grimaced. Advantages or not, he was not ready to swallow it.

Chapter 14

"They say the past always catches up with you, sooner or later. I prefer sooner, because by the time later rolls around, the past has picked up a lot of speed." — Malcolm Fletcher

JIMMY ANDERS WALKED INTO the Lucky Black and took a seat at the bar.

"What's your poison?" the bartender asked.

He put a twenty-credit note on the counter. "Do you have any Ersut Vodka?"

The bartender raised an eyebrow but still reached under the counter for an unlabeled bottle. "You've been through here before, but I don't recognize you."

He watched the glass being poured and licked at his lips. "It's been a while, but I remember my favorite local blend. It still has the root, yes?"

"I don't make it. I just serve it."

"Fair enough."

The bartender took the twenty and pulled out a ten from the register.

"No, kind sir, you keep that."

The bartender smiled at him and wandered off to leave Jimmy in peace with his drink. He took a sip and picked up a trace of that tonja root taste. It was not nearly as effective to drink it as to smoke it, but he knew he would have a nice low-grade buzz for the next hour or so. When he finished, Jimmy called him back over. "Can I get a beer to chase that? Whatever you've got on tap is fine." He laid another twenty on the counter as the mug was delivered. "You keep that, too," he said.

The bartender looked at him a moment. "Is there anything I can do for you?"

"Well, now that you mention it, I'm looking for a friend of mine, thought maybe he'd been through here."

"A friend?"

Jimmy shrugged. "Friend, business associate. He didn't make our meet-up out on Nasar, so I thought I'd check here."

The bartender still held the twenty in his hand. "What's your friend's name?"

"Fletcher," he said. "Malcolm Fletcher of the *Sophie's Grace.*"

The bartender slid the twenty into his pocket. "Then I'm sorry to be the one to tell you, but your friend is dead."

"Dead?" Jimmy asked in feigned shock. "Are you sure?"

He nodded. "We had the wake right here, maybe two months ago."

"Well, damn, that is bad news. He was a good guy."

"That's what I heard."

"I have to say, I didn't know his crew very well, but I knew his boy Michael. Do you know where he is? It would be nice to stop in and pay my respects."

"Sorry, I don't know. The last I saw of him was at the wake."

"Too bad," he replied and lifted the beer to his lips before pulling it away. "I worry about him, a kid like that on his own."

The bartender looked away for a moment. "You know, I think Fletcher had a girlfriend here in port. She might know. Annie... something, I don't know."

"Annie, eh?" He took a sip this time. He was definitely starting to feel the tonja buzz. "Working girl?"

He nodded. "Yeah, you might try over at the Far Meridian after dark."

"Thanks."

Michael sat at the station next to Zane, rubbing his temples. Liberty had ended at nineteen hundred the night before, and they had pushed back and headed out during second shift. The *Wilhelm* had pulled out the day before that, but that had not stopped the party. Michael had thrown away every drinking lesson Malcolm had ever taught him, and as the drone of the tach drive morphed into a steady throb, he deeply regretted it.

"A little too much liberty?" Zane asked.

"More like libation than liberty," he replied.

"Well, I guess that's to be expected. I heard the *Wilhelm* was in port."

He nodded. "How about you?"

"Oh, nice and quiet. My girl and I went groundside for a couple of days. She's got a friend with a little hut down on the beach. It was a tad cold, mind you, but still a very refreshing change from this," he said, waving up at the maze of machinery and catwalks around them.

Michael remembered that last day out on the beach with Josie. He missed her.

"And how about you? Did you have any special rendezvous with anyone from the *Wilhelm*?"

He shook his head, feeling his brain bounce back and forth. He might have had a chance with that Celine girl from their mechanical department, but it did not happen. They talked and drank together for almost two hours on the second night, but he never got up the nerve to make a move on her. Finally, she retreated back to her crewmates, and he later saw her with Walter Brookstone. After that, he settled for making friends and tasting all that Ballison station had to offer. Clearly, it had offered too much.

133

"Well, no shame in it, my boy. There are other ships, other ports, and lots of other girls."

He nodded, mesmerized by the flickering display of the tachyon capture rate. It dipped once, then twice, and then started to decline. "Hey," he said, "I think we've got a sail change coming."

Zane laughed. "I knew you were going to work out. Hungover, and you're already spotting them before the navigator is."

Sure enough, Gabrielle's voice came pounding through the comm. "Navigator ordering sail change, starboard-side dorsal, one degree counter-clockwise, three degrees to port."

Michael saw stars as her voice faded, but fortunately, the sails shifted according to orders.

Zane slapped him on the back. "Yep, you're going to do just fine."

Jimmy Anders sped through the video playback, pausing only at the movements. The camera was remote, tucked beneath a third-story balcony several blocks away. It was not a live feed, since a constant broadcast might draw the attention of some electronic snoopers, but he passed by once every ten hours to download the compressed video. The quality was pretty poor, but it was good enough to get the feel for what happened at Annie Fowler's place.

He had found her easily enough, and she had remembered Fletcher, but as soon as he asked about the boy, she got a faraway look and said she could not remember any boy.

In his line of work, he had been lied to quite a bit. She was not even in the junior league.

So he had feigned confusion and bid her good night. He thought about following her then, but he knew she would already be suspicious. Of course, she was not suspicious enough to not go back to the same club the very next night, go out with another man, and then let herself be followed on her way home after leaving his hotel.

In his younger days, Jimmy would have simply busted down her door after she had gone in, but the prize in question here warranted more caution. So he watched and waited. Forty-eight hours of video surveillance taught him a lot. For starters, she did not live alone. The girl seemed a little old to be a daughter, and after following her one night, he realized she was just another prostitute. They never seemed to bring their business home with them, and from the pattern of window lights, it seemed that the girl had a room of her own. So, she was not a transient couch surfer.

A few more drinks at a few more bars gave him a name: Josie Coron. He had a list of her specialties as well as her usual hangouts. The best information, however, was that she had dropped out of the business for a few weeks the previous month. He checked the dates and saw that this would have been shortly after Malcolm's wake. That was a coincidence worth following up on, so on the third day he followed her out of the apartment building, through the warren of the port's residential district, and into the corner grocer.

He timed his introduction to bump into her rounding the corner of the bread aisle. She dropped her items. He dropped his. Amidst mutual apologies, they knelt to the floor and started sorting out the mess.

As soon as she looked up to meet his face, he feigned recognition. "I'm sorry, miss, but you wouldn't be Josie, would you?"

She smiled. "Yes, I am. Have we met?"

He handed her the last of her items. "Once, maybe twice. I was a friend of Malcolm's. Malcolm Fletcher that is."

"Oh," she said, her smile fading.

"It was just in passing, but Malcolm mentioned you a few times. Shame about him, though."

She nodded. "Oh yeah, tragic really."

"I know. I heard about it over on Nasar and came as soon as I could get away. Mostly I wanted to check in on Michael, see how he's taking it."

She frowned. "Yeah, he took it pretty hard. I didn't go to the wake, but we talked about it after."

"Oh, then you know him. How's he doing?"

"I guess he was okay when he left."

"Left? Where? I heard his ship was still in port."

"His uncle came for him a few weeks back."

Uncle? Malcolm had only ever mentioned one sibling, a dead sister. "Uncle? I guess I didn't know about him."

"Uncle, cousin, something like that... named Hans. He made a big deal about coming, diverting his ship and everything. Kind of a dick if you ask me."

He thought of trying to pump her for more information, maybe the name of the uncle's ship, but she was starting to move towards the checkout scanners. He tried to put on a reassuring smile. "Well, at least he's with family now. That has to be worth something."

"I guess," she said. "I was going to write him soon. Anything I should pass along?"

He shook his head. "No, just one more old friend of Malcolm's wishing him well."

She paused at the scanner and looked back, but Jimmy had already moved into the next aisle. The last thing he wanted was for her to remember him as anything but a passing encounter. After she left, he made his way back to the Guild lounge and starting a search of recent ships passing through.

There it was, three weeks back, the *Heavy Heinrich*, one of S&W's four big container ships. The captain was listed as Hans Schneider. Holy shit, but Hans Schneider? He was the most senior captain in the entire S&W fleet, and it would not be too many more years before he would be pulled up into the CEO slot at Callista Prime. He had never known Malcolm had any brothers, let alone someone like this. More likely, he thought, that Schneider had been a brother-in-law or something even more distant.

That kind of family connection would make any kind of extraction that much more difficult, but on the other hand, who was to say a simple data con game could not end with a little ransom to spice it up? That was outside of his skill set, but he knew the people who could make it work.

The *Heinrich's* next port of call had been listed as Ballison, so he checked out of his hotel and signaled his crew to make ready to depart. They were going to have to push hard to get in front of the boy with the right lure.

Michael was in his quarters after dinner, looking over the navigation math again. Gabrielle had sent him the data log from the navigational computer from that day's first shift along with some highlighted notes on which key pieces of data had told her how to react. It was still fairly dense stuff, but Michael found that this was much more concrete than the standard academic text was. That was all hyper-torus flux rolls and shock-wave rotations, but what Gabrielle had sent him was the missing half from his tach-drive engineering knowledge. Knowing how it fit with what he already understood suddenly made the math much more intuitive.

Well, at least a little more intuitive. After two hours of it, he was going cross-eyed over vector integrals. He decided to give it a rest and look for something more entertaining on the console. He still had not loaded his entertainment modules that he had brought from *Sophie*, but he did not want to attempt that tonight. A couple of the games were a little pornographic, and he needed to talk to Wally Brookstone again about how private the crew data partitions were before he installed any of those.

Other than the navigation studies, he only had easy links to the galley menu, the movie schedule, the planned maintenance work in engineering, and the files he had put together when learning the crew's names. Certainly that was a mere fraction of the ship's network. He simply had not searched beyond that yet.

Search, he thought. There was a search he had contemplated before Ballison that he had never followed through on. He sighed. It may as well be now.

He pulled up the personnel search and typed in the name: Peter Schneider. Two names came up: Peter K. Schneider, S&W founder, deceased 3312, and Peter F. Schneider, captain, deceased 3381. He selected the second name and froze when the file opened.

It was like looking in a mirror. The same hair, the same chin, the same nose, and even the same earlobes. The only differences were the eyes, which seemed more gray than blue, and the mustache. Quincy Williams' words rang in his ears, "the broom of doom." He smiled at it a bit. It was indeed as bushy as one of those push brooms he knew from the docks.

So this was Peter, his biological father. He pictured Malcolm's face in his head, and even from his memory, he was left with no doubt. He had not wanted to believe the records, and even the blood types were poor evidence in his heart. Certainly he had accepted it intellectually, but until he saw that picture, it had not penetrated to his emotions.

Having done so, the facts left him numb. He knew so much about Sophia from all of Malcolm's stories, but Peter was a complete blank. He seemed to be little more than a sperm donor with a face.

Text flowed on beneath the picture. Married to Sophia Grace Ross, 3379. Son Michael William Schneider, born 3380. Ratings: tach drives-3, environment-2, nav-1. Captain's Guild ID #82245-HC-901.

So Peter had been a captain as well. Michael sat up a bit straighter for that. No matter what Hans thought about him going for his captain's license, he had come from a line of captains: Peter by blood, and Malcolm by training.

He read on, seeing graduation dates, links to transcripts, promotion dates in S&W's fleet, his posting to the *Kaiser's Folly*, even a civilian commendation from the Navy in 3378. Then it ended abruptly. Died in border incident CasRb-733.

He selected the link for that last item. It came up as a terse navy report. All it had was the reference number, no title. It was not the Battle of Veraton or anything so glorious. Border incident, Caspian rebellion, file number 733.

The ships were listed in two categories. First were the freighters. *Vannover Markey*, damaged, five deaths. *Corey Tasha*, destroyed, all hands lost. *Kaiser's Folly*, destroyed, all hands lost. A note appeared in red below reading, "Updated 3381-183, survivors four."

Then came the combatants. *Reilly*, privateer, undamaged. *Hammerhead*, privateer, undamaged.

The *Hammerhead*, privateer. That had been their old ship, before *Sophie*. Malcolm had commanded it, both when he was a child, and back during the Caspian rebellion. Michael's memories of the *Hammerhead* were mostly of tall corridors, spin-wheel hatches, and playing hide and seek in the engineering crawlways. But he also remembered that it had been armed.

Malcolm often talked of converting one of the missile bays into a hidden cargo area for "special cargo," and Michael had a clear memory of sitting in the plasma turret pretending to shoot pirates. He had always assumed that the weapons were strictly to defend the ship. The border area had been very dicey at the time, after all, but he never remembered them actually engaging in combat. Then again, the war was over by the time he was four, so who knows what he would really remember?

Privateer. Letters of marque. He had read enough to know their definitions, but he had no idea of what they meant in practice. But at that moment, sitting there in his cabin, he was not sure he truly wanted to know.

His door chimed, so he closed the file down and signaled it to open. It was Karen from down the hall.

"Hey there, Michael. I still have some time before my shift starts. Did you want to go up and catch the movie tonight? It's *Concealed Interest,* one of my favorites."

He nodded. At that moment, anything was better than thinking about Malcolm's past. An evening with Karen would be a most pleasant escape.

Chapter 15

"When I want some distraction, it's easy enough to find something to keep me busy. The only problem with that, son, is that when I'm distracted, I can miss something important."
— Malcolm Fletcher

ARVIN WAS A MUCH larger station, with nine rings plus frequent shuttle service to the navy base sixty degrees forward in the geostationary orbit. The crew of the *Heinrich* had its regular haunts there as well, but this layover was to be a very short one. A time-sensitive delivery of heavy construction vehicles was waiting for Tortisia. The manufacturer had contracted with S&W for delivery according to *Heinrich's* original schedule, but they were still running six days behind. The deadline for a delivery-performance bonus had already passed. Now they were merely hoping to still get the on-time payment instead of discounting the transport fee. As such, the stop at Arvin had been cut from an already short three days to thirty-four hours.

Michael felt particularly sensitive about this because he knew he was ultimately the cause of them being behind schedule. The announcement came shortly after down-tach during lunch. He had gone forward from engineering to eat and fetch lunch for Zane and Nathan, so he was in the galley when

Corazon informed them all over the PA. A general groan swept through the assembled crew, but to their credit, Michael never saw any dirty looks sent his way.

The liberty schedule was further cause for discontent. All of the crew that also had cross-ratings in cargo handling were restricted to the *Heinrich* to expedite the offload and re-loading of the cargo. Michael figured that meant he would have no liberty since he had such a cargo rating, but his name was not on the restricted list. He was slotted for general liberty from sixteen hundred until fourteen hundred the next day. As guilty as he felt about the delay, he could not let that go by unquestioned, so as soon they secured the drives after docking, he headed for the bridge.

Corazon was still sitting in the forward bridge, on comm with someone from the dockworkers' office. "Priority offload," she was saying. "I have additional crew standing by to assist as soon as you can get the loader array moving."

"Understood, *Heinrich*. It's going to be an hour, but I'll get a team over there."

She flipped off the comm and turned to him. "Be brief, Mr. Fletcher."

"I have a cargo-1 rating, but I wasn't listed for cargo duty, ma'am. I'd like to volunteer."

She shook her head. "You've never worked a radial container ship before, Fletcher."

"I'm a quick learner," he argued.

She granted him a smile. "I appreciate your eagerness, Mr. Fletcher, and perhaps we can let you work a shift at a future port, but this time is going to be fast and frantic. I don't want any inexperienced hands out there. Is that clear?"

He sighed. "Yes, ma'am. It's just that I feel responsible for the delay."

He felt a few eyes turn towards him this time, but Corazon only laughed. "Mr. Fletcher, when you command your own ship, then you can feel responsible for the schedule, but if you're eager to give up your liberty, I will gladly put you to work as a runner."

"Yes, ma'am," he said. "Thank you."

"See if you want to thank me when we pull out," she said. "Sleep when you can, and keep your link turned up."

He went back to his quarters intending to at least rest, but he never got past taking off his boots before the first call came in. The captain's manifest declaration had to be delivered to station headquarters before the offload could begin. He laced up his boots as quickly as he could and headed for the forward airlock. The line for liberty was already forming, and he cut through with the packet in hand.

Billy Mason was working the liberty lock watch again, but before Michael could even start to explain, Billy called out to the crowd. "Make way for the runner," he said. Everyone shifted to the left side of the corridor and let him pass. He and Brookstone were the first out through the lock.

"You've got runner duty?" he asked.

"Yes. You?"

"Dockside lock watch." He reached into his pocket and pulled out a red card on a chain. "Here, this should get you wherever you need."

Michael took the card and read it as they floated down the docking tube. "*Heavy Heinrich*: Captain's Runner," it said, complete with an embossed logo and scan tag. "Thanks," he said.

"Are you getting any liberty?" Brookstone asked.

"No, I'm on runner duty the entire stay."

Brookstone shook his head. "I've had that duty. Remember, sleep when you can."

They reached the station lock and passed through. A uniformed officer was waiting for them, but when he saw the tag hanging from Michael's neck, he waved him through. He took off at a steady jog and only then realized he did not know where station headquarters was.

He found a map at one of the section bulkheads and plotted a route. Headquarters was in the central core, but three rings away. He caught a tram into the core and then a lift down from there. On the one hand, it was nice. Everyone stood aside for him as soon as they saw the red runner's tag. On the other hand, he knew that the entire cargo team was waiting for him to get that packet to headquarters.

Once he reached the right level, signs were plentiful, and once he found the main entrance, he saw a bank of windows next to it. The large red sign said "Ship Runners." He picked the shortest line and got to the head of it in moments.

"Cargo manifest for *Heavy Heinrich*," he said.

The man on the other side took it, passed the seal beneath a scanner and placed it on a conveyer belt behind him. "Wait over there for confirmation." Michael looked to see several runners clustered around a few tables, most of them drinking from cups.

He walked over, found the cups and fountain and got some water. He sat down next to two other runners. "*Morgan Ruth*," one of them said. Michael could see from her tag that it was not her name but rather her ship's name.

"*Heavy Heinrich*," he replied.

"Big ship," she said. "You're going to get a workout."

He was going to ask what she meant, but the PA blared out, "*Morgan Ruth*," and she hopped up. Michael turned to the other runner at the table. He was slumped forward, resting his chin on his hands. "You okay?" he asked.

"Three more hours," he replied. "Three more."

"*Heavy Heinrich*," came the call, and Michael went back to the window labeled "outbound."

A woman with her hair pulled back in a haphazard ponytail handed him another packet. "Offload authorization. Put it in the dockmaster's hands."

Off he went again, up three rings, and out on spoke number six. A number of dockworkers were milling around along with a few of the crew. He spotted Wally about the same time he spotted Michael.

"Dockmaster!" Wally called and pointed.

One man turned and Michael waved the packet over his head. He reached out for it as soon as Michael got to him, tore it open and looked briefly over the first page. "All right, boys and girls, let's get suited up and moving."

Movement swirled around him as Michael bent over and panted. Eventually, Wally guided him to a seat. "Drink," he said, handing him some water. "And try to get some sleep. You've got an hour, maybe two."

By morning, he was starting to understand why everyone had been talking about sleep. Over the course of the night, he had made two trips back to station headquarters, one to the S&W corporate office, one to the representative of the construction equipment's manufacturer, and one to the local branch of Fidelity Union Bank.

He was on the way back from that trip, riding the lift down from four rings up. He was starting to look a lot like that tired runner from the day before, but he still had six hours left. Alone in the lift, he leaned against the wall, and he did not even hear the other passenger come on at the next level. His first notice was when he heard the voice.

"Michael, is that you?"

He turned and saw his uncle. His eyes bolted open. This was the first time they had been alone since he first came aboard. "Captain!" he said in alarm. "Uh, yes, sir, it's me."

"Ah, I see she has you on runner duty. Takes me back," he said. "Remember, sleep—"

"When you can," Michael finished for him. "Yeah, I think I was about to do precisely that."

"Heading back to the ship?"

He shook his head. "Corporate office... coming down from Fidelity Union."

"Of course, that would be the performance bond." He checked the time on his link. "Good, we're still on schedule."

145

Michael started drifting again, but his uncle's voice brought him out again.

"Things working out in engineering?"

"Yes, sir."

"Gabrielle tells me you've been studying the navigation logs."

"Yes, sir. I still don't have a rating there."

"Still have your heart set on that captain's exam?"

He came wide awake with that. "Yes, sir. Still."

His uncle sighed and turned to face him directly. "Michael, about the name…"

Michael stood straighter, doing whatever he could to point his name patch at Hans. "Yes?"

"Understand that I can never forgive what…" He paused. "The loss of my brother eats at me even now. It's hard to get past, but given the qualities you have shown the rest of the crew, I can admit that Malcolm Fletcher did a reasonably good job in raising you. It can never erase what he did before, but I can see that perhaps you softened him, helped him turn away from… from his past."

"And the name, sir?"

"You can use whatever name you choose, Michael. I mean that, but I want you to know that your father was a good man. You don't have to take his name, but his is a heritage you can take some pride in."

"And Malcolm's isn't?"

Hans turned away. "I don't want to spar with you, Michael. I only wish you could have known your father as I did. He would have been proud of you."

Michael saw it for the compliment it was, but he could not bring himself to thank him for it. "Yes, Captain. Is there anything else?"

Hans opened his mouth to say something, but closed it with a shake of his head. He got off one ring before Michael, and as soon as the door closed, Michael regretted how it had ended.

He felt that there was much more he wanted to say. He simply did not know what.

Three more errands kept him moving, but he did not run into his uncle again. At the end of his duty, he was all set to go back to his quarters and sleep at last, but he ran into Zane along the way. "Come on, Michael. We're still on first shift duty. We're doing pushback and up-tach before dinner."

Groggily, he made his way back to engineering, lasted through the pushback and up-tach, and only fell asleep at his station once. He was not so lucky at dinner. After he planted his face in the potatoes and gravy, Zane and Charlie carried him down to his quarters and tucked him into bed.

He woke in the morning and swore to never pass up liberty again.

Jimmy Anders rapped his knuckles against the security window twice. A bearded man leaned forward from his chair and slid the glass to the side. "What are you doing in here, mister? This is a restricted area."

Jimmy looked around the dark warehouse with shipping containers stacked two and three high. No one else was near. "Are you Rufus?"

"Yeah, what's it to you?"

"Can you get a message to the Winged Lady?"

Now the security guard looked around himself. "Sure, for a price."

Jimmy handed him an envelope. It contained five crisp hundreds and a data card. "I think that's the going rate for priority traffic."

"Priority, eh?"

Jimmy nodded. "Get it to her quickly enough, and I'm sure you'll be in her good graces."

"All right, I'll make sure it goes out on the next run. And your name?"

He shook his head. "She'll know from the message."

Michael stopped in at the galley past twenty-three hundred. He had dropped Karen off in environmental for her shift and wanted a snack before he went to bed. Very little remained to choose from at this hour, but he did find a leftover dish of raspberry sorbet in the refrigerated case at the end of the line.

"If you were looking for the pudding, I'm afraid I got the last one."

Michael turned to see Corazon sitting at a table in the corner with a tablet. "No, ma'am, this will be fine."

"It looks like you've recovered from runner duty at Arvin," she said, pointing to the seat opposite her.

"Mostly. I think I lost a kilo in the process," he said, taking the seat. "Is it always that hectic?"

She shook her head. "Hardly, but everything was so compressed at Arvin. Plus, the Captain and I usually make about half of those runs ourselves, just to keep up our own contacts."

"That makes sense. I ran into the captain on one of my runs."

"He mentioned it. How are you two getting along?"

He shrugged. "It's still a lot to take in."

"Your parents?"

"Yeah, I looked up Peter. I see why people keep talking about my chin."

"So I've heard."

"You never met him?"

She shook her head. "I didn't join S&W until about twelve years ago, and I understand the Captain's brother died during the war."

148

Michael nodded. "I saw the report, but it was pretty spotty, not much more than a list of ships. I found our old ship there, the *Hammerhead*, listed as one of two privateers."

She nodded. "There were a lot of privateers back during the war."

"How did that work? I mean, were they handing out a free pass to anyone with a missile rack or plasma gun?"

"I never knew their criteria. It probably wasn't the best, but I doubt the Caspians were much more prudent. They gave out their share of letters of marque, too."

"But why? Where was the fleet in all this?"

"They had their own problems. What started as a civilian political problem escalated into a shooting war, and the next thing they knew, over a third of their ships were on the other side, including two whole carrier groups."

"And the merchants?"

"We were trying to pay our bills and make our shipments. I was only a junior navigator on one of Takasumi's ships back then, but it was a mess. No one wanted to carry anything with military value and risk becoming a target, but the Navy didn't give us much choice. In the end, it didn't matter. Soon enough, all the shipping was at risk. I lost a good friend of mine to a hull breach."

"How?"

She shrugged. "She got lazy. I don't know. Maybe she just didn't want to put on her environment suit one more time, and that was the time the other freighter turned out to be a privateer."

"Which side?"

"We were still in the Confederacy, and my captain would have plucked out the eye of anyone who suggested we pull out."

"No, I meant the privateer."

"I don't know. Does it matter?"

He looked at the sorbet, slowly melting. "It's hard to think of Malcolm that way."

"They weren't all bad. I knew a few who were good solid captains."

"A few? But not most?"

She tried to make a smile but it did not hold. "Where do you think Yoshido recruited his fleet?"

Every spacer in the Confederacy had heard of Yoshido. No one knew if he was still around, but dead or alive, he had left a considerable piracy organization behind. If you were wary, you would come through all right, but every now and then, you would still hear about ships disappearing near the borders. It was not nearly as bad as the Neridians of the early Republic, but it was bad enough.

But Malcolm? The way he had always talked about pirates, Michael could never believe he was one of them. "I wish I knew more about that battle."

"You can always request the records. The Navy may not have much more than you've already seen, but you won't know without asking."

"How?"

She frowned. "It's a pity we didn't have this talk last week. Arvin would have been the ideal place for it. Given how short our time was, I don't know if you'd have even gotten to see anyone over at the fleet's station, but you could have at least had real-time communication."

"Oh," he replied. "When are we coming through again?"

She paused to do the calculations. "Seven, maybe eight months, but you don't have to wait that long. You can start the request by mail at our next port. I'll even help if you'd like."

"I'd like that," he replied, but even as he said it, he was not so sure. As long as he did not know for certain, he could still believe that Malcolm was innocent.

But what if he was not?

Chapter 16

"It's good to have friends on other ships as well as friends at each of your ports, but when you really need those friends you have to remember one thing. Ships move. Ports don't."
— *Malcolm Fletcher*

MICHAEL RESTED HIS HEAD against the wall in the shower, holding the valve chain down with one hand as the water beat on his back. It had been a long, exhausting shift. They had had nine axis shifts that day, and the sails sank into fluttering oscillations on four of them. Zane, Nathan, and Michael had been climbing over the generators making adjustments to the sails all day. Finally, at around fifteen thirty, Gabrielle had ordered a course change.

At dinner, she had looked as tired as he felt. "Tachyon storm," she explained. "Looks like a big one coming in from coreward. If I had to guess, I'd say it's the downwind shake out of either a nova or something big hitting the core's accretion disk."

"Aren't you supposed to get forecasts of that kind of thing?"

She shrugged. "Only after someone reports it. Looks like that's our job this time."

She promised to send him the logs and ask the overnight navigators to do the same. He had thanked her, but he had no intention of looking at them tonight. He only wanted to shower and go to sleep.

And showering was exactly what he was doing, letting the water course over him, but after a few minutes a warning light came on. He knew from talking to Charlie that if he kept the water running it would signal an alarm down in environmental, so he released it. He soaped up with the water already clinging to his skin and then rinsed off as quickly as he could. He ran the towel over his head and chest before wrapping it around his waist.

He stepped out and came face to face with Karen in her robe. "Good evening," he said. "Or morning, whatever."

She reached out and put a hand on his bare chest. "Oh, Michael, what are we going to do with you?"

He blinked twice. "I'm not... what do you mean?"

She shook her head. "Three weeks of flirtation and you still haven't made your move? I think this calls for direct action."

He was about to ask what she was talking about when she reached down and yanked the towel from his waist. He tried to cover himself but relaxed when she let her robe drop to the floor.

"Back in the shower, boy," she said. "You can start by washing my back."

He watched her go in and admired what he saw. Karen had quite a back.

Gabrielle had fifteen minutes left on the elliptical when the XO started up the machine next to her. Other than that, the room was deserted.

"This isn't your usual night," Corazon commented. "Normally I have the gym to myself on Tuesday nights, but I don't mind the company."

"After the crazy winds the last few days, I needed to unwind, and tonight's movie isn't quite my thing," she replied.

"*Revenge of the Pharaoh*, right?"

"Yeah, another Paula Stone spandex special, but it's also got Marcus Kearn as the love interest."

"Ah, him I like. I can understand why the galley emptied so suddenly."

"Everyone went?"

"I believe so, though it's possible some were pairing up for other activities."

Gabrielle did her best to suppress a grin. "So, what rumors have reached your elevated office?"

"If you're asking about Miss Larkin and a new crewman called 'biscuit boy,' then yes, I've heard."

"Oh," she replied. "You're not going to tell Father, are you?"

Corazon stepped up her speed. "There's no reason I should, is there?"

"Oh, no, not at all. I just thought, you know…"

"That I might tattle? No, young Mr. Fletcher needs some breathing room, and as long as he doesn't hyperventilate, I'm inclined to let him be."

"Thank you, ma'am."

They pressed on in silence for a few minutes, but when Gabrielle switched into the cooldown stage, Corazon turned to her again. "But let's not let him get too sidetracked."

"Oh?"

"I believe you've been tutoring him on his navigation."

"Yes. He's struggling, but I think he's making progress."

"Good. Keep it up. I don't want to see him driven off by your father's vendetta against the late Captain Fletcher. Understood?"

"Absolutely, ma'am. I confess I've been asking around at port. Father's version doesn't add up to me, and if I can, I'm going to prove it to him."

The XO gave her a short grin. "While I would never want to interfere in family politics, I wholeheartedly approve of you sticking up for a fellow crewman this way."

"Yes, ma'am."

"But feel free to make your feelings known to Mr. Brookstone about the movie selections. I do believe this is the third Paula Stone film we've had in as many months. We should have more variety than his libido can provide."

Gabrielle giggled. "Yes, ma'am, I most certainly will."

They were a day late getting into Tortisia because of the tachyon storm, but they still beat the deadline for performance penalty by nine hours. Liberty was scheduled for three days, and Michael made sure he was signed up for all of it. He was looking forward to some more relaxed time with Karen instead of the snippets they managed to piece together during second shift when he was winding down and she was waking up. He caught up with her in the line for the airlock and gave her a brief hug from behind.

She turned around and tickled him in the ribs. "Hey, you," she said.

"So, what's good here? Any place with a bigger bed?"

She chuckled but quickly shifted to a more neutral expression. "Yeah, about that. It turns out that the *Summer Night* is in port, and I have a good friend on board."

"Well, a good friend of yours should be a good friend of mine," he offered. "What's her name?"

Her face took on more of a frown. "His name is Aaron Forrester, and he's not so much of a good friend as he is a special friend."

"Ah," he said. Gabrielle had warned him about this back at Ballison. Let Karen have her fun in port. He did his best to put a smile on it. "I understand. You two have a good time."

He must not have been very convincing, because she took him by the chin and turned his face directly to hers. "Remember, we talked about this. Neither of us is settling down, just passing the time."

154

He nodded. "I know, but now I'm not sure what I'm going to do."

She gave him a quick kiss. "I imagine I could hook you up. Aaron has friends."

He shook his head and tried harder to look happy. "I'm sure I'll be in sufficient demand as it is."

She laughed and jabbed at his ribs again. "That's my boy."

The truth was he was not in such high demand after all. He trailed along with the rest of the crew, most of whom settled into a faux-historical pub with plenty of dark corners and other drunken crews to fill them. Several attractive women caught his eye, but none of them seemed to pay him much attention as he sat at the bar by himself. Finally, after two hours of this, he gave up and left.

Tortisia station was much smaller than Arvin had been, and its only military presence was a recruiting station on the bottom ring. It was well into the evening ship-time, but the station's local population was heading into midday. He found recruiters for both the Navy and the Marines, but he settled in at the desk for the Navy. The recruiter was an older man bearing the stripes of a non-commissioned officer.

"Ready for some action, young man?" he asked.

"Excuse me?"

"I asked if you're ready to throw off the yoke of your corporate master and see some real action amongst the Confederacy's finest."

"Oh," he replied. "No, actually I'm not here to enlist."

The recruiter crossed his arms. "Then what do you want?"

Michael pulled a data card from his pocket and handed it over. "I want to file an information request under the War Records and Reconciliation Act." He made sure to give the full name, precisely as the XO had given it to him.

"You want to do it here? Arvin's only a hop over that way, you know."

Michael smiled. "Yes, but my corporate master won't be going there for several months."

He took the card. "All right. I'll forward it up through channels. What are you trying to find out anyway?"

"I want the war records of my adopted father, Malcolm Fletcher."

"What branch?"

"He was a privateer."

The recruiter paused. "War records from a privateer?"

"I was told they had some kind of support."

He shrugged. "Support yes, but I doubt you'll find much in the way of records." He started typing on his keyboard. "I'll forward the request, but if you want real answers, you should go talk to some other privateers."

"I would, but I can't find any."

The recruiter chuckled. "They're a lot more common than you think, young man. The *Hamilton James* is in port. Try her."

He headed back down to the docks and checked the registry. The *Hamilton James* was indeed in port, scheduled to pull out in thirty-eight hours. The captain was listed as Leonard Bradley. He went back up to ring two and found the right dock. The dockside lock officer was a woman with graying hair.

"Excuse me, ma'am, but I'm looking for Captain Bradley."

"Sorry, son, he's not aboard."

"Can you tell me where I might find him?"

She looked him over before shaking her head. "Sorry, it's against ship policy to tell outsiders where our crew are. I can take a message for you, but that's the best I can offer."

"Can't you call him for me?"

"Is this some kind of official ship-to-ship business?"

"No," he confessed. "It's personal."

She stood her ground. "Sorry. Did you want to leave a message?"

He paused. What could he even ask the man? Were you a bloody privateer during the war? Did you know Malcolm Fletcher? Did he kill my parents? "Please tell him that Michael Fletcher of the *Heavy Heinrich* would like a word with him."

She nodded. "Okay, but no guarantees."

He thanked her and headed back for the *Heinrich* on ring three. He was getting tired and thought he may as well sleep in his own quarters. Being alone in the Ballison hotel had not been a comforting experience, and he was not in the mood to repeat it here.

Roxy Collier had the dockside watch. "What happened, Michael, did you strike out?"

He shrugged. "No, I just..." he paused, thinking about his failure at the *Hamilton James*. "Yeah, I guess I did."

"No worries, at least it's not as bad a time as you had at Arvin."

The gears started turning in his mind. "Say, who's on runner duty?"

"No one right now. It's a long enough layover that we're letting things batch up."

"Do you have something now?"

Roxy checked the box by her station. "Yeah, two for station administration and one for the bank, but none of it's high priority."

"Do you mind if I go ahead and deliver them?"

She shook her head. "Go ahead, but you're a glutton for punishment."

He took the packets and the runner card. "Yeah, I'm sick that way. I should be back in a few hours."

He went first to station administration and delivered the two packets. Only one got a confirmation, but even once he had it, he hung out in the runners' lounge. It was smaller than the one at Arvin, but it still had a steady trickle of runners coming and going. He sat near the back where he could watch them enter.

It took almost two hours, but eventually he found what he was looking for: a young woman wearing the runner tag from the *Hamilton James*, the old gunpowder cannon marking its distinctive logo. "Hey, *Hamilton*!" he called.

She walked over with a drink and sat down. "Hey, *Heinrich*," she replied. "I've heard of you guys. I've got a cousin on Ballison who's been dating one of your engineers."

157

"Zane?"

"Yeah, I think that's what it was. Small galaxy, eh? So, what's up?"

Michael hefted the packet for the bank. "I've got something for your captain."

She reached for it. "I'll give it to him, save you the trip."

He held it out of her grasp. "Sorry, I'm supposed to put it 'in his hands'. You know how it goes."

She chuckled. "Do I ever! Fucking officers." She hit her link on her wrist. "Suzie, this is Lana. Do you know where the skipper is? I've got a packet for him."

There was a pause, and the voice that came back was that of the graying woman Michael had spoken to before. "He should be up at the Guild hall having dinner."

"Thanks, Suzie. Lana out." Then to Michael, "Look for a white beard above a big belly."

"Fat captain?"

"Not roll-down-the-ramp fat, but he's got his own gravitational field."

Michael nodded. "Thanks, Lana."

"Anything for another runner," she said. "Say, I'll be at Xeno's later if you want to get a drink."

He stopped short, because now he realized that she looked pretty good: short black hair, green eyes, and beneath that *Hamilton James* uniform a pleasant curvy figure. But he had already started off with a lie to take advantage of her, and she was not going to be happy when she found out. Malcolm had taught him better than that, but now he did not see any way to fix it.

He stood. "I'd love to, but I may have duty."

She shrugged. "Maybe another time, Mr. Fletcher."

"That would be nice," he replied and got out before he dug his hole any deeper.

The Captains' Guild was up on ring five, and so was the bank. He dropped off the packet there first and made his way to the Guild hall. He still had his runner's badge, and he figured that he could bluff his way in if need be, but that would probably get back to his uncle. More family grief was the last thing he needed right now, so he found a seat outside and watched the door.

Fortunately, he did not have as long to wait this time. After twenty minutes, he spotted his target. Captain Bradley did indeed have a white beard and his own gravitational field, but he also had a crewmate with him. He wore the same uniform, and his lapel bore the gold triangle that denoted first officers amongst civilians. Well, Michael was in it already, so there was no point in backing down now.

He stepped forward into their path. "Captain Bradley," he said. "May I have a word with you?"

They both stopped, and the first officer's hand slipped quickly into a pocket. "About what?" Bradley asked.

"I wanted to ask you about privateers during the war."

The first officer pulled his hand back slightly. He was clearly holding something. "Do you want me to get security, sir?"

Bradley opened his mouth to reply but paused. He tilted his head and peered at Michael. "You wouldn't be Malcolm's boy, would you?"

Michael nodded.

Bradley turned to his officer. "No, that won't be necessary. Mr. Fletcher here is the son of an old friend."

"Do you want me to stay?"

"No, Jerry," he said. "You go on and enjoy your evening. I'll catch up with you in the morning."

The officer nodded but gave Michael a hard stare as he passed.

"Come on," Bradley beckoned. "Let's go back in and get a drink."

Chapter 17

"You don't have to inspect every cargo container, son. Sometimes it truly is better not to know." — Malcolm Fletcher

MICHAEL HAD BEEN IN a Guild Hall only twice before, both of them with Malcolm. Captains could bring guests, of course, but Malcolm had shared the privilege with him rarely. "You want to go more often," he had said, "then get your own license." In truth, that more than anything had driven him towards getting the necessary ratings. Someday, he had been sure of it, he would reserve a table for himself and Malcolm and pay for their dinner himself. As he followed Captain Bradley in, he realized that day would never come. Licensed or not, he was never going to have that dinner.

"Table for two," Bradley said. "By the window if you can find one."

The waiter led them out to edge of the restaurant. It was situated at the outer edge of the core, and the wraparound window looked out at the rings above and below. In the distance, Michael could see the *Heinrich* docked with the radial cargo loader sitting idle nearby. He tried to remember where the *Hamilton James* would be, but he had lost the orientation somewhere along the way.

"Have you eaten?" Bradley asked.

"Actually, no, but I wouldn't—"

"Bring him a steak," Bradley told the waiter. "A growing boy like you needs the meat."

"Thank you, sir."

"I think we met once, but you were little." He made a dismissive wave near the floor. "This was back when your dad still had the *Hammerhead*, of course."

"Have you heard?"

He nodded. "I'm sorry for your loss. Is this S&W thing a family connection?"

"Yes, it turns out my birth father… did you know I was adopted?"

"I thought it might be, either that or you were some by-blow. All I knew for sure was that Malcolm picked you up sometime during the war."

"You knew him then?"

The older man shuddered. "Bad times, but he was a good friend."

"So what's that whole privateer thing about? Were you… I mean, I have a hard time imagining him going after other merchants, given the way he always talked about pirates."

"How do you think he got that way, Michael?" He shook his head. "Like I said, they were bad times. The Navy wanted to starve the rebellion out, not literally mind you, but they figured if they could cut off enough of their trade, it would bring them down from within."

"Then why didn't they do it themselves?"

Bradley frowned. "They did. They blockaded most of the larger ports, but too much was slipping around the edges. You know, smaller ports, transfer stations. If you grew up with Malcolm, I'm sure you've seen those places. The Navy couldn't patrol them all without spreading themselves out damned thin, and the Caspians had too many ships of the line to risk that. So they got us instead."

"Privateers," Michael said, almost spitting it out.

"Yeah, I know. For some, it wasn't much more than piracy with a government license, but not Malcolm. Know this, Michael, he was a fair man."

Michael shook his head. "What does that even mean in a context like that? Please give me your cargo before I kill you?"

The waiter returned with food for Michael. It looked delicious, but knowing the history of the man who was paying for it, he was not sure he could stomach it.

"Eat it," Bradley said. "A full belly will make this easier."

He frowned, but he cut into the steak anyway. "So, what's fair in the world of privateers?"

"Personally, I always offered them a chance to surrender before I fired the first shot. A lot of them were only trying to fulfill a contract, so they had no taste for the politics. They usually made it easy and dumped their cargo into open space."

Michael started eating. "And you'd collect it?"

"When feasible. The Navy cleared all our recovered cargo and paid good money for it, too. I even hear they made good on some of the merchants' insurance bonds after the war."

"But a lot of people weren't there to collect, right?"

Bradley looked out the window at all the freighters waiting at their docks. "I'm not proud of everything I did, Michael, but I know I played by the rules. Whenever I could, I always went for the drive sections. One good missile shot, and I could disable a ship with minimal casualties, or if they tried to go to tach, a well-placed gravity warhead could rip those generators to pieces. I couldn't always take on survivors, but I always reported their location at the next port. Most of them made it."

"And Malcolm?"

Bradley chuckled. "At first he developed a reputation for wasting ammunition. Warning shots, that kind of thing, and he'd go through twenty or thirty missiles on each outing, trying to box ships in with distant gravity warheads. You know, enough to foul the sails but not enough to feed back into the generators. Foolish stuff like that."

"Foolish?"

162

He shook his head, remembering. "I remember one time, he and I were chasing down this fat whale of a ship, almost as big as that one you're on now. He'd mined the approach to some transfer station with gravity warheads, and fouled up the winds for days, and this big boy was trying to make a run for it. I wanted to snake a missile up his ass, but *Hammerhead* had the lead position, and Malcolm insisted on closing in for a plasma shot. I swear he must have pulled to within ten kilometers before he opened up on them. He had a hot gunner then, and that gal shredded their cargo section front to back, top to bottom. It almost broke the ship in two, but she had left enough structure intact for the spine to hold."

Michael nodded, thinking about what that would look like on the *Heinrich*, with all the cargo containers arrayed radially around the long spine connecting engineering to the rest of the ship. Eighty percent or more of the central width was cargo at that point, and he could imagine how a gunner could wreak havoc with that while still doing minimal damage to the rest of the ship. "What's so foolish about that?"

"You never knew when one of those freighters was going to start shooting back. They weren't armed at first, but as the war went on a lot of them started bolting on what they could."

"Maybe Malcolm didn't want to kill anyone."

"Yeah, I used to think that, too."

Michael froze mid-bite. Is that what happened to Peter? Was his uncle telling the truth?

"You see, we weren't the only ones out there," Bradley went on. "The Caspians had their own privateers as well."

"Well, weren't they doing the same as you?"

Bradley shrugged. "Some of them, but I also knew a few captains who weren't very particular about who they got their letters of marque from, or for that matter, how many they had."

"They fought for both sides?"

He shook his head. "No, not really for either side, just their own."

Michael nodded. Pirates with a license, indeed.

"Malcolm didn't take a kind view to that particular practice, so he started keeping track of things: which ships showed up where, how long they were gone, what cargoes went missing, which ones showed up later on another ship, who crewed which vessels, that kind of thing. Before long, he was building a list of suspects."

"And what did he do with them?"

"Well, at first he was satisfied just reporting them. He presented his evidence to the Navy's review board and let them deal with it."

Michael tried to imagine Malcolm doing that, but it seemed a stretch. It was not that he was against law and order, but to Michael, he had always seemed to care much more about order than law. "At first?"

"I don't know exactly what happened, but somewhere along the way, he lost his patience with the review board. Maybe the wheels of justice weren't fast enough for him, or maybe the Navy was willing to look the other way for certain captains. But about halfway through the war, he started taking matters into his own hands."

"No more review board?"

Bradley shook his head. "No more surrenders, at least that's what I heard. Maybe it was only the ones on his list, or maybe he just stopped caring."

"So he killed Caspian privateers?"

"Yeah, even some of the ones who were supposedly on our side, too. If the war had kept up, he might have gotten them all, but after enough blood it was finally over. Of course, then he had you to look after. I suppose he let it go after that."

"And the privateer program?"

"They maintained it for another two years in modified form, kind of an auxiliary navy while they got the sector back under Confederate control. I got out around then. They asked me back a few years later for some new thing, but I'd had my fill."

"But you still have the *Hamilton James*."

164

He gave a little smile. "She's a good old ship, but she's no fighter anymore. I ripped out the missile bays eight years back, turned one over to cargo and put some hydroponics in the other. The ship smells like spring now. I've still got the old plasma turret, but I don't keep a gunner on board. If it came to it, I'd probably be up there myself trying to remember how to point the damn thing."

He remembered Malcolm talking about something similar on the *Hammerhead*, turning the missile bays into hidden storage areas for "special" cargo. Perhaps he had let it all go. They had sounded like bad times, like Bradley said, but nothing he had learned so far answered his most important question.

"Tell me, Captain Bradley, did you ever hear of the *Kaiser's Folly*?"

"Doesn't ring a bell," he said. "At least, I'm pretty sure it wasn't one of ours."

"No, it wasn't a privateer, just a freighter."

He shook his head. "Why do you ask?"

"I was on it. That's how Malcolm found me."

Bradley shrugged. "He never said much about how he ended up with you, but by then we weren't very close."

"No?"

"Well, after he went on the hunt, he wasn't the best guy to be around. Don't get me wrong, Michael. If it came down to it, I'd have had his back, but you didn't want to be standing next to him when the shots started."

Michael returned to the diminishing food on his plate. "I guess I can understand that."

"Anything else I can do for you, son?"

He started to shake his head, but then he remembered the girl. "Actually, yes. I met your runner today, Lana."

Bradley nodded. "Yeah, Lana Marcellus. She's my junior mechanic. What about her?"

"Well, I told her I had a packet for you. That's how I found out where you were."

"So you lied to her."

"I know. If it's not too much to ask, sir, can you tell her I'm sorry?"

"I'll do better than that, young man. You finish up that steak, and we'll go tell her together?"

He gulped. "You mean, in person?"

"Best way to apologize, don't you think?"

"Yes, sir."

"Besides, maybe you do have something for me after all. Your dad, I mean Malcolm, had a recipe for this chicken and pepper soup that I swear could resuscitate the dead. Do you have any of his old files?"

"I'd have to check, sir."

Captain Elsa Watkins held the decrypted message in her hand. It looked like Anders had been productive after all.

"But there is an end-around to the security on the ship," his message read. "The boy should have access to it himself as soon as he's of age. I have good data on the S&W routes, and I'm attempting to skip ahead to intercept him. Schedule is attached. Join me at Latera if you're interested."

She scanned over it again. "Mr. Neiru," she called out. "How soon can we be ready to leave port?"

"A few hours, Captain," her first officer replied. "Do you have a destination in mind?"

"Tsaigo," she replied. Latera was much too far to reach in one leg, but if they hurried, they could probably catch up with Anders and the boy in time.

Chapter 18

"Sometimes you get sucker punched, and sometimes you just walk into a fist." — *Malcolm Fletcher*

MICHAEL SAT AT HIS drive station alone. Evidently, Terri Schwartz had decided he no longer needed babysitting, so she and Zane were tackling some maintenance on the sublight drives behind him. The tachyon winds were particularly stable as well, so he had little else to do but sit at his station waiting for orders that did not come. He had gone so far as to pull up some of the same navigation displays that would be on Gabrielle's bridge station, but even with his limited knowledge, there was nothing to concern him. In the early afternoon, he thought he saw the leading edge of an eddy coming in from starboard, but it faded rapidly, a mere ripple.

While it was nice to have a relaxing shift, it also left him with entirely too much time to reflect. He had no idea when his request to the Navy would yield results, and given the recruiter's response, he was not sure how much information they even had to give him. Meanwhile, Captain Bradley's tales had left him with even more questions than he had had before. Which side had the *Kaiser's Folly* been on? Had Peter taken them over to the Caspian side of the rebellion? And if so, had Malcolm offered them the chance to surrender? Or had the

Kaiser's Folly somehow ended up on Malcolm's list? Could they instead have been bystanders to a fight between the *Hammerhead* and the *Reilly*? Which side was the *Reilly* on? Who had been her captain?

He shook his head to try to clear it all away. Running through it over and over was not going to get him any answers. He knew that, but it did not help. Variations on the scenario kept coming into his head unbidden.

At least he had something of a date planned with Karen that night. The layover at Tortisia had been a bust as far as that went. Another ship with a "special" friend had arrived on their last day in port, so Karen had begged off plans with him to get in a quick visit with the other crew. He had managed to spend a pleasant evening with Lana from the *Hamilton James*, but it had ended with merely a hug and a promise to be looking for one another in some future port.

A movement on the navigation display caught his eye briefly, but the inflection point reversed itself, the slope holding near zero but positive.

He sighed. The quiet shifts were always the worst.

Gabrielle made several marks on the pad as Michael watched. She scrolled down, made some more marks, chuckled, and scrolled some more. When she finally set the pad down, Michael could no longer contain himself. "Well?"

"Close, but you still didn't pass. Sixty-eight percent. The ratings board requires a seventy, but most commercial vessels want a ninety before they consider the rating valid."

He slumped in his chair. They had the small common room to themselves this evening. Everyone else was up in the theater watching a vid of the xeroball semi-finals. Many had placed bets before they had pulled into the last port, and while the results were already theoretically known, most had kept quiet until they could watch it together. Michael knew he had already lost — Stonefall Comets by three in overtime — so he had convinced Gabrielle to proctor the test for a navigation rating.

"I'm curious, what score does the *Heinrich* require?"

She shook her head. "Dad requires an unblemished one hundred, and he gives his own tests to confirm the public ratings."

Michael frowned. "Any tips?"

"From cases eighteen and twenty-two, it looks like you're using a right-handed coordinate system with your spin calculations. For tachyons, it's a left-handed spin coordinate."

He nodded. He knew that and was not sure how he had missed it on the test. "What else?"

"Well, I have no idea where you went wrong on case nine, but if you had done that in a live test, your sails would have been slammed so hard, they would have fed back into the generator. Even if everything else had been correct, I think most captains would fail you for that one answer alone."

He cringed. "That bad?"

"Sorry. Maybe you're simply not cut out to be a navigator. Sure, there's some overlap with the tach drive rating, but not every engineer makes a good navigator and vice versa. Take me, for example, I'm flummoxed by power systems. Put me in your chair back there, and I'd be as likely to short out the generators as push out the sails."

"I hear you, Gabrielle, but I need to keep working at it."

"Why? Where's it written that you have to know everything?"

He allowed himself a little smile. "In the Captains' Guild licensing regulations."

She pushed herself back from the table. "You know, I'd heard a rumor that you were shooting for a license, but I didn't believe them. Whatever for? I mean, you're seventeen years old. Someday, sure, maybe even I'll try for captain, but why are you wasting your energy on it now?"

The truth was that he had started on the path to prove to Malcolm that he was capable of it, but that hardly seemed a good answer now. "Well, there's *Sophie's Grace*. She's going to need a captain, and it may as well be me."

"*Sophie's Grace*? That's your old ship, right?"

He nodded. "Yeah, though I guess it's really my ship, not my old ship."

She shook her head. "Look, if you want my advice, and you're getting it whether you want it or not, you should sell that ship and put every last credit into ship shares here."

He laughed at her. "Why would I ever do that? Trade an owner's share for the scraps of an engineer?"

"You still don't get it, do you? I cleared eleven thousand on my ship shares from this last run alone, and that was a bad run. If you came in with the proceeds from the *Sophie*, you'd easily get double my shares, maybe triple. How much did Malcolm clear on his runs?"

Michael frowned. Honestly, he did not know how much the *Sophie* had made on its runs. He had helped load the cargo, helped sell the cargo, even did a few side deals on his own, but Malcolm had never shared the finances with him. He had had his allowance, and that was it. Still, he knew enough to know that after fuel costs, docking fees, crew salaries, and whatever other side business Malcolm had been conducting, clearing eleven thousand would have been a decent run. And that was for the entire ship, not the navigator.

He looked at Gabrielle. "Well, less than the *Heinrich*, but that's to be expected. She's a smaller ship, but Malcolm knew what he was doing."

"Yeah, Malcolm knew." She started gathering her things. "It's your own life, Michael, but I hope you figure out that there are better role models out there than him."

"Wait, what do you mean? Are you buying your father's story now?" Michael fumed. "I should have known you'd stick to Daddy."

She closed her eyes and took a deep breath. "You know, Michael, I'm doing my best to welcome you into the family. I wanted to give you the benefit of the doubt, and I wanted to extend that to Malcolm. If you'd lived with my father as long as I have, you'd understand how much I'd like to prove him wrong just once."

"And?"

"And he's not. I've been asking around in port, other crews, other captains."

Michael's interest both picked up and cooled at the same time. "And did they know what happened to the *Kaiser's Folly*?"

"No, but they knew about other ships. I talked to a pilot who had seen your precious Malcolm gut a ship from stem to stern, and when that was done, he started shooting at the escape pods." She shuddered. "The escape pods, Michael! Who does that?"

"I, um... I don't know."

"Merciless Mal, that's what they called him. You may think he was a good man, but from what I hear he was a vicious bastard. And for the record, the role model I was talking about was Peter Schneider, your real father."

He stammered at her as she left, but in the end he had no retort. Merciless was as apt a description for Malcolm as he had ever heard.

Michael did not bother making plans with Karen for the Folsom liberty. He had learned his lesson at Tortisia, and while she did not say anything about it in their brief times together, he was certain she would find someone at Folsom whom she had not seen in far too long. It turned out three such crews were vying for her attention, so he did not even bother trying to keep track of her.

Gabrielle kept her distance as well. At least at Ballison he had been able to use her for introductions, but without her he drifted from table to table, club to club, bumping into various crewmates, looking for anyone he knew. Finally, he settled in at the bar of some club on the ring above where they had docked.

The bouncers had stopped giving him any grief about his age. He was not sure if he actually looked any older or if he simply looked too glum to be that young.

He was into his third round at this particular club when a girl slithered into the seat next to him. He glanced at her once, saw the blond hair, and then did a double take. For a second, he thought it was Josie, but it was not.

"Wow, you look like you saw a ghost," she said.

He shook his head. "Sorry, you just reminded me of someone."

"Someone good or someone bad?" she asked.

"Good," he replied. "Very good."

"Then why don't you buy this good girl a drink, and maybe I can help you relive some old memories."

He waved the bartender over. "Michael," he introduced himself.

"Fini," she said. "I'll have whatever he's having."

"So, Fini, are you a good girl?"

She took a sip from Michael's glass. "Depends, Michael. How good do you want me to be?" She took another sip, her puckered lips lingering on the shot glass.

Michael could not help but to react. What Fini lacked in Josie's sweetness, she more than made up for in raw sexual allure, but given Josie's profession, that was not much of a reference for this girl. *So, are you a professional?* He could hardly ask her that. Instead, he settled on, "Do you live here?"

She shook her head. "Groundside. I'm up on a joyride with a friend of my mom's. She's got a semi-regular squeeze passing through." She made a motion back towards the corner. "He's another spacer like you."

The bartender arrived with her drink, and Fini lifted it up to Michael's mouth and tipped it for him. "I owe you a few sips," she said.

This one seemed stronger than the previous ones, so Michael pulled back before he drank too much of it. "So, what ship is he from?"

172

She shrugged. "I don't know. Wanna meet him?" She reached under the bar and squeezed at his knee. "He's got a suite at the Velocity. Hot tub, auto-massager, the works."

"Sure," he said. After all, Karen was off having her fun. Why not him?

Fini led him over to a corner booth where an older man and woman were locked in an embrace, their drinks forgotten. "Look, Vera, I got one too."

The couple broke their kiss and looked at them. The woman, presumably Vera, smiled at Fini. "Looks like you got yourself a nice one, girl, but I'm going to stick with my captain."

The man nodded. "Jimmy Anders," he said, reaching for his drink on the table.

"Michael Fletcher," he replied.

The man paused, his hand hovering over his drink. "Fletcher… wait, are you by any chance Malcolm's boy?"

He felt his shoulders sag, but he nodded. "Yeah, I am."

The man bounded up from his seat, wiped his hand on his uniform and stuck it out towards Michael. "Damn glad to meet you, son. Your dad and I go way back."

Two men sat at a table. They were early for the meeting as was their custom. The younger one wore a mischievous grin.

"What have you got?" the older one asked.

"A records request for our old privateer program."

"And why are you bothering with it?"

"I had some of the records flagged. This request is of particular interest."

The older one paused, and then a smile crept across his face as well. "Fletcher?"

"You were right, Admiral. His boy Michael requested his war records, with a specific request for all data on one particular battle."

"Second battle of Tanaris?"

"No, some little border incident."

"Why? I mean, what was special about it?"

"Well, it turns out the boy isn't Fletcher's. His parents were S&W employees with family connections, and their ship was destroyed in the incident. It's not clear how the kid ended up with Fletcher, but according to the synopsis Fletcher was there at the battle."

The older man chewed it over for a moment. "Interesting. Maybe it is time to talk to the boy. Is he still out on the border?"

"No, he's on an S&W ship now, the *Heavy Heinrich*. Actually, they passed through here three weeks ago."

The Admiral stroked his beard. "Ok, go pull the records, especially for that 'little border incident.' I want to see them after lunch. There may be more going on here than it looks like."

"And the boy?"

"Don't pack your bags yet, but start checking *Heinrich's* route and look for a courier run you can hitch a ride on. If this is some mess left over from the old program, I think we owe it to Fletcher to pull the boy in."

"I'll get on it right after the meeting."

"No, Commander, skip this. Get going on this Fletcher thing now."

"Aye, sir."

Michael and Anders sat in the front room of the suite, drinking coffee. Michael had still not acquired the taste for it, but Captain Anders was an old comrade of Malcolm's, and he did not want to look like a little boy. At least this brew was not as harsh as what he was typically offered.

"*Kaiser's Folly*," Anders repeated, chewing it over. "No, I don't remember it. What's it to you?"

"My mother died on it," Michael replied. He did not want to get into the whole adoption thing with Anders, especially not with Fini and Vera still asleep in the other rooms. "The old *Hammerhead* was there when it happened. I'm trying to get the details."

"Details? Like who killed her?"

He nodded. "Something like that. I put in a records request to the Navy, but I don't know if they've got any more than I do."

"Well, I'll tell you who would know, and that's Malcolm."

"Yeah, but he's not here to ask."

"No, but you've still got his files back on *Sophie*, right?"

"I suppose," he replied. "But he was on the *Hammerhead* during the war. I don't know if he would have kept them."

"Of course he would," Anders replied. "Your dad was a data hoarder. I do salvage, you see. That's one of the ways he and I did business. I recover cargo and parts from old vessels, some of them dating back to the war. Your dad was able to point me to a few of the older ones, and whenever I found one of my own, he always bugged me to get a copy of their data. A man who wants that much old data never throws any of it away. I'd bet you a container of gold that he's got the full record of every shot he fired on the *Hammerhead*, all tucked away somewhere in *Sophie*'s memory."

"You really think so?"

"Damn straight. It's a shame though. I bet he's got a few old salvages set aside that he never told me about. When you get back to *Sophie*, I do hope you'll let me know if you find any in there."

Michael thought about it. There was no harm in it, after all. These were ships that had been long dead for years. "Sure, as soon as I get back."

"And when will that be? I mean, you'll be of age pretty soon, right?"

He did the math. It had been four months since Malcolm's death, or was it five? He would turn eighteen in January. If the *Heinrich* kept to her schedule, they would be somewhere in the

Gemini Basin by then, almost on the other side of the Confederacy. "Yeah, I guess it is only a few months now."

"Are you going to head back soon?"

He sat back and found he had no answer. He had not thought seriously about the travel schedule since the day Hans had retrieved him. He was stuck on the *Heinrich* for the time being, and they were hardly going to run him back to Taschin on his birthday. He knew they would circle back through this sector later, but by then it would be May or June, with *Sophie* accruing docking charges the whole time.

"I'd like to, I suppose," he said. "But I don't see how I can book passage on my own until January. My... my captain isn't likely to let me out of his sight."

Anders looked around and shrugged. "He doesn't seem to be watching now."

"I can't jump ship."

Anders dismissed it with a wave of his hands. "All I'm saying is that Malcolm had a lot of friends, and it wouldn't be that hard to find one heading back to Taschin. Heck, I'd take you even if I had to change my route."

Michael considered it. It was tempting, but it was not a decision he was going to make while sitting in a station hotel room, wearing a borrowed bathrobe. Still, he realized he did need to start planning his return to Taschin, and the sooner the better. "Well, I can't do it right now, but you've made a good point. I'll definitely be thinking about it."

Anders nodded. "Well, I'm off to Latera the day after tomorrow. Call my ship if you change your mind."

"Latera? We're headed there, too."

Anders raised his coffee mug to Michael. "Well then, I'll extend my offer by a week. Find me at Latera if you're interested."

"Thank you, Captain Anders, I may just do that."

"No more Captain for you, Michael. Call me Jimmy."

—— ◁ ——

Gabrielle pushed the eggs around her plate. The blue Captains' Guild logo repeated itself around the edgework of the china. Across from her, Hans scanned over a few documents next to his plate.

"I guess neither of us is particularly good company this morning," he said.

She sighed. "I guess not."

Hans set the papers down. "Am I keeping you from something?"

"No, I don't have any friends in port this trip, so I'm playing the tourist."

"You could volunteer for a few dock watches, you know. Maybe let Miss Schwartz or Mr. Brookstone have some extra time off."

She grinned. "No, not Walter. He's in trouble with the XO."

"Again? What for?"

"Are you sure you want to know?"

Hans grumbled. "I suppose not, but I swear if that young man doesn't clean up his act, Felicia is going to bounce his ass out the airlock."

At least that got a smile out of her.

Hans glanced back at his papers. "So why aren't you out with another crewmate? I hear Harry's a riot at port."

"She's almost twice my age, Dad."

Hans shook his head. "Nothing wrong with that in my book, but by the fact that you're even awake at this hour tells me you haven't been out carousing with Mr. Norris."

"Dad, I am not sleeping with Jake. I don't do that with crew."

"I didn't say you were, but the rumor is that you two have a wingman routine that rarely leaves either of you in your own beds."

"Dad!"

He held up his hands. "Not judging, though if your mother found out about it..."

"She's not going to. She's too busy pestering Alicia. Besides, Jake's parents are in port, so he's off being the good son."

"Then what about Michael?"

Gabrielle crossed her arms. "Do you not enjoy our breakfasts anymore?"

Hans started to answer, paused, and let out a deep sigh. "Of course I do, but they're not as nice when you're so sour. Is something wrong? Do I need to be dear old Dad instead of Captain Schneider?"

"No, Dad, it's nothing."

"Then if you're playing tourist, why aren't you doing it with Michael? He's still new to the crew. He could use some company."

She started poking at her eggs again. "Michael and I had something of an argument."

"Oh?"

She looked up at him, and could see that she was not going to get away with only that. "It was about Malcolm Fletcher."

"And?"

She shook her head but plunged in anyway. "I've been asking some questions at the last few ports. I wanted to find out the truth about him."

"And you didn't believe me?"

"I wanted you to be wrong... you know, just to be wrong for once in your life."

Hans slumped a bit. "I'm sorry, Gaby. From the look on your face I'm guessing I wasn't."

She shook her head. "It doesn't look like it. And when I told Michael, he got all upset and —"

"You told him?"

She shrugged. "I guess. It started off innocent enough, but then he got all defensive, and one thing led to another. I said something awful, and... we haven't talked much since."

Hans sat silently for a moment. "Gabrielle, it's easy for me to lose my temper over this because Peter was my little brother, the kid I was supposed to be looking out for, and the loss of him... well, I'm never going to be over it. Never. But Peter was just a distant uncle to you, and now Michael is here, and he needs family. He needs you."

"But Dad, if Malcolm was —"

"As reckless and evil as I think he was?" He shook his head. "It doesn't matter how bad Malcolm was. It doesn't even matter how much Michael defends him. Malcolm Fletcher's crimes aren't Michael's. You can't..." He trailed off with a sigh. "We can't keep blaming Michael for something he didn't do."

Gabrielle nodded, lifted her fork one more time, but ultimately pushed her plate away. "Okay, but I don't know how to fix it."

"With time," Hans replied. "We'll have a long layover at Callista Prime in a few months. We can go down to the old family homestead, maybe get some of Peter's things out of storage, and let Michael take in what he can."

"Do you think that will really work?"

He shrugged. "It's the best we can do."

Fini came out of her room, dressed and ready to go. Anders was still in his bathrobe, leering at Vera, but she kept her distance at the other end of the sofa. "You both did very well," Anders told them.

"It was easy enough," she said. "How about you, Vera?"

"I just want to get paid," Vera replied.

Anders pulled a money clip from the pocket of his robe and started peeling off crisp hundred notes. "Seven hundred a piece," he said, counting it out. "And that's on top of the three hundred I gave you yesterday."

Vera reached forward and grabbed at her pile without a word. Fini took hers and counted it out slowly. "So, Captain Anders, why the ruse? I mean, you knew his dad, right?"

"I had my reasons, and you've got your money."

She nodded and tucked the bills into her shirt. It was never comfortable to do that, but she always liked the look she saw on the johns when she did it. "And I do thank you for it, but I'm curious about why it was so important the he find you rather than you finding him. It seems simple enough. 'Hi, I knew your dad.' Why not?"

Anders took a step towards her. She had forgotten how tall he was. "You know, you ask a lot of questions for someone who wouldn't be missed."

Vera was already at the door. "Drop it, Fini. Let's go."

"Listen to your friend, little girl. You don't want to remember me any more than you want me to remember you. Understood?"

She backed away towards the door. "I'm sorry. I don't need to know anything, just um... thanks for the cash."

She followed Vera out the door and made sure it closed behind her before she ran.

Michael lay on his back with Karen's body pressed up against him, sweaty skin to sweaty skin. It was an act of both intimacy and necessity. In his narrow bed on the *Heinrich*, there was room for little else. They still did not have much time together in their second shift window, but at least they had been making good use of it, four times since they left Folsom.

She traced patterns on his chest with her fingernail. It was a delicious balance between tickling and hurting. "I want to do something nice when we get to Latera," she said.

"It's ok," he replied. "You don't have to make special plans for me."

"No, I really want to this time. It's a long layover, and we can get permission to go groundside. There's a string of resort islands near the equator, a couple hours' flight from the main spaceport. We could get a little bungalow, sit out on the beach... go diving even."

"Sounds fun," he said, "but I hate to see you go to all that trouble."

She shifted to look up at him. "I want to make a memory with you, Michael, because it's going to be the last time for a while."

"Last time?" he asked. He shifted to look back at her, but as soon as their eyes met, she looked away.

"I'm transferring," she said. "There's an opening on the *Sailing Siegfried*, and I'm taking it."

"Wait, transfer?" He found himself backing away, which did not amount to much in their confined space, but she retreated as well.

"It's for a department lead. It's a smaller ship, but it's a promotion. I've got the rating, so it's the right step for me."

"But why didn't you tell me?"

She shrugged, but he could still see some guilt in her face. "I didn't know until now. I applied for it before you even came on board. Charlie's a great department lead and everything, but I was going out of my mind sitting that third shift by myself. I did the paperwork as soon as I qualified for the rating, but I didn't hear back about anything until we reached Folsom station."

"And now?"

"It's too good to pass up," she said. "It may not mean as much to you with your family connections, but this is an officer position. I can start making some real money there, a higher cap on ship shares, the whole deal. Here I'm always going to be third shift watch."

"And me? Us?"

She reached out to put a hand on his shoulder, but he rolled back in reaction. "Michael, look this isn't about you. This is about my career. You've been on ships your whole life, so you should know that. Crew come and go. Let's enjoy the time we have left and hope to cross paths again."

He fought against the truth, but deep down he knew she was right. He had lost count of how many crew had come and gone from Malcolm's ships over the years. There had been Geoffrey who had taught him to move in zero gravity, Susan of the long black hair who had been his first crush, Nel who had let him sit on her lap for his first engineering watch, and countless others. "I guess I wasn't expecting it here," he admitted.

She reached tentatively for him again, and he met her hand with his. "I'm sorry, Michael, it's what I have to do."

"And Latera?"

"I have a layover of three weeks before the *Siegfried* arrives. You'll have six days before the *Heinrich* pulls out. I'm sure there will be some kind of farewell party when we reach port, but if we leave that night, we can still have four or five days before you have to return for duty."

He sighed and pulled her closer. "Okay, so let's make good use of our time. You still have an hour before you have to get ready for your shift."

She let a grin crawl across her face. "If only I had your energy, Michael, third shift wouldn't seem so long."

"My Lady?" Bishop asked as he entered the office.

Elsa Watkins sat behind the desk. "Have a seat." Ideally, she would have had this conversation back aboard the *Blue Jaguar*, but this office on Latera station was about as secure as she could make it.

She poured two small glasses of wine. "You're to be commended, Mr. Bishop."

Bishop eyed the glass but did not reach for it. "And why is that?"

She shook her head and smiled. "You were right about that cargo," she said, taking a sip for herself.

He reached out and took the glass, sniffing at it but not yet drinking. "The valuable cargo?"

"Yes. We've been instructed to divert to Arvin to pick it up."

182

Bishop took a sip, swirled the glass around, and then set it back on the desk. "I appreciate the sentiment, Captain, but I believe I will refrain from any celebrations until we have delivered the cargo."

She sighed and set her own glass back on the desk. "Fair enough, Mr. Bishop." She knew she had been premature. She simply felt like enjoying the good news, and Bishop was the only person she could enjoy it with. But Bishop was right, and that was one more reason she was going to recommend him to Father Chessman.

"Will we be stepping up our departure?"

She shook her head. "The pickup window doesn't even open until the seventeenth, and I'm inclined to hang out here for another few days if feasible."

Bishop cocked an eyebrow. "Anders and the boy?"

"You're very sharp, Mr. Bishop."

He shrugged. "The shipping networks reported Anders' ship at Ballison six weeks ago, at Arvin three weeks ago, and at Folsom nine days ago. If he is tracking the boy, Latera is a very logical next stop."

"Excellent deduction, Mr. Bishop. Anders' last message suggested Latera as the best point for a rendezvous. The kid is supposed to be on board the *Heavy Heinrich*."

Bishop nodded. "I thought he might, given that the *Heinrich* was reported to have diverted to Taschin. The *Cerento* and the *Dolicia* were both possibilities as well."

Elsa stared at him for a moment. She trusted him, at least to a point, but she kept details from him mostly to see how well he was able to deduce them on his own. As rare a mind as Bishop had, it was not unique. If he could figure it out, so could others.

"If I may be so bold, my Lady, are you sure you should engage in this diversion when we have the cargo at Arvin?"

"I've considered that."

"And?"

"It's a rare opportunity to close out a troublesome account. Besides, it's been a long time since I tangled with Malcolm Fletcher. I want to see how much of him is in the boy."

"And if there's too much?"

She smiled. "Well, Mr. Bishop, that's where your particular talents come in."

He nodded. "Then I look forward to putting them to good use."

Michael sat alone in his quarters. They would reach Latera sometime the next morning during his shift, and he was still steeling his resolve. The letter on the screen before him effectively sealed his fate, but he knew better than to send it now. He could easily arrange for it to trigger at the end of liberty. That way, if he changed his mind, no one would need to know.

He scrolled back to the top and read it one more time.

"Gabrielle, first of all I wanted to thank you for making me feel welcome and for all the help you've given me on the navigation math..."

Chapter 19

"You've made some pretty bad decisions before, son, but this one deserves a trophy." — *Malcolm Fletcher*

JIMMY ANDERS LEANED FORWARD against the railing, looking at the schools of fish swimming on the other side. Most were grayish, but several sported more colorful orange and yellow stripes. His first warning of Elsa Watkins' approach was her image reflected against the glass next to his.

"Picking out your dinner, Jimmy?" she asked.

"No, merely enjoying the movement. They say that groundside you can go swimming and see them even closer. It's like an environment suit, but for water instead of vacuum."

"The aquarium is good enough for me," she replied. "I prefer things to be boxed up, under control. Speaking of which, how's our boy?"

"Our boy?"

"Yeah, I figured I came all this way. That makes him as much mine as yours."

"Fair enough," he replied. "His ship is due in sometime tomorrow. I already spoke with him back at Folsom, and if I read him right, he'll come looking for me as soon as he hits the dock."

185

"How are you playing it? I'm fine with snatching him, but accessing the data would go more smoothly with his cooperation."

Jimmy smiled. "Oh, he'll cooperate all right. After all, that's his whole point in going back early, to look at that data."

"And where do we come in?"

"Why, you remember what good friends we all were with Malcolm, don't you, Elsa?"

She shuddered. "Good angle, Jimmy, but don't you ever call me that in public again, okay?"

"Sure thing, Lady. Sure thing."

They held Karen's farewell party at the Short End. It was one of the smaller clubs on Latera station, but it was both classy and cozy. As was tradition, they had rented it out for the night, restricting it to *Heinrich* crew and guests. The guests ended up numbering forty-eight, but it still felt tight-knit. Stories were told, toasts made, and farewells said. The station itself was heading into its afternoon when they wrapped up, though it was well into third shift back on the near-empty *Heinrich*. Karen, of course, was still going strong when the last of her comrades faded, but Michael stuck it out to the end.

Drunk, but not staggering, they picked up their luggage and made their way down two rings to the groundside shuttle docks. They ate a few snacks while waiting for their flight, and Michael focused on drinking as much water as he could.

"They'll have water on the flight," Karen teased him.

"Yeah, about that... I'm sorry, Karen, but I'm not going."

"What?"

"I'm not going down to Latera with you."

She stared at him with dizzy eyes. "You're kidding, right?"

He shook his head. "I'm sorry."

Her eyebrows pinched together. "Well why the fuck not?"

"I can't explain," he said. "Not now, but there are things I have to do. This really isn't about you, and that makes it that much harder."

"It's not you, it's me?" she shot back at him. "That's pretty lame, even for a kid."

He stood. "I'm not a kid, Karen."

"Well you're acting like one, dropping this on me at the last minute. I made plans with you, you little spoiler."

He picked up his bag. "And I'm sorry. I'm sure you'll have a good time anyway. I've never seen you alone when you didn't want to be."

"And what the hell is that supposed to mean?"

He shook his head and took a step back. "I do wish you the best, Karen, and I honestly hope to run into you again at some future port of call, but I have to do this now."

She scowled at him and started to say something, but she held it back. She finally settled on a nodding frown. "Yeah, okay Michael. You do what you have to do, but the next time I see you, you'd better have a damn good explanation."

"I will," he told her. "I promise."

She pulled her feet up onto her seat, crossing her arms across the top of her knees. "Then you go do what you're going to do. I'm a big girl. I'll be all right."

"Until next time," he said with a wave that was almost a salute.

She turned her head away and rested it on her crossed arms.

He turned away and walked out of the dock. He found a public terminal and punched up the code he had been given twelve hours before. Captain Anders answered right away. "Good to hear from you, Michael. Are you ready?"

"I've said my goodbyes."

"Excellent. I'm waiting at ring twelve, dock eighteen. It's the *Blue Jaguar*."

"Wait, I thought you said you were on the *Diving Belle*."

"I'll explain when you get here. See you soon."

187

He was not sure what to make of the change, but he was committed now. True, he could still go back to the ship and cancel his letter to Gabrielle, but after breaking it off with Karen, he felt he had already paid the entry fee. He was going to get what he came for.

He shifted his duffel to the other shoulder and made his way up seven rings and out to dock eighteen. He spotted Captain Anders standing by the dockside watch desk talking to a striking woman with pale skin but dark black hair. He waved, and they beckoned him forward.

"Good to see you, Michael. I'd like to introduce you to Captain Jana Lewis. She knew your father back in the war."

The woman extended her hand. "Glad to meet you, Michael. Your father was a good captain. I'm sorry to hear what happened."

Michael took her hand and shook it. It was warm but somehow felt delicate. He played the name over in his head but did not recognize it. Then again, Malcolm had rarely talked about his war years in any detail. "Thank you, Captain Lewis."

"So, Michael," she said. "I understand you want to get back to Taschin to claim your dad's old ship."

"Yes," he replied. "The *Sophie's Grace*."

She looked surprised. "Not the *Hammerhead*?"

He shook his head. "No, she had a major drive failure a long time ago."

"Still, I'm sure Malcolm would have chosen a good ship. I also understand there's some question of records?"

"Yes," Anders spoke up. "Michael wants to go through some of Malcolm's old war records. I figure they would have transferred over from his old ship."

Captain Lewis nodded. "I wouldn't believe otherwise. Malcolm was meticulous like that." She turned back to Michael. "Well, I happen to be heading back towards Taschin. Would you like to hitch a ride?"

He turned back to Anders. "I had thought I would be going with you."

"Well, as I was explaining to Jana here, I was hoping to tag along with you. That is, if you would be all right sharing the data on old battle sites."

"I suppose, but what about your ship?"

He frowned. "Well, truth be told, I got confirmation on an old wreck near Pinot's Hammer. The cargo won't have any commercial value, but it's old enough that it may have some historic appeal. Antiques, that sort of thing. My first officer manages most of the actual salvage operations, and he's licensed, so I was planning to send him on and catch up later. This one's going to take a while."

Michael nodded in gradual acceptance. It made a sort of sense, and he knew what Malcolm had always said about picky beggars. "They suck vacuum — you don't want to suck vacuum, do you son?" He turned back to Captain Lewis. "Then I humbly accept your offer of passage, Captain Lewis. I do have a number of ratings, so I may be able to offer some help."

She grinned. "You sound just like him. I'm sure we'll find something for you to do. Come on, Jimmy, you too. My pushback is set for two hours. Let's get moving."

Commander Samuel Collins stepped onto the dock of Latera station. Normally he would have had to take the shuttle over from the navy's station, but he politely encouraged the "captain" of the fleet courier to drop him off directly at the civilian station. After all, the captain was only a captain in the context of his ship, as couriers usually only rated a lieutenant for their command slots. Still, it was always considered rude to pull rank on another officer's ship, so he had been polite. His boss's reputation did not hurt matters either.

He had already accessed the docking registry on their way in, so he headed confidently down six rings and out to dock four, the *Heavy Heinrich*. A middle aged woman was sitting at the dockside watch desk. She set down her pad as he approached.

"What can I do for you, sir?" she asked.

He read the name tag: Roxanne Collier. "I am trying to get in touch with one of your crew, Miss Collier, a young man by the name Michael Fletcher."

"And what would you want with this Michael Fletcher? I don't think he's looking to join the Navy."

He smiled as pleasantly as he could muster. "I'm not a recruiter. Mr. Fletcher filed an information request under the Records and Reconciliation Act. I'm here to give him that information."

The woman raised an eyebrow at him. "Must have been some request to rate a Commander."

He sustained his smile with effort. "It caught my eye. Now, is Mr. Fletcher aboard?"

"No, he's on liberty."

He nodded, letting his smile slip a bit. "Can you tell me where I might find him?"

"I'm sorry, but it's against company policy to give out that kind of information. Crew security, you understand."

"I see. Can you possibly get him a message for me?"

"Normally I might," she said. "After all, I suppose he asked for you, but this liberty is a little special. We have a crewman departing at this port, you see, and she and Michael had become close. I would hate to interrupt their time together for anything short of an emergency."

His smile slipped away entirely. "Well, I can wait a few days. You'll leave him a message that I called?"

"Certainly," she said. "How can he reach you?"

He had not even selected a hotel yet, so he had few options. "I'll be in the port registry," he said and handed her his card: Commander Samuel Collins, Naval Intelligence, Arvin.

Michael sat at the pilot's station on the bridge of the *Blue Jaguar*. They were already sailing under tach, so the pilot's job was over, but Captain Lewis had offered to let him monitor the navigation readings. Felipe Toro sat beside him at the actual navigator's station. He was much quieter than Gabrielle had been, but he clearly knew his navigation.

"We're much nimbler than your big freighters," he told Michael. "We don't waste our time with all those off-axis sail calibrations. We weave through a lot of turbulence that would collapse the bigger sails you're used to."

He nodded knowingly. That was similar to how the *Sophie* had been run, but until he had been on the *Heinrich*, he had never understood why. The *Jaguar* was not quite as maneuverable as the *Sophie*, or perhaps Toro was simply not as deft a navigator as Malcolm had been. Michael knew better than to speculate out loud on which was more true.

They were two days out of Latera en route to Magella. It was a smaller station than any that the *Heinrich* would visit, but it was exactly the kind of world he and Malcolm frequented during his childhood: small, rough, and a little off the beaten path. It was also more directly on the path back towards Taschin than retracing *Heinrich*'s path would have been.

He saw a wiggle on the cross-spin third derivative, but it did not hold. He looked over to Toro, but he did not seem to pay it any attention. Then it happened again, and an alert popped up on both of their stations. "Wake Detection," it read. "Crossing course, eight by three degrees, closest approach four light hours."

"What's that?" he asked.

"Nothing," Toro replied, and dismissed the alert on his display.

Michael read it again and hit the icon for more information. It brought up a display with their present position, an animated display of the current winds, and a ragged gray line projecting across their path, growing broader and fainter the further it went. Its direction and length corresponded to the course projected by the initial alert message.

"Is it that damned wake warning again?" It was the first officer, Marcus Nieru, standing over his shoulder.

"Yes, sir, but I've never heard of a wake warning before."

"Oh, it's some cocked up theory about tach sails leaving an imprint in the wind, like the wakes of those groundside ships, the ones that run in the water."

Michael raised an eyebrow. "I've never read that in any of the navigation texts."

"Well, if it actually worked it might have made it in."

"It doesn't?"

Nieru shook his head. "These supposed wakes are indistinguishable from other noise. Isn't that right, Mr. Toro?"

Toro stirred next to him. "Yep, nothing but noise."

"They tried to make it work back during the war," Nieru continued, "to give us some kind of proximity detection to look out for other ships, but it never worked. I swear, the next upgrade we do is going to rip that shit out of the system."

"That would be nice, sir," Toro replied. "It's damned annoying having that pop up all the time and not being able to do anything about it."

"Well, perhaps soon, Mr. Toro. Soon."

Michael looked back at the display on his station. The gray line remained, and a small note appeared next to it: two-sail configuration, 780 tau, 83% confidence. For noise, it seemed awfully specific, but with Nieru standing over his shoulder, he decided it was not worth the trouble. He closed the display and canceled the original wake warning.

"Good to be on the bridge, isn't it?" Nieru asked him.

"Yes, much better than engineering," he replied.

He got another wake warning two hours later, and this time he cleared it as quickly as Toro did.

Felicia Corazon stepped onto the bridge of the *Heinrich*. "It's an hour from end of liberty. What's our count?"

Walter Brookstone checked the display as his station. "Fifty-nine aboard."

"Is that counting the dock officer or not?"

"No, ma'am. Karl Roth has dock duty, so we're only missing three at this point: Feldman, Fletcher, and Tennyson."

She nodded. Charlie Feldman and Michael Fletcher had become reasonably good friends and would probably show up together, and Tennyson was notorious for hitting the shops up until the last minute. But then she remembered Karen Larkin.

"Wait, didn't Fletcher go groundside with Larkin?"

"I believe so," Brookstone replied.

"Do you have contact information for her?"

"No, ma'am, but I can look it up."

"Give her a call. I want to make sure Mr. Fletcher isn't still asleep in some beachside hammock."

"Yes, ma'am."

She checked the cargo and fuel status and went back to her ready room. Fifteen minutes later, her door chimed. It was Brookstone.

"Ma'am, everyone has reported in except Fletcher."

"And did you find Miss Larkin?"

He licked his lips and gulped. "Yes, ma'am. She says Mr. Fletcher did not go with her."

"What?"

"According to her, he dropped her off at the shuttle dock, said his goodbyes, and left her there."

She felt the room spin as she took a few deep breaths. "Shit," she managed at last. "Put out a general announcement to the crew. I want anyone who has seen or heard from Mr. Fletcher since that farewell party, and get Miss Larkin back on the line for me."

"Yes, ma'am. Do you want me to alert station security?"

"No, not yet, but call the local branch of Fidelity Union. Have them send all of Michael's transactions since we got here. Tell them the captain asked for it."

"The captain, ma'am?"

"Just do it."

She fought the rising panic. The party had been five days ago. If he had jumped ship or gone groundside, there was no telling where he could be by now. Her monitor jumped to life. "I have Miss Larkin for you, ma'am."

"Karen," she said. "You said Michael didn't go with you."

"No, ma'am," she replied. She could hear the ocean waves in the background. "He left me at the docks, said he'd changed his mind or something."

"Or something?"

"I'm sorry, ma'am. I was pretty surprised and, honestly, still a little drunk at the time. He said that he had to do something and that I should understand."

"That was it? He had to do something?"

"Yes, ma'am. He didn't take the news well, my transferring and all. I figured he was angry at me. Is he all right?"

"I don't know. We're trying to figure out where he is. For all I know he's heading for the dock right now."

"Do you want me to come back up?"

"No, but if you think of anything else, call it in."

"Yes, ma'am. Definitely."

Brookstone chimed in as soon as the call ended. "The bank says the last transaction they have is at a food court near the shuttle docks, thirty-one minutes before Miss Larkin's shuttle flight."

"Nothing for the five days since then?"

"No, ma'am."

Her door opened without a chime. It was Hans Schneider. "Felicia, I heard the announcement about Michael. Do we have a problem?"

She stood. "Yes, sir. I'm afraid we do."

194

Chapter 20

"Take the help when it's offered, especially if you think you don't need it, because honestly, you're not smart enough yet to know the difference." — Malcolm Fletcher

COMMANDER COLLINS HAD BEEN across from the *Heinrich* dock all morning, watching the crew return. He had pulled a photo of Michael from the port registry the night before, but none of the crew had matched it. The stream had dwindled to a trickle, and now only the dock officer remained. He seemed increasingly nervous, as well he should. It was almost noon, and the *Heinrich* was scheduled for a pushback at thirteen hundred.

He approached the dock officer. "Excuse me, I'm looking for a member of your crew."

The officer stood, his name reading Karl Roth. "Which crewman?"

"Michael Fletcher."

Roth's eyes went wide. "I see. Have you been in contact with Michael?"

"Not recently. He made an information request a few weeks back, and I wanted to speak to him about that request. I've already left a message for him."

"I'm sorry. I wasn't aware of that. Your name please?" He handed over another one of his cards. Roth took a brief look at it. "Could you excuse for me for a moment?" He stepped away and whispered into his wrist link. Collins did not like the way this was progressing, but Roth returned a few minutes later.

"Is there a problem with Mr. Fletcher?" Collins asked.

"I'm sorry, Commander. We're having a momentary security issue. Would you be willing to wait here for a few minutes?"

"Would this security issue have anything to do with Mr. Fletcher?"

Roth's eyes gave him the only answer he needed.

"It doesn't matter," Collins assured him. "I'll wait."

"Thank you, sir."

Gabrielle headed down to her quarters on deck two. Pushback had been cancelled, or at the very least, it had been delayed past the end of first shift, so she was not going to be there for the up-tach. All for Michael! She stormed into her cabin and gave her duffel a solid kick.

"When I get my hands on him," she growled.

She sat on her bed and looked at her duffel over by her desk. She might as well unpack. She started pulling dirty clothes out and transferring them into a bag to take down to Harry. A few things were still clean, so she hung them to get the wrinkles out. Finally she pulled out a few souvenirs and set them on her desk temporarily.

That was when she saw the message light blinking on her monitor. She signed in. Twelve messages. Four were automatic updates that should not even be sent during liberty. She had been on Wally's back about that for months. Three were navigational forecasts for the upcoming leg. The data went directly into the charts on the navigation console, but the summary was traditionally copied to all the navigators. Two were from friends on other ships whose messages had caught up with her here at Latera. One was the agenda for tomorrow's senior staff meeting. One was a copy of Wally's general announcement about Michael.

And one was from Michael.

It was dated from before they docked, but it had only shown up now at the bottom of her message list. She opened it immediately and scanned through it. Then she read it again more carefully.

Gabrielle,

First of all I wanted to thank you for making me feel welcome and for all the help you've given me on the navigation math. I know it's been a little rough between us this last couple of weeks, but I want you to know that my decision to leave was not because of you or anyone else on board. I can see that you all have the kind of bond I had with Malcolm, and I know you tried to form that bond with me as well.

But I'm not ready for that, not until I get the truth about Malcolm. I would like to think that your father is full of crap, but I've learned enough to realize that he might be right. It's not enough to know that Malcolm was a privateer or that he was there when Peter and Sophia died. I have to know his role in all of this. Until I do, I cannot find my place in the world, whether that be on the *Heinrich* or not.

So I'm leaving. There's a way for me to definitively find out what happened, so I'm going to do that. I'm sorry for not saying more or telling you ahead of time, but to be honest, I worried that your father would try to stop me. I won't let him. I'll try to catch up with you again after I know the truth. I'm sorry for all the problems that this is likely to cause, and I hope you and the rest of the crew will forgive me for doing what I have to do.

I expect you to share this with your father once you realize I'm gone. That's all right, but please don't let him try and stop me. If he does, I'll only leave again when I'm of age.

— Michael

"Fuck," was all she could say.

The four of them sat in the officers' wardroom. Corazon had brought the navy officer up, and Gabrielle had held Michael's letter hostage as her leverage to get into the meeting. Her father had given her a particularly lethal glare over that, but she had stood her ground.

The officer was the last of them to read the letter. When he was done, he set the hardcopy down in the center of the table between them. "Thank you for sharing that with an outsider. I only wish I could have found him beforehand."

"You said you were here because Michael requested some information," Corazon prompted. "This was about Malcolm Fletcher's war history, yes?"

Her father turned sharply to the XO. "You knew about this?"

Corazon held up her hand. "He had spoken to me. I suggested he file under the Records and Reconciliation Act, but I didn't think it would net us an intelligence officer. Is that, in fact, why you're here?"

"Yes, Ms. Corazon. That is indeed why I am here, at least in part."

Gabrielle raised her hand. "Then do you know what happened?"

Collins smiled briefly. "I brought the information specifically for Mr. Fletcher. Forgive me, but I am not inclined to share it with anyone else before I can give it to him."

Her father snorted. "Then what good are you?" He turned to the XO. "Why did you even let him on board?"

Corazon kept her cool. "Because I believe he can help us track Michael down." She turned back to Collins. "Am I right to think that?"

Collins gave a slight nod. "I do have certain resources that neither you nor station security are familiar with. Michael's case is of particular interest to me, so yes, I will help you track him down. However, to the point of his letter, I am not interested in stopping him. Rather, I want to get him the very answers he seeks."

Her father stood. "I already know what happened, and I don't need you to tell me again who killed my brother."

"Father!"

Hans glared at her.

"Dad, don't turn this into a repeat of Michael's homecoming. If you want to find Michael, let this man help you do it."

He took a deep breath and returned to his seat. He waved his hand towards Collins, but did not speak.

Collins accepted it and turned back to Corazon. "I presume you've already notified station security."

She nodded. "But I doubt he's even on station anymore."

"I agree," he said. "I can only think of three definitive sources for the incident in question, the records we have at Arvin, the records from the *Hammerhead*, and the records from the *Reilly*. The *Reilly* was destroyed near the end of the war, and the *Hammerhead* was scrapped nine years ago. However, I would expect Malcolm Fletcher copied the *Hammerhead*'s records to his new ship."

Hans nodded. "And that ship is back on Taschin."

Corazon picked it up from there. "So you think he's headed either to Arvin or Taschin?"

"Very likely, but the question is how is he travelling?"

"What does it matter?" Gabrielle asked. "Can't we just go there and look for him?"

Hans shook his head. "A station the size of Arvin? Or groundside on Taschin? If he didn't want to be found, I doubt we would find him. We need to know which ship he took." He turned back to Collins. "You can actually determine that?" Collins smiled. "No promises, but I'll see what I can do."

The *Jaguar* dropped out of tach at Magella two hours early. It was a much smaller station than any the *Heinrich* had visited, except perhaps Taschin, so traffic control was minimal. They pulled in at the one and only ring and docked without incident. Captain Lewis declared "restricted liberty" of forty-one hours.

As soon as he could, he asked what she had meant by restricted.

"I keep more of my crew on-board than many ships do," Captain Lewis replied. "I find it helps with faster turnarounds, but I make up for it with some longer layovers at more hospitable locations, actually getting some vacation groundside."

It made some sense to him, though Malcolm had never run things that way, even on the old *Hammerhead*. "Will I be able to go aboard?"

"I don't see why not, but keep your head down. This isn't as nice a place as Latera. In fact, why don't you go with Anders? He can help you out."

He thanked her and grabbed a few things, most importantly an empty duffel. He had not packed much in the way of personal gear, and the available stores on the *Jaguar* were not nearly up to the standards of the *Heinrich*. He was looking forward to doing a little shopping.

Jimmy Anders was waiting for him in the airlock, but he did not seem to be in any hurry. "Ah, Michael. You look ready for the hunt."

He hefted the duffel. "Just looking for a toothbrush and some extra socks, that sort of thing."

"Well, that should be simple enough. Let's go."

Magella station was not what he was expecting. It was not that it was merely small. It was run down, even dirty. It was not anything so obvious as trash on the deck or rust on the pipes. Rather, it was in the details: an old stain on a section of wall, an unpainted structural joint, that kind of thing. He would not have even noticed these things a few months ago, but he had grown used to the *Heinrich*, where almost everything was either spotless white or polished chrome.

The shopping was perfunctory. Anders found them a drab shop called simply Crew Supplies. Their wares were still not up to what he had had aboard the *Heinrich*, but at least it was better than what he had found on the *Jaguar*. Cotton seemed to be the safest bet here, so he loaded up. The toothbrush situation was not good at all. They didn't have any of the pulse jet brushes, so he settled for one of the old vibrating kinds.

He made his way to the register, but Anders intercepted him. "Let me pay, Michael."

Michael allowed it, but after they got out, he piped up. "Thanks for that, but I do have some money."

Anders patted Michael's shoulder. "I know, son, but I figure the less you show up on the station radar, the better. Now, if you've got actual cash, you can buy me a drink or perhaps a skin dance or two."

He did actually have some cash. He had pulled six hundred from his account before Karen's farewell party back at Latera. "I do, but why do you think I should stay off the station's radar?"

Anders paused near a support column at the edge of the corridor and glanced around. "Look, Michael, I know you said you settled up with your old ship on Latera, but I have to ask. Did you really settle it, face to face, crewman to captain?"

"Not quite face to face, but I think I did enough."

Anders shook his head. "I can't blame you. I was young and impulsive myself, and I sure as hell avoided my captain whenever possible. Still, if you left with only a note or something, he might very well be looking for you."

Michael frowned. "They're not going to divert from their route." At least, he did not think they would do it a second time. Not even Uncle Hans was that committed to the long-lost nephew. "Besides, I made it clear that they should not come looking for me."

Anders chuckled. "And I'm sure that your captain has a long history of doing what you tell him to do, eh?"

Shit. "Well, not so much."

"Look, all I'm saying is you should lay low these next few weeks. Don't leave a wake for them to follow."

"I guess, but I had thought I might send a message to their next port. You know, to let them know I'm doing all right."

Anders shook his head. "Not yet. Why don't you wait until you're back on board your own *Sophie*. Tell them then, when it's a done deal."

He nodded. "I see your point."

"You don't want to call the Confederates down on us for transporting a minor after all."

"Yeah, I guess I hadn't thought about that, and I definitely don't want to cause any trouble for you or Captain Lewis."

"No trouble at all, my boy."

"So, you mentioned something called a skin dance?"

Anders grinned. "Oh yes, I know a place. Hold your money tight, Michael, or you'll leave broke and broken."

It had been twenty-two hours since the four of them had last sat in the *Heinrich's* wardroom. Ms. Corazon and her father were there as a matter of course. Gabrielle had not been invited, but she had been shrewd enough to be waiting in the inner lock to guide Commander Collins through the ship. She led him into the room and took a seat before anyone said a word.

Her father raised an eyebrow at her, but she stared him down with a glare of her own. Yes, Father was captain and uncle to Michael, but she at least had been his friend.

"Thank you for getting back to us, Commander Collins," Ms. Corazon said, motioning him to the seat opposite her. "We still have no updates from station security or our inquiries to the planetary authorities below. We're hoping you have better news."

He smiled politely. "I do have news, but I don't particularly think it's better news." He opened his briefcase and passed out hardcopies of a report. They were all stamped with "NI Classified" and were printed on a strangely slick paper. Gabrielle had heard about this stuff once: auto-degrading paper. The ink would be gone within the hour, evaporating as the paper slowly oxidized and disintegrated.

Collins laid his out squarely in front of him and flipped past the cover sheet. "One hundred twenty-nine ships left dock from the time of Mr. Fletcher's last sighting to the time you issued your security alert. These are listed with their flight plans on pages one and two, organized by vessel class.

"Nine were passenger liners, and their passport policies are strict enough I don't believe he could have bluffed his way on board. Another twenty-eight were corporate freight ships that had advertised passage, and nineteen of those reported taking on passengers. The N.I. office here has crosschecked all the passenger names reported by those vessels against next of kin and other contacts, and they seem to be legitimate. An additional eighteen ships had posted open positions, and fifteen of them filled those positions here. Those fifteen additions to the crew manifests were crosschecked against arrival dates and financial records, and they all appear valid, starting over the last several weeks and stopping around the various departures."

He glanced briefly at the three of them and turned the page. "Another thirty-eight private vessels offered neither passage, post, nor cargo. They are also quite small, many of them purely sublight craft, and it would be unlikely Mr. Fletcher could successfully stow away for the duration of a flight. With his history on smaller vessels, I believe he would know this. This leaves us with thirty-six vessels, a mix of yachts, surveyors, and independent freighters. Any of them could have given him free passage and not reported it."

Her father shook his head. "Thirty-six ships scattering to the winds. I appreciate what you've done, but we still don't know enough to find him."

Collins smiled briefly and cleared his throat. "The favor of free passage to an unrelated minor is not one to be granted lightly. An aggressive prosecutor could make a kidnapping charge out of it, so this would almost certainly have to be someone Mr. Fletcher knew, either that or someone that Captain Malcolm Fletcher knew."

Her father took on a scowl and was about to launch into one of his rants. Gabrielle could see it in his eyes, so she cut him off. "Are you saying you know who Captain Fletcher knew?"

Collins nodded. "What I'm about to tell you is not generally known, and were it not for the sterling reputation of Schneider & Williams and its officers and owners," he said with a nod to her father, "I would not even be discussing this. I must ask for your word as loyal citizens of the Confederacy not to repeat this information."

His gaze swept across them as they each nodded in turn.

"Thank you," he said, turning the page. "Since the Caspian rebellion and the rise of the Yoshido pirates afterwards, we in Naval Intelligence have begun tracking people's movements: the ships they take, the places they visit, the times they visit them, purchases they make, and so forth. I don't want to say too much about our methods, but suffice it to say, I could pull a report on each of you for the last ten years that would startle even your memories."

Gabrielle thought about it. They reported crew manifests at each port. Passports were checked at each of the stations, to say nothing of all the financial transactions on station. Hell, the hotels could probably even track who she had slept with based on the patterns of passkey usage. She gazed down at the page, a long list of names, dates, locations, and ship names.

"For normal citizens such as you," Collins continued, "the tracking is simple and quite accurate. You tend to stay in the more populated areas, stick to the orbital stations and sanctioned ground ports, and don't play with false identification. As privately as you conduct your affairs, much of it is actually an open book to us."

Her father stared at Collins. "And do you report this to anyone?"

"Like the taxing authorities?" Collins grinned as her father's eyes went wide. "No, this is strictly for Naval Intelligence and requires a security clearance to run even the most basic of pattern-matching queries. Believe me, there are a number of government officials and their mistresses who would not appreciate the existence of this database."

"Then what do you use it for?" Ms. Corazon asked. "This looks like a random assortment of names and places to me."

"For pattern matching, personnel overlaps, times when one identity disappears and another one reappears... that kind of thing. It's not meant to keep track of people like you. It's meant to keep track of those we cannot trust."

Gabrielle was scanning the page, and the next, and so on. One name kept coming up over and over. "Who is James Anders?"

Collins nodded to her. "The young lady wins a prize. Of all the common intersections between Mr. Fletcher, Captain Fletcher, and the present and past crews of those thirty-six ships, Captain James Anders comes up more than any other, and most suspiciously, his last port of call was Folsom station."

"We were there last week," Gabrielle said.

"At the same time Anders was," Collins replied.

Her father nodded firmly. "So he's on Anders' ship, the *Diving Belle*, right?"

"That was my first reaction," Collins replied, "but now I think not. The *Diving Belle* did not depart for twenty-nine hours after Mr. Fletcher's last sighting, and when she did depart, her flight plan was for Pinot's Hammer, which is in the wrong direction. The *Diving Belle* is primarily a salvage vessel, and I do have reports of a recently discovered wreck in the outer orbits of that system."

"But he still could have gone," Hans insisted. "Maybe you're wrong about him heading back."

Collins shook his head. "The flight plan was filed by Anders' first officer, which is quite an anomaly in the *Diving Belle's* records. So, I crosschecked Captain Anders' history against the other ships in port." He turned to the final page.

Gabrielle did as well. Only one ship showed up, again and again: the *Blue Jaguar*.

"The *Blue Jaguar* left Latera station two hours after Mr. Fletcher's last sighting. Her flight plan was for Magella, and I believe both Captain Anders and Mr. Fletcher are on board."

Her father scanned around the table. "Then that's where we go, to hell with our cargo."

Ms. Corazon swallowed hard, but she did not say anything. So with a sigh, Gabrielle was the one to speak up. "We can't, Father."

Her father turned to her. "This is your cousin, young lady, not some errant watch stander."

"I know," she answered him. "I'm saying the *Heinrich* can't catch them."

Collins nodded to her. "Your daughter is quite correct, Captain Schneider. Our best estimate puts the *Blue Jaguar* at three point seven lights to the day. Even with the best navigation, the *Heavy Heinrich* cannot quite reach three. With the *Jaguar's* head start combined with her median turnaround of thirty-two hours, she's probably on her way out of Magella even now."

Hans sagged against the table. "I cannot simply sit here and wait."

"As it happens," Collins said, "I have a priority claim for passage on Naval couriers, and I intend to take the next one back to Arvin. Even if that is not Mr. Fletcher's destination, it is an excellent information nexus to see where the *Jaguar* is heading. I could possibly take one or two of you with me if you decide you want to."

Hans began to nod slowly, building steam. "That's an easy decision."

Gabrielle reached out and took hold of his arm. "Yes, Father, I think it is."

Chapter 21

"The only reason for putting a rat in a cage is because you plan to do something worse to it later." — Malcolm Fletcher

FOR TWO DAYS OUT of Magella, Michael sat watch on the bridge without seeing another wake alert. He could almost believe they were a rare software glitch. After all, he had never heard of such a thing in all his years in space, but late in the shift, he began to question it.

The tachyon winds shifted slightly to port with an aggressive clockwise spin, and this time he correctly used the left-handed coordinates for calculating the adjustment, but he was still off from the orientation change Felipe put in. When he asked, Felipe merely said, "You're overcorrecting. You don't have to meet it head on, just close enough to keep you at speed without getting pushed out of the lane. It's not only the wind; it's where you are."

He nodded silently, hoping he understood. Still, he wanted to run the numbers again after his shift, so he opened the log to copy the data to his personal storage. That was when he saw them: three wake alerts in the last hour. They had not shown up on his terminal, but they were still in the log. He grabbed them as part of his data selection and sent them along, mumbling something about "checking my math after dinner."

Three in an hour was not exactly a rare software glitch, and he began to wonder if it was a glitch at all. A cluster like that did not seem to be random noise either. He thought about where they were, roughly halfway between Magella and Deshmon. They were moderately close ports, but they were small enough to not have much traffic between them. At least, not so many that he would expect to roll through that many wakes in such a short period. Maybe it was a glitch after all, but he was determined to look at them much more closely, just not under the watchful eyes of the first officer Nieru.

Dinner was immediately after the shift ended, and he ate it with Anders. Unlike the *Heinrich*, the crew of the *Blue Jaguar* had not made a point of getting to know him. It stung a bit, but he could understand. He was passing through, a transient guest. The fact that he had been allowed to watch the navigation did not truly change him from passenger to crew.

Still, he found himself examining the name and departmental patches of every crewman who walked past. The drive and environmental patches were fairly recognizable, but he found the cargo patches puzzling. At least, he presumed they were cargo with the blocky box shape, but the hammer threw him off.

"What are you looking at?" Anders asked him.

"The patches," he said, pointing towards one of the men in the food line. He was big and muscular with a crooked scar across his chin. "That one, with the box and hammer, what is it?"

Anders turned and looked. "Cargo."

Michael nodded. "I figured, but I wondered."

"Wondered what?"

"There are an awful lot of them. I've counted nine since I came on board, and I'm sure I haven't met everyone."

"Nine, so?"

He shrugged. "Well, the *Heinrich* had only six, and she was easily three times the size of the *Jaguar*."

Anders chuckled and frowned. "I could believe it. That's one of the reasons all the smaller traders are being squeezed off the main shipping lines. Those radial loaders are too damned efficient. Most of us can't compete."

Michael thought about the disastrous financial discussion he had had with Gabrielle. Radial loaders like the *Heinrich* really were that much more efficient. Plus, the *Heinrich* only docked at orbital stations, and they had their own dock workers. Ships like the *Blue Jaguar*, and for that matter his own *Sophie's Grace*, could land on the ground, and ground ports did not always have their own cargo teams. "I see your point," he said at last. "I guess I didn't think it through."

He went to his quarters after dinner. He had little else to do on the *Jaguar*, but instead of queuing up a movie, he pulled up the navigation data he had copied. He started to work on the course adjustment he had overdone, but the wake alerts called to him.

He opened the first and looked at it. It was a crossing course, almost perpendicular to the line of their own trajectory, though the computer was fuzzy on it given the distance, over twenty light days to the galactic south. The second was also a crossing course with a heading similar to the first, but closer. The computer had estimated it to be a much larger sail, moving more slowly. The third, again, was a crossing course, but this time going the opposite direction and only two light days away.

The three wakes clustered together like that seemed too much to be a random coincidence. That kind of traffic was only found in established shipping lanes, and even then, the Magella-Deshmon shipping lane was unlikely to see that kind of traffic over a day, let alone an hour. Thinking back to what Felipe had said, it was also about where you are. He pulled up a star chart and plotted the *Jaguar's* location in the hour when the wake alerts had fired.

Three dots appeared on the screen. He then plotted the estimated vectors from the wake reports, both forwards and backwards. The plot from the first wake detection did not seem to go anywhere very interesting, but it had been the most distant and weakest. The second and third had had almost exactly the same course but in opposite directions. One went to Tsaigo, and the other went to Tortisia. Tracing the vectors in the opposite direction led back to Tortisia and Tsaigo, respectively. Those ships had been in a shipping lane all right, just not theirs.

The paths between two nearby stars were mind-bogglingly empty, not merely of stars or planetary masses but of other traffic paths as well. Still, on rare occasions those paths could be close. He looked it up in the official chart listings, and the Tsaigo-Tortisia route listed a yellow-two warning about the Magella-Deshmon crossover, urging navigators to divert at least ten light days to the galactic south. Actual collisions would be astronomically rare, so many captains ignored such advisories, following the more direct paths, crossing traffic be damned.

Perhaps there was something to these wake detections after all, but if that were true, why were the alerts now being shifted to the log files instead of the active boards?

Elsa Watkins ate lunch in her quarters. They truly were her quarters, even though the name on the door read Captain Jana Lewis. All her crew knew her by that name, even Bishop and her first officer, though they also knew her as the Winged Lady. The one other person who knew her by that name also knew her by an older name she would prefer to see forever purged from the records.

And he sat across from her, eating pork tenderloin: Jimmy Anders.

"This is good — much better than you've got down in the galley."

She shrugged. "Captain's privilege."

"I appreciate it, but I don't think you invited me because you had extra."

She shook her head. "Your boy has been asking a lot of questions."

He took a sip of the juice and made a face at its tartness. "Well, he's curious."

"He's getting too curious for my taste, too curious by far."

Anders shrugged. "Well, he's never been on this kind of ship before. Things are different here. More cargo workers for starters."

She smiled at him. "Cargo workers?"

He chuckled. "Well, I could hardly call them boarders, could I?"

"No, I suppose not."

"So, what kind of questions is he bothering you with?"

She shook her head. "Not me, my bridge crew. I was willing to tolerate his interest in navigation. It seemed a reasonable distraction for him, but now he's digging through the logs looking at wake reports."

He made another face, this time not from the tart juice. "Watch reports?"

"Wake reports," she repeated. "Tachyon winds, sails, trailing wakes. That kind of thing."

He frowned. "I guess I've heard about them. Those don't actually work, do they?"

She shot him a feral grin. "Let's not get too deep into how I run my business. It's enough that he's been looking where he shouldn't, and I want it to stop."

"Why don't you cut off his access?"

"I already have, but now I'm worried about how much he's seeing on the bridge in general. We're keeping clean on this run, for more reasons than your boy, but I can't turn this into a peace-loving vessel at the flip of a switch. He's got an eye like Malcolm had, and I won't have that eye wandering around untended."

"So what then, toss him in the brig? I remind you that we're trying to keep his trust, or at least keep it long enough to access the *Sophie*'s computer core."

"I think we can avoid the brig for now, but I'm growing pessimistic about him handing over those codes in good faith. My security chief agrees."

Anders shrugged. "Your Mr. Bishop seems unnaturally dour if you ask me."

"I don't pay him for his optimism."

"Obviously. So what do you want to do about Deshmon? We get there tomorrow, right?"

"The boy stays on board. He jumped ship once. I don't intend on giving him that opportunity myself."

"What do I tell him?"

"Restricted liberty. He went last time."

He nodded. "Just as well. You know, he was actually thinking about sending a message back to his ship. Hey, I'm all right and all that."

She sighed. "I don't know how I let you talk me into this, Jimmy. I really don't."

"Restricted liberty, my ass!"

Michael sat up on his bed and bounced a ball against the wall partitioning off the closet. The only other time he had been denied liberty was when he had disobeyed Malcolm, but apparently on the *Blue Jaguar* this was a matter of course. And this turnaround was even faster than the last, nineteen hours.

He threw the ball again, hitting the exact same spot over and over. It made a nice hollow thump against the partition and fell back towards him as a dead weight. His head and shoulders were leaning against structural bulkheads. He had tried bouncing the ball against that, but it had retained too much energy and bounced wildly around the room. He had a private bath across from his bed, but that was a maze of uncatchable ricochets.

So he threw the ball again. By this point, he could see he was leaving a mark on that one spot.

213

Yes, he knew different ships were run different ways, but the *Jaguar* was almost alien to any ship he had even heard about. He did not have a lot of ship-born peers, but he did run into them at port every now and then. They sometimes complained about things Michael liked, or they raved about things he hated, but by and large, they were all living similar experiences — not so much on the *Jaguar*. How Captain Lewis kept her crew happy was beyond him.

"Better not be restricted next time," he grumbled. "Or I might have to find another berth."

Gabrielle pushed the remnants of her lunch around the tray. She hardly expected the food on board the CFS *CP-2133* to be up to the *Heinrich*'s standards, but even for instant food, this was pretty weak. The so-called galley was little more than a refrigerated locker, a speed heater, and a table with four chairs. Then again, with an active-duty crew of five, they probably never needed more than that.

The three passengers had been ordered onto a shifted schedule, two hours off from the crew. "It minimizes the shocks to the support systems that way," their skipper Morris had said, a lieutenant who seemed far too young to be that fat. Father was using the one shower on board at the moment, while she had breakfast. Her turn would come in an hour, after the water systems had recharged.

She heard footsteps and looked up to see Commander Collins ducking through the hatch. "Good morning," she said.

He nodded and went to the coffee dispenser. He sniffed at it and added a squirt of cream. "How are you holding up?"

She put on the best smile she could manage. "It's not home, but it's okay."

He sat down opposite her. "At least it's fast."

"How fast?"

He shrugged. "Emergency speed is classified, but we're moving at a good clip. We should reach Tortisia tomorrow and Arvin four days after that. You do the math."

She already had. It was almost four times faster than the *Heinrich*'s usual plodding pace. Even then, they weren't sure they would reach Arvin before Michael did. Collins had hinted that the *Blue Jaguar* might be faster than they expected, and they had lost another day and a half at Latera waiting for the next courier run.

"What do we do when we get there?"

"Well, I wish I could have sent word ahead to flag the *Blue Jaguar*, but of course, that message would have gone on this ship. If we get there first, we can be waiting when she docks. If not, hopefully we can hold her before she leaves."

"You hope? They've got Michael. Isn't that enough to hold them?"

He sipped at his coffee and chuckled. "We think Michael is on board, but that's a far cry from 'they've got him.' Captains don't take kindly to having their ships boarded and searched."

"Even by the navy?"

"How do you think your father would react?"

She frowned. "Yeah, he wouldn't like that much." In fact, she was pretty sure she knew exactly which sections of the commercial shipping code he would quote while standing steadfast in the airlock.

"Then what's your backup plan?"

He took another sip of his coffee and scowled. "I'm not sure I have one yet, but we have another five and a half days. Do you have any ideas?"

"Other than throttling him when we find him? No, I don't." She pushed her own tray away. "But I guess I should start thinking."

Michael stepped out of his quarters and stood for a moment, counting silently. After twelve seconds, he heard footsteps. Maya Zoland rounded the corner and spotted him. "Hey Michael, what's up?"

He shrugged. "I was thinking about getting a snack from the galley."

Maya grinned at him. "That's a capital idea. I'm pining for one of those brownies myself. Let's go."

Michael repressed a sigh and followed along. As if the restricted liberty had not been bad enough, after Deshmon he had been denied access to the bridge for monitoring navigation. Anders had explained that he had been causing too many distractions for the crew and suggested that he simply enjoy the rest of the trip as a passenger. "Get some rack time," he had said. "Catch up on the latest vids."

So for two days he had been stuck in his room, a virtual prisoner. Every time he went out into the corridor, another crewmate just happened by and was eager to accompany him on whatever he wanted to do. Last night had been Leo Perez for dinner. This morning had been Chester Walsh for breakfast and then Vince Weston for a trip to the gym. They were all either cargo handlers or mechanical specialists. The *Blue Jaguar* seemed to have an endless supply of them, all with sharp stares and strong arms. He had thought Karen had been muscular, but this Maya put her to shame.

Maya led him to the mess with frequent over the shoulder looks, chatting with him about the most inane topics. Michael followed obediently. Upon their arrival, he looked at the brownies but settled for a muffin instead. He headed back immediately, hearing Maya follow him all the way to the final corridor intersection. "See you around, Michael," she said.

Michael closed his door behind him and tossed the muffin onto his bed. He leaned against the door, pressing his ear hard against the surface. He listened. Eventually, he heard a pair of departing footsteps. He waited another minute, still listening. Nothing.

So he waited another minute more, and then five more. After ten minutes, there had still been no sound.

He went back into his bathroom and turned on the exhaust fan and then went back out to his door. He opened it but did not go out. He simply stood there by the door and counted. By the time he got to fifteen, he heard footsteps.

This time it was Leo walking by. He stopped outside his door and nodded to him. "You okay, Fletcher?"

"Yeah, I'm airing out the bathroom."

He sniffed at the air and peered past him. "Ah, I see you've been having some of Cookie's notorious muffins. That'll stink up any bathroom. I'd stick with the brownies if I were you."

"I'll remember that."

Leo nodded and started down the hall. "Holler if you need anything," he said.

Like a straitjacket? Michael shook his head and closed the door. He went back into the bathroom and turned off the fan. He stood before the sink, staring at himself in the mirror.

A fucking prisoner! He kicked the wall beneath the sink. It felt good, so he did it again, and a third time for good measure. That last one had made a lot of noise, so he gave up on it and returned to his bed.

"Catch up on the vids," he said to the empty room. "How about *Forty Days in the Pit* or maybe *Mariner's Escape*? Yeah, that would be a good one right now. Practical, plus lots and lots of Paula Stone's cleavage."

He shook his head and sat up. That was when he saw it. The wall panel beneath his sink was hanging loose. He got up slowly, stepped over, and knelt before it. It was not riveted onto the structural frame like the panels on *Heinrich* had been. It was clipped into tabs in the wall's metal frame. In his kicking, he had knocked two of the tabs out of their brackets.

He pulled at the loose end while pushing at the fixed end, and before long, the fixed end popped loose as well. The sink pipes came in through a gap between the panels, but the opening from there to the floor was largely clear. He laid down and cautiously put his head through. It was a collection of pipes, vents, and electrical conduits, almost exactly like the spaces he had worked in back on the *Heinrich*.

There were two exceptions, though, two very critical exceptions. First, all the wall panels he could see were attached using the same flimsy tab and bracket, even the panel out to the corridor. On the *Heinrich*, these would have been riveted into place or bolted down tight, making it impossible for him to open them from the cabin side of the wall. And second, the pipes did not go up or down through custom cuts in the solid deck. On *Heinrich*, the decks had been as thick as structural bulkheads, and the seals around the pipes and ducts had been air tight. But here, both above and below were simple grates with gaps every half-meter to allow access. The grates, at least, were screwed in, but both nut and bolt were wing nuts. He played with one to test it, turning it easily with his fingers.

On the *Heinrich*, he would have been trapped without a full toolset and a welding torch. But here... he smiled to himself. No tools required.

Chapter 22

"I agree. You are indeed well and truly fucked. So what are you going to do about it?" — Malcolm Fletcher

COLLINS STEPPED INTO THE gym. At least, that is what the hatch was labeled. It was a tiny compartment, three meters square, with a treadmill on one side and a resistance machine on the other. Hans Schneider was on the treadmill, watching a recorded news report on the screen before him. He muted it as soon as he saw Collins.

"Commander," he said, huffing a surprising amount for the speed he was walking at.

"Mr. Schneider," he replied. In most other settings, he would have referred to him by his merchant rank of captain, but by long naval tradition, only the master of a ship was referred to by that rank, even if in this case, their "captain" was a lowly lieutenant like Morris. Naval commands, no matter how small, came with certain privileges. "Is that your exercise of choice back home?"

He shook his head. "Rowing machine, but I like to walk the ship." He lowered the speed to a more leisurely pace. "And you?"

"Weights are fine," he replied, and set the lower grips for a hundred twenty newton bicep curl. He took them firmly in his hands and started the slow pull. "I go for a ladder climber when I get the chance."

Hans nodded. "Used to, but my shoulder can't take it anymore."

Collins watched the counter increment until it reached eight. He paused, resting for a moment. "I do have some news."

"Good news?"

He shrugged. "Hard to say. I got a report on the way out of Tortisia. The *Blue Jaguar* was sighted coming in to Deshmon three days ago."

Hans stepped hard and lost his balance for a moment. He grabbed hold of the handrails and kept going. "Then we're on the right track."

Collins started his next set. "Maybe. Arvin could be next." His voice strained as he worked through each pull. "But if Taschin is the goal... easily four other layovers instead. Backwater worlds like Deshmon."

Hans sighed. "But if it is Arvin, can we catch them?"

"Depends," Collins grunted, finishing off his second set. "The report didn't say when they left Deshmon. If they stayed a day or more, then we're good." He started setting up for a triceps push.

"And if not?"

He started the push, keeping it at a hundred twenty newtons. "I've already asked Captain Morris to see if he can get a little more out of the sails. I can't order him to emergency speeds, but he's sympathetic to your plight."

Hans nodded. "I'll be sure to thank him, one way or the other. I'm glad to hear he understands about family."

Collins paused, halfway through his set. "Is that what this really is about for you, family?"

"Of course it is!" he replied, his steps accelerating until the treadmill checked him. "What else would it be?"

Collins resumed his set. Four more. "I don't know. You seem... intent on proving Malcolm Fletcher... to be the bad guy."

Hans laughed. "And you believe otherwise, I gather. Did you owe him some favor? Is that why you're in this?"

"No," he said, finishing out the set. "But I had an interest in Malcolm, and I suppose that interest extends to his, um, to Michael. I don't have any particular interest in proving Malcolm's guilt or innocence. Why do you?"

"It's not just that," Hans replied, finally hitting the cooldown mode on the treadmill. "Have you ever lost family?"

"No, I haven't," he replied. Mom and Dad were still working away on Callista Prime, and Callie was getting her doctorate on Latera.

"Shipmates then?"

"Yes." He had been commissioned a year after the end of the Caspian rebellion, but he had been in two nasty fights with the zealots of the Shiantic Ribbon. He had earned a Silver Shield for distinguished service in one of them, but he never wore it. His survival had been his only distinguishing action. The man who had saved him had only gotten a letter written to his family. "Yes, I have, but if it's revenge you're after—"

"No," Hans cut him off. He shook his head as his pace slowed further. "Michael is my last link to Peter. My little brother Pete... he's been gone seventeen years now, almost eighteen since I last saw him." The treadmill finally came to a stop, and Hans leaned forward against the rail. "I wasn't there for him, Commander, not for him, not for Sophia, and not for Michael. I was off chasing profits instead. It doesn't matter anymore whether or not I'm right about Malcolm. This time," he paused to face Collins, "at least I'm going to be there."

Collins opened his mouth to reply, but Hans walked out before he could think of what to say.

If he was going to get off the ship at the next port, the cargo path was Michael's best chance. The main airlock would have watch standers around the clock, and even if he could get one of the other maintenance airlocks to open without faking some kind of emergency, he did not have a proper EVA suit for maneuvering around on the hull. For that matter, he did not even have a survival bag in his quarters — a serious safety oversight in his book.

It was also a serious setback, since going through the cargo path would mean exposure to vacuum. His plan was to hide in one of the cargo containers, but they were rarely airtight, and the trip from cargo bay to dockside cargo lock was typically zero gravity and zero atmosphere. He could try to hold out for a groundside port, but the next stop was supposed to be Arvin station. Given how his passenger status had been steadily declining, he did not want to risk waiting any more. So, if he was getting off, he needed that survival bag, and that was precisely what he was going to get.

It was three hours after dinner, and beta shift had already settled in. Like the *Heinrich*, most people worked first shift, called "alpha" on the *Jaguar*. All the maintenance was done then. The other shifts were little more than bored watch standers, doing their best to stay awake while watching the monitors, though he knew at least one watch stander would be watching his door. He had found the security camera in his previous night's exploration. Tonight, he intended to give them nothing to see.

He popped the sink panel off with ease using a makeshift tool. It was ostensibly a bottle opener Karen had given him for their vacation on Latera. It only gave him a hand's length of leverage, but it was made of titanium and did not bend under the heaviest loads he could manage. He slipped it back into a sleeve pocket, but kept it tied to his wrist with a bit of string. He did not want to risk losing it crawling through the walls tonight.

He began by slipping through the hole and into the plumbing access space behind his bathroom. It was a tight fit, but he could curl around to the side and then tuck his legs in and roll onto his back. He wiggled around some more, trying not to make enough noise to be heard in the bathroom next to him, until he could finally stand up.

The quartermaster was up on deck one, where the bridge would have been for the *Heinrich*. He could climb up the two decks from where he was, but his one trip up to the quartermaster before had been under escort, and not simply by one of his cargo-handling tag-alongs. There had been a legitimate guard, a Mr. Bishop, armed with a menacing shock stick. That would not be so much of a problem, except that the quartermaster storage had been on the port side of the ship. He was on the middle hall, starboard-side, deck three. While he was pretty confident in being able to pop open one of the hallway panels quickly, he could not think of a safe place to do it. Clearly, his hallway on deck three was being watched. Deck two would have been right between the Captain's quarters and the bridge. And finally, deck one had the formidable Mr. Bishop with his shock stick.

No, the only way was down, and down was a simple drop into environmental. As best as Michael could see, it was an out-of-the-way corner behind an algae tank. In the brief exploration he had done the night before, he had never seen anyone step under him, let alone look up. From what he remembered of his few shifts in environmental, crew did not like to stand around the algae tanks. No matter how tight the seals, you always wanted a shower afterwards.

So after waiting a few minutes to confirm no one was nearby, or at least no one was making noise nearby, he unscrewed the mounts for one of the floor grates. He wedged it between two pipes as quietly as he could and stuck his head through the hole to look around. No one was near, and he could fairly easily step down onto the nearest tank and get down to the floor from there.

He pulled his head back in, repositioned to hold tightly onto a couple of the wall frame struts, and lowered himself down onto the tank. Part of him wanted to simply drop as fast as he could, but he also did not want to make a noisy landing.

Remembering Karen's overnight detection of the bad air gaps in *Heinrich's* plumbing, he knew that a lot of environmental problems were found by nose and ears rather than by simply watching the monitors. If this overnight watch officer was as diligent as Karen had been, he would have to be very quiet.

With his feet lowered onto the tank, he then knelt with his hands still braced against the ceiling. He did not see or hear anyone. Carefully, he slipped his legs over the side of the tank and eased himself down to the deck below. It was another collection of metal grates covering other pipes and vents, so he stepped gingerly, testing each one for wobbles or creaks before putting his full weight on.

Here in environmental, the layout was entirely different than the upper decks. There was no central corridor, only pipes, tanks, and filters. The wet wall that would have been directly across the corridor from him was covered by an array of air ducts moving aft towards filters. That did not matter much, because that was still too far forward for the quartermaster's storage.

So he moved aft, but not in a straight line. First he had to go to port to get around two more tanks and an air scrubber. Then he made his way aft about twelve meters, passing by more scrubbers, a somewhat noisy pump, and a water heater. He grew even more cautious because even though he had the pump's noise to mask his movements, he could see that he was getting closer to some control systems. Even if it was not the main watch station, you could never know when the watch stander would make a trip past to check something on the equipment itself.

He shifted back towards the center of the ship, squeezing between a couple of reserve water tanks and stopped to take his bearings. By looking through the maze of pipes and equipment, he could see the pale green algae tank that he had originally come down on. It was about nine meters forward and three to starboard. He should be in about the right position, and when he looked up, sure enough, he saw the floor grates of the cabin utilities access space above him.

He braced himself between one of the reserve tanks and a pipe and wiggled his way up until he could reach the wing nuts holding the grate in place. He knew this was the most dangerous part of his path. He was stuck there, with his head and shoulders above most of the machinery for over a minute, very visible to anyone who just happened to look. But he also knew that worrying about it would not make him any less visible, so he hastily undid the nuts and dropped them into his pocket. He shifted the grate aside and grabbed hold of the wall frame above it.

He was most of the way up when he heard the voice.

"Is that you, Case?"

He pulled his feet up and promptly stepped to the side, but the gap in the grate was wide open.

"Case? Buddy?"

He did not recognize the voice, but at least it was not one of his usual watchers. Then he heard the clomp-clang of boots on the deck grates below him. A leg came into view, and then a hand. It ran over the pipe he had used to climb up, but then it left. He heard more steps, another pause, and then finally a more casual clomp-clang of boots receding into the distance. Thankfully, whoever it had been had never looked up.

Michael thought about putting the grate back in place, but he thought better of it. He would be coming back through here soon enough. He turned his attention upwards, and bracing himself between wall frames and pipes, he started his climb. The grate to deck two came off easily enough, and so he made his way up to there without incident.

Very few pipes rose up to this level. From the looks of it, it was a single sink. He was not sure if it was part of the captain's quarters, or if it was perhaps the officers' wardroom. Either way, he was very careful to move slowly and quietly. The last thing he wanted was to slip and bang against the captain's bedroom wall.

Only air ducts and electrical conduits went up to deck one. That made sense. After all, the quartermaster's storage room had no sink. He carefully wedged himself higher up between the wall frames, unbolted the grating above him, and slid it aside. The access space above him was different, but he was still able to climb up into it.

When he got there, he saw just how different. The walls to the aft were the standard partition walls he had been dealing with all along. The forward wall, however, was solid metal. Whatever that nasty Mr. Bishop had been guarding was put together more securely than the rest of the ship. He wondered what it could be but did not let it distract him long. The aft wall was the wall to quartermaster's storage, and that was his goal.

He popped out a section of the wall from the floor to his chest and slid it to the side. It was dark on the other side, and he considered that good news. No one should be staffing the storage closet at night. When he had enough room to move through, he stooped down and through.

It would have been nice, of course, to have the survival bags on a shelf right next to him, but he was happy to spend his luck elsewhere. As it was, he came out behind a stack of pillows, and when one went crashing to the floor, it barely made any noise at all. Taking advantage of the opening, he slid through the gap on the shelf and stepped into the room proper.

He moved past the bedding and uniforms over to where the environment suits were. He did not see many. In fact, mostly it was only parts of the suits, and they looked very odd to him. While most environment suits are fairly light and supple, the chest piece he saw was heavy and bulky. Even for a thruster suit, it looked over-engineered. His curiosity called to him, but he pushed it away. He needed the survival bag, and with another minute of searching, he found it.

Here he counted himself lucky. Survival bags are packed in one of two ways. More often than not, they come in a box, about half a meter cubed. It had a pull cord that began an inflation of structural members. The idea was that it would turn itself into a nice sphere for you to step into through the open seam and then seal it up behind you, using the rest of the oxygen tank to keep you breathing. He had been worried about only finding those, because he was not so sure he would have been able to fit them through the gaps between the decks.

Fortunately, all of the *Jaguar*'s bags were of the other variety. They were packaged in longer tubes, about a meter and a half, with a carrying strap as well as a couple of hooks. The idea behind these was that a suited rescuer could carry several of these strapped to himself to give to any trapped survivors he found. They did not have as long of an air supply, but they would easily fit through the space he had to move through tonight. He took one, moved back to the open wall, put the pillows back in place, and slipped quietly back into the wall, closing it up behind him.

Moving down was much easier, even with a load, but he forced himself to go as slow as before. Josie had warned him that day they had gone climbing the mountains. "Going down is much more dangerous than going up. It feels so easy, you get sloppy, and the next thing you know you've busted your pretty little ankle."

So he was lowering himself into the access space on deck two very carefully when he heard the thump of the water slamming into the air gap in the pipes above the sink. Someone had just used it. He froze, knowing that someone was close by on the other side of the partition. After several seconds, he dared to shift into a more comfortable position, still halfway down to the floor.

And that was when he heard Jimmy Anders laugh.

Cautiously, he pressed his ear to the wall and listened.

"It's not funny," Elsa said. "There are warrants out for that name."

Anders shrugged. "Yeah, old warrants, from back in the war. I don't see why they scare you so much."

She shook her head. She was amazed someone as careless as Anders had survived this long. "Some of Elsa's so-called crimes have no statute of limitations. War or not, few judges would be lenient. So hear me on this. Elsa Watkins died in the war, and if you don't want to end up in her empty grave, you'll leave that name alone from here on out."

He frowned but nodded. "I guess Malcolm's not the only one with secrets."

"Yes, but hopefully Malcolm's secrets will die with him. Or at least they'll die with his computer."

"Die?" He looked her cautiously. "I thought we were going to extract the data."

"Sure, I'm going to make a copy, but once I get it out of there, I'm wiping that core, wiping it again, and then slagging the whole thing before blasting it apart." She slammed back her vodka, and slid the empty glass back towards Anders. "And after, if I'm feeling generous, I'll let you have portions of it."

"If you feel generous? Aren't you forgetting that I'm the one who brought you this little deal?"

"This deal? This headache, you mean."

"What headache? He's asking a few questions, that's all."

She pointed to the bottle, and Anders poured her another vodka. She sipped it more slowly this time. "It's not the questions. He's an unchecked security risk on my ship. My ship, my business, does not like security risks."

"But you said he's staying in his quarters."

"That's not the point. Maya's getting a bad vibe off him. The kid's suspicious, and that makes him a risk. Bishop agrees." She shook her head. "I wanted to see how much of his father he had in him. Well, he's got too much for my taste, and now we're heading into Arvin with him."

"Keeping him on board again?"

"Damn straight," she replied. "This is the last place I'd want to let him loose. We'll see how he handles another restricted liberty, but I lay you odds that he'll be in Mr. Bishop's brig before we're done." She took another sip.

"Hell, El-, er, Jana, if you're that worried, why are we even going to Arvin?"

She shook her head. "Believe me, if I had a choice, I wouldn't be, but orders are orders."

"Orders? Ha! Who in the universe does the Winged Lady take orders from?"

She chuckled. "If you can believe it, Father Chessman."

He leaned in against the table. "You're kidding. You know Father Chessman?"

"Of course not," she replied. "No one knows Father Chessman." She saw him open his mouth, but she cut him off. "No one knows him. That's what they say. Supposedly it's all dead drops and encoded orders, but when you get an order from him, you follow it or you start looking over your shoulder for the rest of your very short life."

"Okay, I get it," he said. "He's not interested in the boy, is he?"

She shook her head and took another sip. "I doubt he ever knew Malcolm even had a son. No, this is about cargo, plain and simple. He's got something special for me to pick up and deliver."

"What is it?"

She finished off her vodka and set the glass down on the table between them. "Now you're starting to ask too many questions, Jimmy. Do I need to put you in your quarters for the rest of the trip?"

"No, Captain. That won't be necessary."

Michael lay stretched out on the floor of his quarters, the survival bag beside him. The final climb had done him in. At least that was what he told himself. The climb was what was making his heart race.

229

It had nothing to do with the talk of security risks, of slagging computers, or of a brig. He thought about the hard metal wall next to the quartermaster storage, Mr. Bishop, and his ominous brig.

He had to get off the ship, and it had to be at Arvin. There was no question about that.

No, the only question he had was this: Who the hell was Father Chessman?

Chapter 23

"They say that a prisoner's first obligation is to escape, and I suppose they're right. But if it's at all practical, do try to piss in the jailer's coffee on the way out." — Malcolm Fletcher

MICHAEL DID HIS BEST to look surprised by the news. "Again? Just how long am I supposed to stay cooped up in my cabin?" He pushed his lunch back in unfeigned anger.

Anders glanced around the galley, but no one else was sitting that close to them. "Look, Michael, I understand. For that matter, I'm not that keen on staying on board either. It's Arvin, after all, and I could do a little business here, touch base with a few friends... maybe even check in on a lady friend or two," he said with a wink. "But each captain has her own way of doing things, and Lewis runs a tight schedule."

"Yeah, I bet her schedule isn't the only thing that's tight."

"Come on, Michael, show a little respect," came Anders' rebuke, but Michael noticed hints of a grin.

Ultimately, he shrugged it off. "Whatever. All I know is that this isn't how I'm going to run things when I'm back on *Sophie*."

Anders nodded. "Well, it'll be your choice then. For now..."

"Yeah, for now I'll be a good little boy and wait it out."

"I could come by for a visit, maybe teach you a new card game?"

Michael shook his head with feigned sulkiness. "Maybe tomorrow. I'm gonna grab a sandwich or two for my dinner. I won't be good company tonight."

He took his tray back to the counter and fished through the sandwich bin for some turkey or ham. On his way out, he grabbed a water bottle and nodded to Maya who followed him from a discreet distance. She at least let him get back into his quarters without watching him the entire way, but once he was into his own corridor, he knew he was on Mr. Bishop's monitors.

He still had about two hours before they dropped from tach, so he packed methodically, then unpacked and packed it again, trying to squeeze in a little more. He could not take much, and the truth of the matter was, very little mattered. He had Malcolm's old utility knife, some food, a bottle of water, and every scrap of cash he had down to the last half-credit.

His timing was little more than an estimate, but he figured his best chance to get into the cargo bay was in the minutes after the down-tach, during the pre-docking maneuvers. It was a hectic time, and while the artificial gravity did a good job at compensating for their various thrust changes, most crew sat out the jerkier moments belted into a locked chair.

"Prepare for down-tach," came the announcement over the speakers. "Stage one in ninety."

That was his signal. He tossed together some dirty laundry and a pillow to simulate a body under the covers. He did not know how much time that would actually buy him if they came looking for him, but that was what they always did in the movies. He figured it could not hurt.

He was popping the panel out from the under the sink when the first down-tach hit. It was smooth, but he could hear it, a subtle change in the background hum of the *Jaguar*. He pushed his bag through and laid it next to the survival bag. He had stored that in there almost from the beginning. After all, how would he explain it if someone saw it in his closet?

He was halfway through the wall himself when the next announcement came. "Down-tach, stage two in sixty."

He squirmed his legs through and pulled the panel back snug against the brackets. He was not going back through, and he wanted to leave no trace of how he escaped. Then he went to work on the floor grate. He had refastened it with only two of the nuts, so it was quick work. He had finished setting it aside when he felt the next down-tach. This one had a bit of a thump that rocked him back and forth in the tiny access space, but he did not care. He was probably as secure as he would be belted into a chair.

The *Jaguar* had only a three stage down-tach, so he knew the next one would be the last. He stood and balanced himself over the missing grate, one foot on either side. He held his bag and the survival gear dangling in front of him, ready to drop them down onto the top of the algae tank below.

"Down-tach, reentry in thirty... mark."

He took a deep breath and started counting it down in his head. What he was about to try was crazy, but he knew that staying was even crazier. He suddenly remembered some of his early pilot training in *Sophie's* little flyer with Malcolm along as co-pilot. "Don't be scared of the landing," Malcolm had said. "Visualize your path, commit to it, and keep your stick on it."

They had been in flight at the time, with the ocean-front runway coming up. Even with what must have been a low-angle approach, he had felt like a falling rock. "But what if I come down too hard?"

"Better too hard than too late," Malcolm had said, looking out towards the sea beyond. "If you worry yourself into waiting too long, you'll miss the runway, and this flyer can't swim."

Back aboard the *Jaguar*, he felt the transition and dropped the bags. They hit softly and slid off. He went next, landing feet first and then sliding down on his backside towards the edge of the tank. By the time the call for status reports went out, he was already on the deck with a bag slung over each shoulder.

233

He shuffled across the metal grates briskly, worried more about the time than about making noise. The environmental techs would not be nearly as busy as the engineers were, but they would still be checking their displays. He made his way port, then aft, then port again before turning aft once more.

He could see his goal from there, a straight shot twenty meters back, a hatch that led into the bottom of the cargo hold. It was not a proper airlock, just a pressure door. According to the ship schematic, the *Jaguar* had three pressure hatches into cargo but only one airlock. In practice, the pressure hatches were almost as safe, since they could not be pulled open with a vacuum on the other side, but he had felt safer on the *Heinrich* where no potential atmospheric boundary was crossed with anything short of double-safety airlock.

But here on the *Jaguar*, it was his salvation. They ran with a pressurized cargo hold here which meant that until they docked to unload, those pressure hatches could be opened. In fact, he had even seen one left standing open, back when he still had the run of the ship. He recalled Zane's warning going through the core airlocks back on *Heinrich*. "If both doors are open, it signals an alarm on the bridge." Despite the menacing Mr. Bishop guarding whatever it was up on deck one, hatch security was clearly much more lax on the *Jaguar*.

The only problem was that between him and that hatch was the environmental control station. It was not directly in the path, fortunately, but it was immediately to starboard. Three stations were arranged in a horseshoe bay, the open end facing out into the path Michael had to traverse. All three of the watch standers sat at the controls there. He could hear them, and with a careful peek over a scrubber unit, he could see the tops of their heads.

He thought about throwing something in the opposite direction to distract them, but the last thing he wanted was for one of them to get up and start investigating. This would have been so much better if they had down-tached on an off-shift. Seconds ticked away.

Fuck it. If they see me, they see me. Commit to it.

He stayed low and dashed aft crossing the gap as quickly as he could. He did not pause at the other side to see if they had reacted. He did not know what he would have done if they had, so it was wise that he did not stay near to find out. In another fifteen paces, he made it to the hatch. It was closed, but not secured. With a simple tug on the handle, it opened up.

He stepped through and closed it behind him.

Now for the easy part, he thought. All he had to do was find a container that was going to be unloaded at Arvin and climb inside. Easy, right?

The *Jaguar* did not carry nearly as much cargo as the *Heinrich*, but it carried enough. She had five cargo decks, spaced evenly across the vertical space of the four crew decks. The central spine corridor ran the length of it back towards the engineering section, but otherwise, it was simply a large array of containers on sliding tracks.

They could be emptied out to the sides, which was more efficient than *Sophie*'s smaller rear-loading cargo bay, but it was still not as efficient as *Heinrich*'s radial pattern, mostly because the radial loaders could unload as well as rotate and resort. On *Heinrich*, it meant that the cargo to be offloaded was almost always positioned out and forward. On the *Jaguar*, he had no idea how they optimized their cargo load.

So he started down the length of the deck and promptly lost his footing. Of course, like the *Heinrich*, the long cargo section of the ship was without gravity. He shifted closer to the side and floated back along the handrails, looking for labels. Most were marked with square holo-codes. They did him no good without a scanner and a copy of the manifest. A few had business names on them, but he did not recognize any of them as belonging on Arvin. They could very well be, but his only memory of Arvin station had been running wildly through the corridors and lifts, ferrying packets from one office to another.

He heard a muted announcement, but he could not tell what it was. It was not the kind of alarm he would expect if they had discovered his absence, or worse, if they were about to vent the cargo hold.

Determined, he drifted up to the second cargo deck and started working his way back forward. Again, it was mostly holo-codes. He found one labeled for Marius Mills. He could remember a Marius Mills, but he could not remember where it had been. For all he knew, it could have been all the way back on Taschin.

He was almost back to the forward end when he missed the next handrail, almost as though it had moved away from him. He reached further forward to grab it, but it was still moving.

Grasping at empty air, he realized what was happening. They were decelerating, only he was not. He started to fall. It was almost a hundred meters to the back end of the bay. Even at half a gravity, such a fall would be fatal. He panicked, but a life on ships had left him with good reflexes. As soon as you start to fall, grab at the take-holds, and in an emergency, any take-hold will do.

In this case, he had grabbed onto the hatch handle of one of the containers. He had grabbed it with his left hand, while his right flailed pointlessly at open air. He swung around to take it with both hands, but in the process, his carrying bag slipped off his right arm and fell bouncing down the long cargo deck. He knew better than to try to go after it now, so he grabbed onto that handle with both hands as gravity built up. He still had the survival bag, and that was what mattered most.

He wedged one foot against a railing as the deceleration increased past one gravity, and rapidly built up towards two. Back in the crew areas, he was sure they were not feeling this at all, but there was no acceleration compensation in cargo. If he could have spared the motion, he would have kicked himself. He should have been expecting the deceleration problem, what with *Heinrich*'s long zero-gravity core shaft, but he had not.

Deceleration held steady at almost two gravities, and while he had the strength to hold on, his palms were starting to sweat. He did what he could by bracing with his feet, but it did not help much. Hanging on for life, he flashed on his navigation math. Was he hoping for an inflection point in the second derivative or the third?

After an eternal twenty-two minutes, deceleration faded, and before long he found himself floating free. He was hesitant to let go of his safe handhold, but he knew he would need to eventually. The push had been long enough to put them on a good trajectory, but surely he still had time before the tugs started pulling them for final docking. He thought about his lost bag. He could live without the food and water, but he would much rather have them. He glanced back down the long space between the containers. It would have fallen down in that direction. He had time to look for at least a few minutes.

He launched himself on a slow drift aft again, glancing between the containers, looking for any possible ledge it might have landed on. A few minutes turned to several minutes with no sign of it. He reached the far end of that level without finding it. Might it have slipped to the next level up or perhaps down? He checked his watch. It had already been over an hour since they down-tached. He did not have time to backtrack, so he moved up to the next level, hoping for luck.

And luck he had, though he did not realize how much at the time. He spotted his bag dangling on a container about a third of the way forward, its strap hooked over a handle. He launched himself towards it, but about halfway there, he heard a deep metallic groan, and his path curved suddenly. He grabbed at the first thing he could, and within seconds, he was dangling again, this time from one of the rails.

It felt different this time, not nearly as smooth. That meant it was the tugs already, their gravitational grapples oscillating in strength as they pulled *Jaguar* into position. His bag was still four containers away, but at this point, that was of little concern. If they were already under pull by the tugs, then he was almost out of time. He could not move safely during the maneuver, and once it was over, they would be on a thruster-only path towards the final dock. That last bit was rarely more than a few minutes.

Then they would have arrived and would start unloading cargo to the docks. That meant opening the cargo bay, and that meant vacuum, and he was still dangling free from a cargo rail, unprotected.

Shit.

He looked around to see if he could possibly climb around. They were only pulling half gravity now. It would be risky, but there had to be enough handholds here and there, right? He frowned. The best handholds he saw were easily three meters apart. If he missed one, that meant six or seven meters of free fall. By then, he would be moving too fast.

No, it was too risky. He would be better off forgetting about the containers and flying out the bay doors in just the survival bag. The station crews would spot him before his oxygen ran out, right?

His weight suddenly disappeared. The tugs had gone. He had a few minutes at best. All the containers around him were marked only with holo-codes and serial numbers. But then he saw one a little different, maybe something in the font.

He jumped for it, sliding smoothly across and forward. Yes, the font was different, and he recognized it. The serial number was in a forward-slanting stencil-friendly font, and he knew where he had seen it. Everything in the Navy's recruiting office on Tortisia had been labeled in that font. And to top it off, the label had the familiar spear and sail logo of the Navy at all four corners. This was almost certainly a Navy container, and Arvin was the biggest naval port in the sector.

He yanked open the inspection hatch and saw it was partially empty. It was filled mostly with large plasteel girders and bracers, the kind of structural materials you would expect for station construction. This was as good a bet as any. He clambered inside and closed the hatch after him.

He opened up the survival bag and pulled the first release tab. Hollow tubes around the edge of it inflated rapidly to give it shape, so within seconds he was holding onto a ribbed sphere a bit over a meter in diameter. He slipped his legs into it and heard a series of three quick alarms. He was not sure if that was the vacuum warning, but he was not going to keep his head exposed to find out.

He pulled himself entirely inside and sealed himself in, first with double zipper and then the final peel and stick seam. These bags were single use. When the time came, he was going to have to cut his way out. Fortunately, not everything had been in the lost carry bag. He still had his cash and Malcolm's old utility knife.

The bag started expanding even before he pulled the release on the internal air tank. Pressure outside was dropping. He shook his head and activated the oxygen and scrubber units. He had been lucky indeed.

Elsa Watkins headed aft from the bridge and ran into Anders coming out of his quarters. "I'm heading in to make some arrangements. How's our boy?"

"Sulking in his cabin," he replied. "I was going to hit him up for a card game, but he put me off until the morning."

"You sure about that?"

"Yeah, he's a moody teenager. Don't you remember being like that?"

She smiled. She remembered others being like that. As for herself, her teen years had been a little different. "I suppose," she said at last. "Just keep an eye on him. Call in Maya or Leo if you need help."

"No problem, Captain. I've got this boy figured out."

Commander Collins stood next to the skipper on the bridge during the down-tach. He would have liked to have had

Gabrielle and Hans with him as well, but two things prevented it. First, it was technically against regulations for passengers to be on the bridge, even those with the kind of VIP status Collins had granted them. Collins was only allowed on because he was an active-duty officer.

The second reason was that the bridge, if you could even call it that, was so small that they could not have fit all three of them in. The compromise was that the two civilians stood in the hallway behind Collins with only the open hatchway marking the boundary between sacred bridge and a common access way.

"Uploading fleet traffic now, sir," Morris explained. That was his primary mission after all, ferrying information between Navy ships and stations faster and more securely than the civilian networks. Everyone knew how eager the passengers were to make contact, but fleet priorities came first.

"I understand, Captain Morris. Please let me know when you get the station report."

"Certainly, sir."

"Any word?" That was Gabrielle out in the corridor.

"Not yet. It'll be a few minutes. Light lag, that kind of thing."

She sighed.

It turned out to be less.

"I've got something, sir. Arvin station lists the *Blue Jaguar* as being in port, current status as unloading."

Collins turned back to relay the news, but clearly they had already heard it. "So, we go with Plan B, right?" Gabrielle asked. Hans looked reserved behind her.

Collins nodded. They had gamed out four scenarios. Plan A was that they beat the *Blue Jaguar* to Arvin, got onto the station first, and lay in wait for it. Plan B was that they got there while the *Jaguar* was in port. Plan C was that they arrived after *Jaguar* had left, and Plan D was that they were entirely wrong and that the *Jaguar* was not passing through Arvin at all. Plan A had been the ideal scenario, but since it was initially indistinguishable from the Plan D failure scenario, he counted himself lucky to be only a little late.

"When your channel is clear, Captain Morris, I would appreciate it if you send packet Bravo to Arvin station and packet Falcon to fleet command."

"Yes, sir, Bravo and Falcon."

Falcon was his own backup plan. Calling Michael's tag-along with the *Jaguar* "suspected kidnapping" was admittedly a stretch. Inflating that to "suspected piracy" was a work of fiction, but one way or another, he was not letting the *Jaguar* out of port until he had searched it himself.

Michael's teeth were still chattering, long after his container had been transferred through the cargo locks and onto the dock. The one feature of the vacuum he had not been expecting was the extreme cold. Environment suits had heating and cooling for a reason, but his minimal survival bag had not. After all, its design assumed that the occupant was being carried by an urgent rescuer, not that he was waiting for three hours as cargo was slowly shifted and unloaded.

Another surprise from the design of the bag was that it carried no gauge for external pressure. After all, the rescuer would know when to open the bag. Michael had no such information. The return of gravity was his first clue that he had made it, but tentative tugs on the bag's support ribs told him that the other side was still vacuum. Only when he could pull it inwards was he certain that atmosphere had returned. Even then, his first cut through the skin was tentative, a tiny incision while he held one of the three emergency patches in his other hand. When he was confident the air was not gushing out, he widened enough for a sniff. The strong scent of machinery told him he had made it.

He shed the bag and pressed his ear to the side of the container. He heard voices and the distant whine of machinery, but he could not hear anything distinct. With no other option, he opened the inspection hatch to let a tiny sliver of light in.

Two things caught his attention immediately. The first was that he was up off the ground, his container stacked on top of another. The second was that he had heard his name.

"I'm sorry, Michael Fletcher?" He could not place the voice, but it sounded familiar, quite possibly one of *Jaguar's* many cargo handlers.

"Yes, though the note says it's possible he might be using the name Michael Schneider."

Michael repressed a laugh. Like that was ever going to happen.

"I'm not sure I've heard of him," the familiar voice replied. "What is it you want with him?"

"He's wanted for questioning."

"Questioning? That's pretty vague for station security." It was Chester Walsh, Michael realized at last, one of his coincidental followers. That was one of the last people he would want to run into, but on the other hand, security did not sound like such a good option either. The only reason he could be wanted for questioning was that uncle Hans had come after him anyway. Maybe that was not such a bad idea after all, but Michael grated at the idea of being rescued by the very man he was trying to escape.

"Look, I don't write the orders," the security guy continued, "I just follow them. Do you have the guy or not?"

"Well, it's against ship policy to discuss specific —"

"Yeah, I know. Article seven and all that. You going to help me out here, or do I have to kick this upstairs?"

"I'll have to check with my captain."

"Sure. We can wait."

"I don't suppose you have a picture of this guy, do you?" Walsh asked.

"No, but if you need it, I can probably get one."

"Maybe later. First let me check with my captain."

He heard footsteps, and he peered out through the cracked hatch. It was indeed Chester Walsh. Michael could see him walking back to the airlock, but he could not see the man from security. For that matter, he could not see anyone else, and that meant he had a decent chance of not being seen.

He opened the hatch the rest of the way and looked around. The closest person he saw was someone driving a forklift, but he was over at the next dock. He swung his legs out through the hatch and lowered himself down until he was hanging on by his fingertips. He could not see how much further he had to drop, but he had come too far to let this stop him. Closing his eyes, he let go.

And dropped less than a meter to the deck.

Well, that was easy.

From the way he had seen Walsh walking, he figured the dockside post had to be on his left, so he headed out to his right towards the neighboring dock. The forklift driver waved to him and continued his work. Michael nodded and kept on walking past two more docks and turned into the first open door he found.

He was not sure if the man he saw was a host or a bouncer, but he looked him up and down and pointed behind him with his thumb. "No tables, but there's room at the counter."

Michael thought of the long-gone sandwiches, now floating somewhere in the *Jaguar*'s cargo bay. Food sounded like an excellent idea.

Elsa Watkins closed the security door behind her with the guard sitting dejectedly in a chair outside. "I don't care why they're looking for him," she said into her wrist comm. "We admit nothing."

"But now the Navy guy is talking about searching the ship, says he can get something called a naval inspection warrant."

She looked down at the floor and ground her teeth. "Don't do anything until he's got paper, and make the local security guys confirm it before you let one boot on board."

"What about Fletcher?"

"Put him in the brig, no... wait, not the main brig. Tell Bishop to stun the little shit and put him in the engineering brig."

"The coffin?"

"Yes, the coffin!"

"Uh, ma'am, Mr. Bishop wants to speak with you."

"Captain," Bishop came on the line. "The boy's gone."

Her fist came down hard on the desk. "What do you mean, he's gone?"

"Not in his cabin. I checked it myself."

"How did he get out? Wasn't someone watching?"

"Yes, ma'am, I've had Leo on the monitor since down-tach. I did find a loose wall panel in his bathroom. It's possible he got out through the access space."

Fuck! How much trouble could one kid be? She took a deep breath and focused. "Ok, Bishop, send Leo and Maya to meet me at the warehouse and then lock the ship down. No one in or out without my authorization."

"And the boy?"

"If he's on the ship, throw him in the coffin."

"And if he's not?"

"Then I might have to fit him for one."

Chapter 24

"When they've got you backed up against the wall, you start thinking about surrendering peacefully. Live to fight another day and shit like that. Not me. I say fuck them. Fuck them hard." — Malcolm Fletcher

"WELL, WHOEVER HE IS, he must have stepped in something stinky, that's for sure."

Michael turned to see two dockworkers coming into the diner, settling themselves at a table behind him.

"What you boys going on about?" the waitress asked.

"Station security is crawling all over dock twenty-two looking for someone," the first one replied.

"Twenty-two... is that the *Wandering Rose*?"

"No," he replied. "They left yesterday. This is the *Bloody Jaguar*, something like that."

"Not bloody, blue," his friend said.

"Yeah, that's right, the *Blue Jaguar*. So what's the special today?"

Michael froze in his seat. He was wearing a *Blue Jaguar* utility uniform, the logo of the blue cat's spotted profile on his shoulder patch. Quietly, he set a twenty on the counter and walked out. Looking back towards the dock, he could see a crowd of onlookers and a fair number of gray-clad security men standing posts.

Again, he thought about turning himself in, but the question kept coming up, turning himself in for what? Was this merely his uncle throwing his weight around to haul him back in, or had Hans gotten mad enough to press charges against him for something? He never remembered signing any contract, so jumping ship should not have been illegal, technically. But walking into a locked box with guards after he had just escaped from one did not seem to be his best option.

He turned away from the docks and kept walking. What he really needed was some neutral party to intercede for him, someone to find out what all this was actually about. It would have to be someone not attached to his uncle and not attached to Captain Lewis or Jimmy Anders. An old crewmate from the *Sophie* would be ideal, someone like Isaac, but the odds of him being at Arvin were too low to even investigate. Besides, someone with some authority would be better, a captain maybe. Captain Wallace would be a great candidate, and he did sometimes come as far in as Arvin.

He started looking for a public terminal, and after passing two more diners, he found a bar with the little keypad symbol by the door. He walked up to the entrance, but the bouncer stood up to block his path. "Let's see some ID, kid."

He shook his head. "I only need to use the terminal."

He looked around the walkway and sighed. "Look, normally it's a two-drink minimum, but since you say you're not going to be drinking, how about you just give me a twenty?"

Michael grumbled but got out his wallet. He handed over the twenty and started to go inside, but the bouncer held out his arm.

"Hey, you said twenty."

"Yeah, and twenty more for the bartender when you get in. Otherwise I come in and haul your ass back out, got it?"

He nodded and finally entered. For such a dive, he was amazed they could even sell two drinks to the regulars. He stepped up to the bar, laid a twenty on the counter, and asked, "Where's the terminal?"

The bartender was a woman, a little worn around the edges, but still the prettiest thing in the whole room. She picked up the twenty, looked at with a tilted stare, and motioned towards the back. "Next to the john."

He made his way back and found it. It was not the most up-to-date model, but at least the keys all worked. He went to the station registry and searched for Wallace's ship, the *Johnny Rose*. It offered up the date of her last visit, nine months before.

Crap.

He tried Isaac Rubin anyway, and it offered up six Isaac Rubins, none of whom were the right Isaac. Besides, none of them were in port anyway. He went through the list of *Sophie's* old crew: Wendy, Henry, Liam, James, even Marty who had been gone for over a year. The only valid result was Wendy who had passed through last month.

He tried to think of some other friends of Malcolm's, but the problem was that even if they were here, they would not have any real authority. If only he knew someone in the Navy. They could wield real authority, especially on a station like Arvin, but the only naval officer he could remember had been that recruiter on Tortisia. And he could not think of any that Malcolm had known either.

Except... he had met one himself somewhere along the line.

Michael tried to remember. He had come to the wake, said his ship had been passing through the system when he had heard. Monty something, of the *Alger*? *Algiers*? Or was it *Alva*? He switched to the naval directory. He did not have much to go on, so he asked for an alphabetical list of ships based at Arvin.

There it was, a third of the way down the first screen: the CFS *Alvarez*, listed as being in port, dry dock seventeen. He clicked on the ship's icon to pull up the details. It was listed as down for repairs, something about a generator alignment. He knew a thing or two about those and figured that the *Alvarez* was not going anywhere for a few weeks. The screen also listed the dockmaster and the senior officers.

Second on the list was Lt. Commander Montgomery Wheaton. He brought up the picture, and he could remember him now. "Don't believe all the stories," he had said. "He was as solid as they come." He had also said to look him up if he ever needed a favor. Well, today Michael could really use one.

He punched the call link, but it was not Wheaton who answered. "Naval operations, how may I help you?"

Michael swallowed hard. Commit and focus. "I'm trying to reach Lt. Commander Montgomery Wheaton of the *Alvarez*. Can you patch me through?"

"One moment please."

That was easy, he thought, but the next man was not Wheaton either. "*Alvarez* comm, Martins speaking."

"Hello, I'm trying to reach Lt. Commander Wheaton."

"Sorry, he's not on board at the moment."

"Can you tell me where he is?"

There was a pause. "According to his schedule he's meeting with the yard master."

"Is there any chance you can forward me to his link?"

"No can do. He left very explicit instructions not to be interrupted. He's breaking balls if you ask me."

"Please? It's kind of an emergency."

"What kind of emergency?"

He thought about it. Adopted son of a long-lost friend emergency? That was not going to get far. "Family emergency."

The icon for video request lit up, so he turned it on. The sailor on the other end of the line did not look much older than Michael, but at this point, Michael had no idea what he looked like. But however he looked, it was clear from the other's reaction that Michael's desperation must have been obvious on his face. "Family, eh? Look, buddy, I want to help, but old Monty said that if I..." he trailed off with a sigh. "Look, here's what we'll do. I'm going to forward you to his mailbox. You

DAN THOMPSON

record a message, and I'll flag it as high priority. I can't guarantee he'll look at it right away, but he will see that it's there."

Michael tried to think of what could change his mind, but came up with nothing.

"Sorry, bud, it's the best I can do."

The screen shifted to a recording interface, so he pushed start and hoped he was going to make sense.

"Lt. Commander, my name is Michael Fletcher, and I sure hope you remember me. We met at... my skipper's wake... on Taschin a few months back. His name was Malcolm Fletcher. You said if I ever needed a favor, I should look you up, and I'm in trouble. So I looked you up.

"Umm, anyway, I got onto a ship that I probably shouldn't have. It's the *Blue Jaguar*, and we're here at Arvin station now. I had to sneak off the ship to even call you, and I'm sure they're looking for me. And that's the other thing. It looks like station security is looking for me too, but I don't know why. I'd rather turn myself in than go back to the ship, but I don't know what they're after. They may want to send me back to my uncle, and the whole point of this was to get back to Taschin.

"I know it all sounds very complicated, and I guess maybe it is, but I could really use some help. I'm at a bar... I didn't catch the name, but it should be on the message id. I guess you can try to get hold of me here. Just..." he trailed off, not sure what else to say. Summing it all up for Monty made his plight seem that much worse. "I hope to hear from you soon. Thanks."

He disconnected and went back to the bar. "Do you have any orange soda?"

The security guard still sat in a chair outside his normal station. Elsa was still issuing commands from his little room.

"Are you sure he's not on board?" she asked.

"I cannot be sure," Bishop replied, "but I'll stake my reputation that if we can't find him, no naval inspector is going to find him either."

"All right. Tell Mr. Nieru to let them in. Cooperate, but get them off my ship. No more than one hour. That should be more than enough for them to satisfy their curiosity."

"Aye, ma'am. Did Leo and Maya find you?"

"Yes, I've got them out searching for the boy."

"Pardon me, ma'am, but won't that attract attention?"

"No," she replied. "No attention at all."

Collins let the station security detachment go in ahead of him. They had been given a basic schematic of the ship, and the regular men could search all the obvious places. With a final nod to the Schneiders waiting beyond the dock, he went in. It would be up to him to search the less obvious places.

He started by going directly to deck one. He went into each of the store rooms of the quartermaster and paced the floor. He then did the same in the hallway. At the aft end, he came up two paces short. The wall looked like any other, but what lay beyond was not the quartermaster's storage. He started to run his hands around the edge seam, looking for purchase but found none.

"May I help you, Commander?"

He turned to see an iron-faced man. His name tag read R. Bishop. "Yes, Mr. Bishop. You can open this compartment."

"I don't understand. What compartment?"

Collins sighed. "Mr. Bishop, I am familiar with this class of ship. I know it down to the placement of bulkheads and the alignment of struts. There is an empty space on the other side of this wall. You will open it for my inspection or I will call in a cutting team to take it apart."

Bishop grumbled but tapped out a command on his data pad. The wall moved out into the corridor smoothly before splitting in two to slide back across the adjacent wall sections. Collins peered inside and saw crate after crate stacked floor to ceiling with a narrow aisle running down the center.

"This certainly looks interesting," he said. "I'm curious as to how this cargo shows up on your manifest."

"I'm sure you are, Commander," Bishop replied, "but as your inspection warrant is for a person and not cargo, I think you will leave the captain's private cargo alone."

He peered in, taking a step forward, but Bishop matched his step with two, cutting him off at the shoulder. "You must agree, sir, that none of those containers is large enough for your man."

He nodded. They were not large enough by half. Turning, he then faced the wall on the opposite side of the corridor. "And this one? More cargo? Perhaps a brig?"

"No, sir."

"Arms locker?"

Bishop hesitated.

"Open it."

Bishop complied. The wall opened to reveal long racks of rifles, handguns, and heavier powered weaponry.

"Quite the collection, Mr. Bishop."

"The captain and crew... you see, we like to vacation at hunting preserves."

"Hunting preserves?"

"Yes, sir. Talloway, for example, out past the spinward border."

"I see." He turned back up the hallway. "And this is your security office?"

Bishop followed along and opened the reinforced hatchway. Beyond it was a small office with monitors all around and two seats on either side. On the monitors he could see throughout the ship where station security was walking the halls, looking into various rooms, taking up positions at key intersections, and being generally useless.

Collins eventually settled himself in front of the monitors opposite the secure door. "I like what you've done here," he said. "The active monitors do a lot to erase the suspicion of a space beyond, but I know there's at least twenty meters of usable volume ahead of us. Open it."

Bishop's shoulders sagged, but he complied. With a few keystrokes at the left console, the wall moved forward and separated. Beyond it laid a stainless steel corridor with rubber skids spaced along the floor.

"Secure cargo," Bishop offered, extending his hand forward.

Collins looked him in the eye. "I know a brig when I see it, Mr. Bishop, and I know better than to step into one without the jailer in front of me at all times. Are you going to give me the tour?"

Bishop stepped forward into the hallway, while Collins kept back at a distance. A dozen windows lined the hallway, six on a side. Collins recognized them as cell doors. In fact, it felt eerily like a Naval brig block like he had seen on a number of cruisers.

"Any occupants?" Collins asked.

"No, sir. We are not carrying any secure cargo at this time."

"Open them, one at a time."

They did, and each time, Bishop walked into the cell so that Collins could safely step up to the door and look around. These were exactly like the navy's brig cells. In fact, they were some the harshest ones he had seen: steel walls, floor, and ceiling, with rounded joins, and no furniture. There were only three breaks in the walls: an air vent coming in, an air vent going out, and a drain at the bottom of the floor. He had personally put a number of people into cells just like this one. The fact that this freighter had a dozen of them made him want to lock Bishop in right then and there.

But even the twelfth cell was empty and spotless. Bishop smiled coolly at him from the far side of the cell. "Where else would you like to look, Commander?"

Ned sat outside his aunt's bar and watched the people go by. It was the typical mix of crew and dock workers, but today there was a surprising amount of station security. He had already put his usual ready-to-sell wares back with his larger stash in the office, but security did not seem to be hassling anyone. They were mostly passing by.

He finally spotted a couple that were moving more slowly, sometimes stopping to ask a question. The man looked pretty mean, even for security, but the woman was a hot little morsel. From the way her jacket hung tightly across her shoulders, she must have been built for action underneath it. Hopeful, Ned waved her over.

"Good afternoon, sir," she said. Close up, Ned found her even more attractive. He would have liked longer hair, but her short-cropped bob would probably feel nice against his chest.

"I see a lot of you security folks down here today. What's up?"

"We're looking for some kid, a real troublemaker."

He gave her a little grin. "You got a picture? Of the kid, I mean."

She held out a tablet with an image.

His grin grew into a broad smile. It was the boy who had bribed his way in almost two hours before. "You know, I think I may have seen this boy."

She cocked an eyebrow. "Did you? Where?"

He gave his lips a little lick. "Well, if I help you out here, maybe you'll come help me out later? You know, when you're off duty."

She set the pad down on his little table and moved in closer. "For a good looking guy like you, why wait?" She pushed him back into the shadow of the bar's entryway, her hands playing across his chest and waist. "Let's see what you're offering me here."

He gulped as her hand slipped beneath his waistband and her fingers wrapped themselves around his testicles. "You're the friendliest security gal I've ever met," he said.

But then her face changed, and he felt her nails start to dig into his scrotum. "Maybe," she said, "or maybe I'm the meanest. So how about you tell me what you know, and maybe I won't keep these," she emphasized with a painful squeeze, "as a souvenir of our little encounter."

He swallowed hard. "He's inside," he waved his thumb to the door behind him. "Got here over an hour ago. Wanted to use the terminal. Hasn't left. That's all I know. Honest."

She gave him one more squeeze and then pulled her hand out, wiping it back and forth across his face. "Now that's a good boy. You remember that, if you ever see me again, got it?"

"What do we have here, Maya?" her partner asked.

"Kid's inside, Leo. You take point."

"Will do."

They left him, and Ned slipped down gingerly into his chair. No way that kid had been worth a twenty.

Michael was on his second bowl of pretzels and his third orange soda, but there was still no word from Lt. Commander Wheaton. How long could that meeting with the yardmaster take? Then, out of the corner of his eye, he saw a uniformed man slide onto the stool next to him. He turned to see, but the first thing he noticed was not the gray security uniform the man wore. Rather, it was the face of Leo Perez looking back at him.

"Good afternoon, Mr. Fletcher."

He jerked around the other way and did his best to leap from the stool, only to stop just as suddenly. Maya Zoland stood four meters back with a pistol leveled at him. She was also in a station security uniform. "Going somewhere, Michael?"

He felt Leo grab his arm and twist it behind him. "We're going to do this nice and quiet, Mr. Fletcher. If you try to run, Maya might have to use that."

"You can't just kill me," he said.

Maya leered at him smugly. "We're security, Michael, and I believe the phrase you're looking for is 'shot while resisting arrest.' Now let's move."

Leo started walking him forward. He looked around in panic, catching the eye of the bartender wiping down one of the tables. "Tell Monty I've been kidnapped!" he shouted.

"That's it, you're under arrest," Leo roared, and underscored it by punching him hard in the left kidney.

He went out silently. The bouncer gave him one brief glance and then looked away.

Collins stood over the empty metal tub, no bigger than a coffin. It had been tucked snugly in a hidden space between the two sail generators. It was the right size for holding a body, though the constant vibration of the generators under power would have made it a living hell for anyone hiding there. Still, it was an effective hiding place. He had almost missed it.

But no one was hiding there now.

A small gathering waited nearby. The sergeant from station security stood patiently. The XO, Marcus Nieru, was less patient. He stood with arms crossed and eyes threatening to shoot flames. The unflappable Mr. Bishop stood with hands behind his back and a hint of satisfaction on his face. Admitting some measure of defeat, Collins stepped over to join them.

The sergeant spoke first. "We've finished our sweep, sir. No sign of the boy."

Collins chewed on it, trying to think of what he could have missed. "I'd like to look through your cargo bay next."

"I'm sorry, Commander," Mr. Bishop said, "but it's been depressurized for several hours now."

The XO stepped forward. "And we don't have the time in our schedule to repressurize it for you, so that's it."

"Well, I'm sure I can find an EVA suit."

"Then you'll have to find another warrant," Mr. Nieru replied. He held up the sheet Collins had presented him with before. "This doesn't say anything about our cargo."

"Well, I'm not looking for your cargo. I'm looking for Michael Fletcher in your cargo."

"I'm sorry, sir," the sergeant spoke up. "But he's right. The warrant does specify the crew areas of the ship. It does not include the cargo bay."

Nieru shifted to a more relaxed posture and stepped to allow Collins a clear path to the exit. "I do wish you the best in finding your man, Commander, but you've taken up enough of our time. I formally request under article seven of the CSC that you and your security leave the *Blue Jaguar* now."

The sergeant nodded to Collins. He did not like it, but at this point, he knew he had no choice in the matter. He followed the sergeant out.

Bishop brought up the rear, and he kept his silence until they had reached the final airlock. "Did you enjoy your tour, Commander?"

Collins turned and faced him. "We're not done, you and I."

Bishop smiled. "Perhaps not, but we're done for today."

He sealed the inner hatch before Collins could think of a reply.

Michael's legs were bound to the chair with some kind of sticky plastic sheeting. His hands were cuffed behind him, the links fed around and through the chair back. In theory, he might be able to stand on his toes, but he was not going anywhere without the chair.

Not that he even had that much choice. Leo stood behind him, while Maya watched him from the door, her hand never far from her pistol. At least he was still on the station. They had taken him to a back room in a poorly lit warehouse unit. He must have asked a dozen questions, but his captors ignored him.

After about twenty minutes of this, Maya raised a hand to her ear and said, "I'll be right out." With a nod in his direction, she left.

He considered for a moment that this might be a good time to try something, but that line of thought was cut short by a hard smack to his temple. Through the pain and disorientation that followed, he heard Leo say, "That's for even thinking about it."

It would not have mattered anyway. Maya returned within a minute, and she brought Captain Lewis with them. Lewis, Watkins... whatever her name was, her arrival was as dreaded as it was inevitable. She paced over, grabbed his face by the jaw and forced him to look up at her. "Well, at least now I don't have to pretend anymore."

"Fuck you, bitch!" he said, trying to fill it with all the bluster he wished he had.

She smiled and pushed his face away. "At least you're in a talkative mood. Let's start with Monty. Who is he?"

He feigned confusion. "Monty?"

She smiled at him and nodded. The blow to his temple came from the other side this time, and Leo's left was even worse than his right. He shook his head slowly until the stars faded. The captain had pulled up a chair opposite him. "Let's start again. Maya tells me that when you all left the bar, you shouted to tell Monty that you had been kidnapped. So, my question is, who is Monty?"

He thought about it for a moment, trying to think of someone he could know that might be looking for him, someone who was not actually Montgomery Wheaton. "My uncle," he said at last.

"Your uncle?" she replied. "I don't think so. Malcolm didn't have any family." She looked up to Leo and nodded again.

Michael cringed, bracing his neck, but this time the blow came low and hard to his ribs on the right. It took his breath away, and he gasped for a few moments, each intake another stab where Leo's fist had struck.

"So, uncle?" she asked.

"Well, he's only sort of an uncle," he answered, amazed at how raspy his voice had become. "It's a long story."

She shook her head. "Long story, eh? Well, when we get you back to the ship, Mr. Bishop and I are going to put you in a very small room, and you're going to tell us all of your stories, long and short."

"Do you want to move him now?" Leo asked from behind him.

"No," she replied. "I want to wait until the dock has settled down a bit more, but it won't be long. First the cargo, then him." She peered at him a moment. "So for now, how about you tell me where your uncle is."

"The last time I saw him was Latera."

"On the *Heavy Heinrich*?"

He nodded. That much at least was true.

"But the *Heavy Heinrich* isn't here. Why were you using the terminal?"

"I was sending him a message." Again, it was true enough.

"What? I'm sorry I left? Please come save me?"

He shrugged. "Something like that."

"And what were you planning to do for the six or seven weeks it was going to take before he could make his way back here? Hang out in that bar drinking soda?"

He frowned. "I, um… I hadn't thought it out that far yet." That, he realized painfully, was entirely true. He had only gotten as far as hoping Lt. Commander Wheaton would actually call him back. It had not been, as Malcolm would have said, a shining example of good thinking. He should have known better, but he had been stupid. From the moment he had walked away from Karen to the moment he got off the *Jaguar*, it had been one stupid decision after another.

He looked up at his captor and saw her grinning. "I would have expected more from Malcolm's boy, but I guess you're not up to his standards. Too bad for you."

He sat there, knowing he was likely doomed and was tempted to simply give up. But then, Malcolm had a saying about that, didn't he? Oh yeah... fuck them. Fuck them hard.

So he looked up at his gloating captor. "Well, once Uncle Monty tells the Navy that Elsa Watkins is alive and well on the *Blue Jaguar*, I'm sure he'll be back with friends."

She stood and took a furious step towards him. "What did you say?"

He grinned up at her and taunted her with his words. "Welcome back, El-sa."

Her face went red, and she hauled her right fist back.

Michael did not remember much after that.

Chapter 25

"They say the cavalry often arrives five minutes too late. In my experience, five minutes is optimistic." — *Malcolm Fletcher*

GABRIELLE COULD SEE THE failure written on Commander Collins' face when he came into the lounge. They were about a quarter way around the ring from the *Blue Jaguar*. She had wanted to wait on the docks where she could watch the *Jaguar's* airlock, but Father had agreed with Collins that they should wait somewhere with privacy.

It was just as well. She would not have liked to have gotten the news in public.

"He was not on board," he said, making it official.

She felt her lip quiver. "Any sign of him?" she asked.

He shook his head. "But I will say this, that ship is going on my list."

"What do you mean by that?" Father asked.

"Whether or not they ever had Michael, that ship is up to no good. They're either outright pirates, or at least privateers, but if it's the latter, they're not one of mine."

"One of your what?" Father pressed.

Collins waved it off. "It doesn't matter now. If they don't have him, then I have to confront the likelihood that my

260

analysis on Latera was wrong. Michael could have gone another direction or on another ship."

Gabrielle shook her head and forced her breathing to steady. "No, it made too much sense. Maybe he got off at one of their earlier stops."

"Then it would have been very easy for them to simply say so. Yes, we had him, but he left. See how well we're cooperating. No need to inspect our suspicious ship." He sighed. "It's far more plausible that they never heard of him in the first place."

"Or..." Father trailed off.

"Or what?"

"Or they still have him."

Collins shifted his jaw. "It's not likely, but I confess it is possible. I wanted to search their cargo. I thought maybe they could have a functioning life pod tucked away in one of the containers, but I didn't have the authority, and station security wouldn't back me."

"Well, you're Navy," Father suggested. "There's a significant fleet presence here. Maybe you don't need station security."

Collins nodded. "Maybe. Nothing I saw in there was technically illegal, but it was damn suspicious. I might be able to convince someone to do an intercept, but that's getting awfully risky. If they do have him and manage to get away from the station, then I'd hate to think of what they might be tempted to do in open space."

Gabrielle shuddered at the image. "But you could do it?"

He stared at the table a moment before realizing that an uncertain head bob had slowly morphed into a growing nod. "I have some calls to make."

Father looked over to her. "Then I guess we wait here."

She shook her head. "You wait. I have to get out of here. I'll search the docks myself if I have to."

Elsa sat in the warehouse's security office again. Its nominal occupant had been sent to keep watch outside in the station corridors. "Ship status?" she asked into the scrambled communicator.

"Fully fueled, all but six aboard," Nieru answered.

"Six?"

"Two cargo grapplers are outside supervising the station's loaders. Then there's you three, and the um... your guest."

She nodded to herself. "Good. How about the cargo?"

"Twelve more to go in the current array, then eight more on the docks."

"And the special cargo?"

Nieru paused. "I'm not sure what you mean, ma'am."

"Twelve of the specials have already been loaded, my Lady," Bishop said, coming onto the line. "Four more are still in the array, with six more specials still on dock."

"Good," she said. "How much longer to get them all?"

"Another hour, tops," Bishop replied.

"I concur," the XO added. "When can we expect you on board?"

She glanced around at the security monitors. They did not show the *Blue Jaguar*'s dock, but things appeared quiet around the warehouse. The security surge she had seen before had dissipated. "What's it like out on the dock? Do we have any more visitors?"

"No, my Lady," Bishop replied. "It's been quiet for the last hour."

"Good. I see there's an opening in the station's launch schedule in a little under two hours. Nieru, do you think we can make that?"

She could hear the XO checking with the bridge crew in the background. "Yes," he said at last. "It'll be tight, but if the cargo keeps its pace, the ship will be ready. What about you? Station regs require the personnel tube to unhook one hour before we pull out. Can you make it in time?"

"It shouldn't be a problem. We'll be moving in about fifteen minutes, as soon as our guest cleans up."

"Cleans up, my Lady?"

"Don't worry, Bishop. There's plenty of work left for you. Nieru, pin down that launch window. If they give you any flack, tell them that Stationmaster Richards said you could pencil it in pending the cargo schedule." It was a lie, of course, but it was late evening according to the local station's clock. While plenty of workers were spread around the clock, the main administration staff was already climbing into bed. Given Glenn Richards' reputed temper, no night watch controller was going to wake him to confirm such a request.

"Aye, ma'am."

"Bishop, be waiting for me in the ship-side airlock. We're not taking any chances this time."

"Understood, my Lady. I'll see you shortly."

She hung up and headed back into the offices. Maya had already found a wheelchair. It was time to mount up.

"But Admiral," Collins pleaded, "I know there's something wrong with that ship."

"I don't doubt you, Commander. No legitimate merchant has a brig that secure, but that doesn't change the fact that you don't have evidence of a crime, naval or civilian. So if they're as dirty as you think, it's that much more reason to let them go and keep a closer eye on them. If they're one of Yoshido's civilian-facing ships, then we can use it to track down the rest of them, maybe even get a location on some of their closer staging areas."

"But the boy —"

"Isn't on that ship. You're one of my best bloodhounds, Collins, and if you couldn't find him, it means he wasn't there."

Collins grumbled agreement. The theory of a lifepod in the cargo containers was far-fetched, but the look in Mr. Bishop's eyes was telling. Something was being hidden. He simply did not know what.

"Admiral, you know I'm not one to ask for favors..."

The line was quiet for a moment. "You're that sure?"

"Yes, sir. I can't point to any analysis or evidence. It's all in my gut. You know what that's like."

He could hear the Admiral sigh. "All right, I'll see what I can do, but don't expect much. I'm NI, not Fleet Command, but at the very least I'll post an intelligence alert to the local defense patrols."

"An alert?"

"I don't know... volatile situation under development, stand by for possible intercept, something like that. You know as well as I do that a hunch won't get me through proper channels, but the officers on those ships will pay attention to what I say. There should be someone close enough to do an intercept if need be."

"That's what I was hoping, sir."

"All right, now you try to track down Major Nellis on your end."

"Old Nancy?"

"Yeah, her battalion is rotating through the civilian station for shore leave. If you end up needing boots on the deck, she's your best bet. Tell her I'm calling in my marker."

"Thank you, Admiral."

There was another sigh. "Just be right, Commander. Be right, and all of this will look good in the morning. Otherwise..."

"I know, sir."

"Then get to it."

Collins pulled up the station registry. Major Nancy P. Nellis, XO 208th CM Batallion, personal link active. It buzzed three times before she answered. Music and chatter filled the background.

"Nancy, it's me, Sam."

"Well hell, Sam. You finally caught me on leave. You want to meet up?"

He swallowed hard. "Sorry, Nancy. I'm calling on behalf of the Admiral."

"No shit?"

"No shit. He said he's calling in his marker."

The background noise dropped off sharply. "All right, Sam. What do you need?"

Michael woke as the wheelchair turned a corner. He was not sure where he was, but he hurt all over. The lights overhead were distant but bright, and a blanket covered his arms and legs. He tried to move a little but found that his ankles and left wrist were chained to the rails of the wheelchair.

Elsa Watkins walked in front of him. Someone else was pushing his wheelchair, probably Leo Perez from the length of his stride. He could not see Maya, but she had to be around somewhere. The deck below them was metallic and heavily scratched, with frequent strips of rubber grips. In his foggy brain, he knew this kind of decking.

He was on a dock, a station dock.

He rolled his head to his right and saw rows of shipping containers. At the next bump, he rolled it back to the left. He was rolling alongside the cargo airlocks. The stenciled numbers read twenty-two. They were back at the *Blue Jaguar*'s dock.

Without thinking he tried to stand up but never got past moving his one free arm. A strong hand came down on that shoulder. "Take it easy there, boy. Almost home."

He nodded his compliance. Somewhere in his head, he knew that getting on the *Jaguar* was a slow death sentence, but as the airlock drew near, he did not see he had much choice.

"Wait," a voice called. It was vaguely familiar, but he did not even try to place it. "Who's that there?"

"Just a drunken crewmate," came the answer. It was Elsa.

"I'd like to see him if you don't mind."

"I think not. Privacy in our worst moments... you understand?"

"I want to make sure it's not my friend Michael."

Michael perked up at that.

"What? This Fletcher thing again? How many flunkies is the Navy going to send down here for him? Ask your security. We don't have him. We never heard of him. So kindly go away and let me tend to my crewman. He's had a hard enough time after brawling with your marines."

At this point, Michael turned his head, craning his neck to see who it was, but he could not quite get a good look, at least not through his right eye.

But it showed enough of his face for it to be seen. "Shit, that is Michael!"

Now he leaned forward, twisting away from Leo's grasp. The tall man in uniform looked very familiar indeed: Lt. Commander Montgomery Wheaton. "You got my call!"

Wheaton stepped forward, flanked by two guards in the gray of station security. "What happened to you?"

Elsa cut across his path. "Look, bud, I don't know who you think my crewman is, but he's my man, and I'm taking him home."

"But I don't want to go!" Michael cried. "They're kidnapping me!"

"It's not kidnapping," Leo said from behind him. "He got into a brawl up on ring seven. Captain Lewis here agreed to pay the damages, so station administration released him to the captain's authority. Can you help us get him through the lock so we can all go home? I'm already an hour into overtime."

Michael shook his head, which seemed to make the entire deck spin. "No, these guys aren't... they're not real security."

Maya stepped into view, laughing. "He's funny, I'll grant him that, but I'm getting tired of this."

Michael looked to Wheaton and then to the guards. "Come on guys, you don't recognize them, right?"

The guard on the left shrugged and looked to the other. He frowned but did not say anything.

Maya kept chuckling. "Hell, I don't know you guys either." She stepped forward towards them with a hand out. "I'm Susan McKenzie, stationed up on seven. That's my partner Billy Borden — B.B. we call him."

The guard on the left took her hand. "Walter Quinn. I just got transferred in, but Victor here's been on station for what, two years, Vic?"

The other guard nodded slowly. "Yeah, two years. Up on seven you say?"

Michael wanted to shake his head again but thought better of it. "Jesus Christ, people, they're smugglers! Pirates!" He waved at the container next to him. "They're picking up a shipment from Father Chessman. Look in there if you don't believe me."

Everyone laughed, all but Wheaton.

"What so funny?" Michael asked.

Elsa looked back at him. "Chessman is a myth, a story we tell fish like you to scare them."

"God yes," Victor said, still chuckling. "I remember those stories. He's up with there with monsters in the tachyon field. No one believes in that nonsense."

"I do."

All eyes turned to Wheaton. "What?" Elsa asked.

"And even if I didn't, I believe the boy," he said. "So we're going to take a look in these containers."

"By whose authority?" Elsa demanded. "I've got the articles on my side."

"By my authority," he answered, walking towards the far end of the container. "And I've got the Navy on my side."

"And when I call for your court martial, what name should I give them?"

He stopped mid-stride and turned to face her, pointing to the tag on his chest. "It's right here. Lt. Commander

Montgomery G. Wheaton. And no bitchy little civilian captain is going to intimidate old Monty."

"Monty?"

"Yeah, Monty!" he replied, walking off.

Elsa closed her eyes and dropped her head. "Shit." She turned to Maya, still standing by the other two guards, and nodded.

Michael saw Maya's gun coming out too late to do anything but shout, "No!" Then too many things happened at once. Victor went down first, a bullet erupting out of his chest. Michael went flying forward as Leo pushed the wheelchair over and started firing at Walter Quinn. Elsa ran for the airlock ramp, and Wheaton dove for cover behind the nearest shipping container.

Michael struggled to crawl on the floor, but he was firmly attached to the wheelchair. Even lying on his side, he could barely move, twisted around with only his right hand free. He could see Victor lying nearby, his gun still in his holster, so he struggled towards it. Maya was firing towards Wheaton who was shouting something about marines. He heard shots continuing to fire behind him, but he ignored them.

Maya circled out into the broad expanse of the deck, still firing. Wheaton's voice spiked mid-word into a pitiful yelp and then subsided into gasping whispers. Michael could not see him, but he could see the furious satisfaction on Maya's face afterwards.

Michael kept pulling himself forward. Alarms were going off overhead, but Michael paid them no attention. Maya was headed in towards Wheaton, and Victor's gun was still a meter away. He almost had it when he heard another voice, this time familiar enough to cut through the haze.

"Michael!"

It was Gabrielle.

He looked up and saw her running towards him, but he also saw Maya stop and turn. She raised her pistol, pivoting as she tracked the moving target. Michael yanked the pistol from Victor's holster, aimed at Maya, and pulled the trigger.

Nothing happened.

He fumbled around looking for the safety but did not see anything obvious.

Maya braced her gun with both hands. She was standing very still.

To hell with it. He grabbed the pistol by the barrel and gave it as hard a throw as he could.

A sick little grin was creeping onto Maya's face when the butt of the pistol's handle smacked into her temple. She turned slightly towards Michael, opened her mouth, and dropped to the floor. Her own pistol fell from her limp hand and clattered across the deck.

Gabrielle skidded to a stop, dropping to her knees beside Michael. He twisted as best as he could to look up at her. "I thought I told you not to come after me."

She nodded. "Yeah, you said a lot of stupid things."

A gray uniform appeared overhead. "Hey, kid, you okay?" It was the remaining legitimate guard, Walter Quinn.

He smiled and gave a thumbs up. "Aces."

"I got the other one. What the hell was all that about?"

"Get some more people down here, and I'll tell you. Get people you know."

"You got that right, kid. Stay here."

Michael looked back at Gabrielle. "So, stupid, huh?"

Whatever she answered was drowned out by a terrible cracking sound and then a sudden and strong wind. It was strong enough to knock Gabrielle onto him and pull them both across the deck towards the open airlock — the open airlock which was now suddenly venting to space. But just as quickly as it began, it cut off with an ear-shattering metallic clang as the dockside airlock door slammed shut under the outbound pressure.

Gabrielle righted herself and looked around. "There they are. It's Father and Commander Collins."

"Your dad's here?"

"Of course."

He looked. Sure enough, Uncle Hans was running towards them with a Naval officer and twenty or thirty marines. Several of them branched off towards Monty and began calling for the medics.

Michael lay back on the deck. "I think I'll go with security after all."

Chapter 26

"You can lie to me all you want, but someday I'll learn the truth. When that day comes, know that there will be a reckoning." - Malcolm Fletcher

MICHAEL INSISTED ON GIVING his statement to Walter Quinn as he was being transported down to the hospital on ring one. Several marines tagged along with them, but Michael ignored them. Some navy officer asked a few clarifying questions, but mostly Michael kept blabbering into Quinn's recorder. He thought he had a lot to say, but it ran down surprisingly quickly: jumping ship at Latera, funny business about wake scans, becoming an unofficial prisoner, Elsa Watkins, the Winged Lady, Father Chessman, mysterious cargo, and fake security uniforms. Still, it drained the rest of his energy to say it all.

The emergency wing of the hospital was a confusion of lights, scanners, and unknown faces behind masks, but by the end of it, they declared him reasonably well. "The concussion seems mild, but I'm going to keep you here overnight for observation. The bruising around your ribs looks bad, but you got away without any breaks."

"What about Monty?" he asked.

271

The doctor looked confused. "The Navy officer? They took him to surgery. I'll find out what I can, but in the meantime, you've got some visitors. Shall I send them in?"

He nodded and regretted it only a little. Whatever they had given him for the pain was effective. Pity it would not be effective against angry uncles.

But it was not Hans that came through, nor was it Gabrielle. It was another Navy man. He was not in a ship uniform, but more of a semi-formal affair you might expect to see around base. As he approached, Michael recognized the gold crescent of a Commander. The patch read Samuel Collins. He walked in slowly and stood by the bed.

"Hello, Mr. Fletcher. Are you feeling well?"

"Well enough," he replied hoarsely. His throat was dry. "You were at the docks, weren't you?"

"Yes."

"Have you heard anything about Lt. Commander Wheaton?"

"I believe he's still in surgery, but the last I heard was they had stopped the bleeding. It's going to take some work to repair his lung, but it sounds like he's going to be all right."

"Good. Are you a friend of his?"

He gave his head a noncommittal tilt. "He's something of an acquaintance, but the truth is I'm here for you."

Michael's eyes went wide. "What did I do?"

Collins smiled. "It's not like that, not at all. No, Mr. Fletcher, you made an information request some time back for Malcolm Fletcher's war records, and one incident in particular."

It came back to Michael slowly. With all the insanity of the *Jaguar*, he had forgotten filing the request on Tortisia. "Yes, a border incident... I can't remember the number."

"CasRb-733," Collins replied. "I came looking for you."

"Well, lucky for you I came back through Arvin."

Collins shook his head. "Quite the opposite, actually. I went looking for you at Latera. That's how I met up with your uncle and cousin. In truth, you led us on quite the merry chase."

As exhausted as he was, Michael still felt his face redden in embarrassment. "Sorry about that, but why would you go all that way just to answer an old records request? I mean, all I was hoping for was some mail."

Collins smiled down at him. "I'll explain soon enough, but it is enough to say that the request caught my eye. They told me you'll be here overnight for observation. We'll talk again tomorrow."

Michael nodded. "Tomorrow then. You'll have the records?"

"Hopefully more. The marines are already on board the *Blue Jaguar*, so I'm going to go check in with them."

And with that he walked out, only to be replaced by Gabrielle rushing into the room. She flew to his bedside and hugged him fiercely. "Dear God, Michael, when you get better, I am going to thrash you so hard."

He hugged her back feebly. "I hear you."

She sat up. "I was so worried about you, and that was before I heard what kind of ship you ended up on. And look at what they did to you!"

He chuckled, vaguely aware that Hans had come through the door. "Well, you should see the other guy. Your friend Collins tells me they're entertaining the marines right now."

"Well good," she said. "I'm just glad you're back."

"I'm just glad you're safe," Hans said from foot of the bed.

Michael looked out at him. "I'm sorry I left you like that, sir. I didn't mean to cause all this trouble."

Hans shook his head. "No, Michael. I'm sorry I gave you cause to leave."

Michael nodded. He did not know what to say.

Hans took it for what it was. "Well, we'll talk more when you're better."

"Yeah, and thanks for coming."

Hans shrugged. "You're family," he said. That was it. He gave a brief smile and left.

Gabrielle watched him go, and then turned back to Michael. "Oh, don't worry about him. He's being stoic. So tell me, what's all this I'm hearing about Father Chessman? Who is he?"

Michael shook his head. "I have no idea."

Michael never saw the doctor the next morning, but the nurse said that the doctor had cleared him for discharge. He got up and dressed. Gabrielle had thoughtfully brought along one of his old *Heavy Heinrich* uniforms. He noted, however, that she had not brought his old *Sophie's Grace* uniform.

He was searching the console for news on the previous day's events when the nurse came in with a wheelchair. He took one look at it and said, "No. Absolutely not."

"Sorry, hospital policy." She wiggled it back and forth, giving it a little tilt. "Come on, it could be fun."

He shook his head twice. "The last time I was in a wheelchair, it was not fun, so policy or not, I think I'll walk."

She shrugged and put it back outside the door. "At least let me walk you out."

"What's the news on Lt. Commander Wheaton?" he asked, following her into the hall. "I heard he came through his surgery, but nothing else."

"He's doing well," she answered. "He's over there in room two-twenty."

Michael did not wait for her to offer. He simply changed course: three doors down and left. Inside, the man was reclining in bed, looking dejectedly at the remains of his breakfast.

"Lt. Commander," Michael called from the door.

He looked over. "Ah, Michael. Come on in."

Michael walked to the bed, leaving his nurse at the door. "How are you feeling?"

He shrugged. "Pretty good. Not hungry enough to eat that, but pretty good. And you? You got beat pretty good I hear."

274

"Beat, yes, but not beaten. I'm sorry I called you in on this, but thanks for coming anyway."

Wheaton shook his head. "No, you did the right thing. It was smart."

"Well, thanks anyway. I guess that makes us even."

"Even?" He looked away for a moment. "Maybe, maybe I still owe you, or at least the Navy does."

"What do you mean?"

"That cargo, you know, the Father Chessman stuff? It was stolen Navy missiles, a hundred sixty of them. Top of the line, ship-to-ship stuff."

Michael's jaw dropped. "What, like gravity warheads?"

"Sorry, classified."

Michael shrugged. "It's okay. I understand."

Wheaton waved him off. "It's not like that. They wouldn't tell me either, but when your intelligence friend got the news, he went nuts."

"Intelligence?"

"Yeah, that Commander Collins fellow. Naval Intelligence, but pretty sharp for a desk jockey. He came by this morning, said he was waiting for you."

Michael nodded. The records request, Malcolm's history, the death of his mother. It was about to become much more real. "Then I had best not keeping him waiting. You get better soon."

The shuttle ride over to the Naval station was longer than Michael expected, but it did give him time to tell the details of his adventure to his family and Collins. The shuttle had a large block of general seating filled with personnel of varying rank, but the four of them had one of the two private compartments to themselves.

Commander Collins listened quietly, only occasionally asking for clarifications on the names. Gabrielle on the other hand was quite animated, especially at first, telling Michael how foolish he had been, but after the third time, Hans told her to stop. "That's quite enough," he said. "It's not your place to judge your cousin's choices. You weren't there."

Hans' reserve surprised him, so he took note of how quiet his uncle was being. In fact, his only other comment during the entire tale was during Michael's explanation of how he was able to move through the walls of the *Jaguar*. Hans merely shook his head and muttered, "Shoddy construction. Fools."

He had just gotten to Maya taking aim at Gabrielle for her mid-battle arrival when the docking notice sounded. "But why didn't you shoot her?" Gabrielle asked.

Michael ducked his head in embarrassment. "I couldn't figure out the safety. Tried pushing it, tried turning it." He shrugged. "I never learned to use one, but I can throw pretty well."

They made their way out of the shuttle and through the station with Collins as their guide. Michael was impressed at the size. It was perhaps as large as the civilian station. It had fewer rings, but they were much larger. "It's for the carriers," Collins explained. "They need more elbow room than even the *Heavy Heinrich*."

At last they reached the Intelligence office, and Collins signed them in and handed them visitor badges. "Why here?" Michael asked. "I thought this was a records query."

"It's more secure here."

He led them further down a corridor to a smaller lounge where a steward waited. Collins paused outside a door labeled "Projection Four" and turned to Michael.

"What I'm about to show you is from our archives, not part of the general record. I can get you a written report that offers more details than the public record, but we don't release copies of these archives."

"Are they classified or something?"

He shook his head. "Not in this case, but there are privacy matters, respect for the dead, that kind of thing. You made the request, so I'm offering them to you. Your family is only here as a courtesy. Whether they join us is up to you."

"But—" Gabrielle began her objection, but Hans put a hand on her shoulder.

"No, dear, this is for Michael. We can wait out here."

Michael thought about it a moment before answering. "No, I think I want my cousin with me."

"Damn straight," she said.

"As for my uncle," he said, turning to face Hans, "Peter was his brother, and I guess he knew Sophia better than I ever will. He can join us if he wants."

Collins nodded and opened the door. "Then let's get started."

The room had six seats arrayed on one side of a curved table, all of them focused in on a large screen on the opposite wall. Collins positioned himself at a podium at the far corner and motioned the others to the seats. The steward closed the door behind them, and the room grew dark but for the soft glow of the screen.

It lit up to read, "CasRb-733, Archive Compilation."

"The review of ship-to-ship battles is a tricky affair," Collins began. "There are multiple vessels with varying degrees of limited information. In some cases this limit is due to distance or interference, and in other cases, it is because the ship was destroyed. Ships often maintain a hardened records core, and after a battle, it is sometimes recovered, but not always. There are also ship-to-ship communications, and they can often shed additional light on the battle. Put it all together, and it can be mere wisps of information in some areas with terabytes of data in others. These compilations are how we tend to view them."

Collins clicked the screen forward, and Michael saw the same summary page he had found months earlier. It presented two columns of ships. On the left were the freighters: *Vannover Markey*, damaged, five deaths; *Corey Tasha*, destroyed, all hands lost; *Kaiser's Folly*, destroyed, all hands lost, updated 3381-183 to note four survivors. On the right were the combatants: the *Reilly* and the *Hammerhead*.

The *Hammerhead* had been Malcolm's ship.

The screen advanced again to show a large tactical display with four icons: VM, CT, KF, and Rl. The *Hammerhead* was not represented.

"For the initial phase of the battle, our best records are from the *Vannover Markey*, but as you can see, she was quite distant from the rest."

The VM icon blinked. While the others were hardly clustered, the distance to the *Vannover Markey* was easily triple the distance between any two others.

"The *Markey* reported falling out of tach after running afoul of a significant disturbance in the tachyon winds. This disturbance was not on the charts and was not subsequently observed, making it consistent with the use of one or more gravity mines to cause short-lived but intense tachyon disruptions."

A soft glow appeared amidst the various icons. "Our best guess is that the mines were set off in this region, near the center of the Nasar approach to Ballison. The *Markey's* port sail generator blew out on impact, and the resulting fire claimed five of her seventeen crewmen."

The display began crawling forward, the timer showing minutes going by in seconds. The *Vannover Markey* continued to drift further away, while the *Corey Tasha* remained almost still. The *Kaiser's Folly* seemed to have the greatest velocity, but it was heading more towards the *Reilly* than anything else. Collins froze the display temporarily.

"At this point, the *Markey* reported the automatic distress signals of both the *Corey Tasha* and the *Kaiser's Folly*. The *Corey* was reporting multiple engineering fires and two hull breaches in crew areas. No voice call was ever received from the *Corey*, and it is possible that few if any of the crew survived the violent down-tach. The *Kaiser* was reporting a fire in her port

278

engineering section, but she was otherwise operating well and thrusting at full acceleration."

"But I don't understand," Michael said, raising his hand. "Why is she accelerating towards the *Reilly*? Was the *Reilly* one of ours?"

Collins shook his head. "Officially, yes, she was on our rolls as a privateer, but in truth, she was operating independently. As for the acceleration, it was a reasonable move on the part of Captain Schneider. The *Kaiser* had come out of tach with a fair amount of velocity, and by adding to that velocity, he most likely hoped to make it difficult for the *Reilly* to match course."

"But it's still taking her closer to the *Reilly*."

Collins started the display again. "Regrettably yes, it took her too close to the *Reilly*." He froze the display with a triangle highlighting the *Reilly*. "At this point, the *Markey*'s scopes detected weapons fire from the *Reilly*, specifically plasma cannons. At that range, they are not considered effective, but either their aim was better than normal or the damage to the *Kaiser* was greater than their automated beacon suggests. At any rate, at this point, the *Kaiser* stopped transmitting her automated beacon."

Michael looked down at the table. "Then that's it. Malcolm was never even there."

"Actually, no, that's not all of it," Collins replied, starting the display forward again. The *Kaiser's Folly* sped past the *Reilly*. Ignoring it, the *Reilly* closed on the dead *Corey Tasha*. It went on like that for almost twenty minutes according to the timer, and then a new icon appeared: Hh, the *Hammerhead*. It dropped out of tach about halfway between the *Kaiser's Folly* and the *Reilly*. "As you can see, Malcolm Fletcher got there eventually, just not soon enough."

The screen divided to show the status display for the *Hammerhead*: sail generators unstable but undamaged, thrusters at full, weapons ready. The timer slowed sharply, matching real-time, second for second. The *Hammerhead*'s display expanded to include a video display. A face appeared there.

It was Malcolm, except this was a Malcolm that Michael had never known. He was younger, not a wrinkle on his face nor a single gray hair in his beard, but more than that. His eyes were intensely wild, almost feral. "Damn you, *Reilly*. I knew you were bad. Either turn and present, or run now."

Malcolm's image turned, and he addressed someone else. "Put that on repeat until you get a response."

An off-screen voice replied, "Aye, sir. I have a transmission from the *Kaiser's Folly*, asking for you specifically."

"*Kaiser's Folly*, this is Captain Fletcher of the *Hammerhead*. What is your status?"

The voice came first.

"God, Malcolm, is it really you?"

That voice. Michael thought he had never heard it before, but he knew it immediately.

Mom.

It was strained. Clearly she was under stress, but even then, something lyrical rang through. The details of the room faded for a moment as memories of songs rushed through his mind. Soft hands. Lullabies. A kiss on his forehead.

"Where is your captain?" Malcolm's voice interrupted, a harsh splash of aged reality.

"Peter's dead," his mother answered. Her image was now on the screen as well. She was as young and beautiful as he had always seen her, but her blue eyes looked out at them in desperation. "They're all dead. Just starboard engineering left. We only got two pods away."

"Sophie, listen to me. Our scopes show you have fires. What is your status?"

"The pods," she went on. "My little Michael is in one of them. You have to get him."

"I hear you, Sophie. My guys are scanning for them, but you have to stop the fire before it gets to your reactor. Do you have damage control?"

She shook her head. "You've got to get Michael. Promise me you'll take care of him."

"Yeah, of course. Can you vent the intervening sections?

"That's not good enough, Malcolm. I need your word on this. Don't let Hans take him. Promise me you'll raise him yourself. Promise me you'll be the father I always said you could be."

The image of Malcolm grew still. "I promise, Sophie. I promise. Now, if you can't vent—"

"I love you," his mother said. "I've always—"

And that was it.

Sophia's picture faded, her words left hanging in the years between them.

The *Kaiser's Folly* icon disappeared from the display.

Michael looked down to the table, unable to make himself watch anymore. He felt a hand on his, gentle and loving, and he broke down. The tears came freely. He had never known his mother, or at least he thought he never had. But when he heard that voice, he knew. He did remember her. She had been real, not just a story Malcolm had told.

And she was gone.

She was gone almost as soon as he had seen her. And she was never coming back.

No song, no soft touch, and no sweet kiss.

He wept, for it had not been seventeen years. It had just happened.

Now.

Eventually, the lights came back up, and he saw that the hands that held him belonged to Gabrielle, and the images on the screen had faded to memory. He looked around. Commander Collins was quietly busying himself in the corner. His uncle was no longer in the room. A box of tissues had been placed nearby.

He reached for one, shedding Gabrielle's touch in the process. He blew his nose a few times and wiped at his eyes. A small pile of crumpled tissue was all that remained of his grief.

281

Collins appeared before them. "If you will excuse us, Miss Schneider, I would like to have a private word with Mr. Fletcher."

She gave Michael one last squeeze on the shoulder and left without a word.

Collins waited a moment after the door closed. "Do you have your answers now, Mr. Fletcher?"

He met the Commander's stern eyes. "Mostly, I guess. What happened after...?"

"After the destruction of the *Kaiser's Folly*? The *Corey Tasha* suffered a similar fate four minutes later, her reactor gutting the rest of the ship. The *Reilly* got enough distance from the tachyon disturbance to reengage her sails and left the scene."

"Didn't Malcolm go after them?"

Collins shook his head. "No, Michael. He spent the next three hours tracking down your escape pod. Then he spent another twelve on a search for more. By then, the *Vannover Markey* had gotten its damage under control and was requesting an escort for the rest of the way into Ballison."

"So the *Reilly* got away," he said, too drained to be angry. "Whatever happened to her?"

Collins' face broke into a brief grin. "Well, it took him almost another year, but Malcolm did finally track them down."

"And?"

"Well, Malcolm's action report to the privateer board was... significantly less detailed in that incident. But as the stories go, he brought them down with an array of gravity mines so dense that it pulled the *Reilly*'s sail generators out through the hull before they could even blow. And then when he closed in, he opened fire with plasma cannons and gutted her from stem to stern."

Michael looked away. The phrasing was eerily familiar. "Any survivors?"

"No," Collins replied. "This is second or third hand, of course, but the rumor goes that he shot the escape pods as well. Seven pods, all told."

Michael nodded, remembering Gabrielle taunting him with such a tale. "Merciless Mal."

"Ah, I guess you've already heard the story."

He struggled to put a smile on it. "Sounds different in context. I guess he wanted his revenge, and he got it."

"Mostly."

Michael turned back to face him. "Mostly?"

Collins pulled up a chair and sat across the table. "Well, it had been almost a year by then. There had been a few crew changes, even a command change, we believe."

"Then he didn't... but the people he killed on the *Reilly*..."

Collins shook his head. "Were no more innocent than the ones who attacked the *Kaiser's Folly*. By then, the *Reilly* was a well-known but elusive pirate vessel."

"And the ones who transferred, they got away?"

"Well, the war ended shortly after that, and with it the privateer program. We hung on to a few of them of course. It took us a while to reassert control over this sector, and men like Malcolm were useful. As part of that, he did some investigating for us, strictly off the books, of course."

"What kind of investigation?"

"Among other things, tracking down what became of the crews of ships like the *Reilly*."

"And did he find them?"

Collins nodded. "Seven, in fact. Four we had the pleasure of putting on trial."

"And the other three?"

"At least he brought us the bodies."

"Was that all of them?"

Collins shook his head. "No. We believe four others may have remained at large, but I don't think even Malcolm knew for sure."

"Who were they, these four?"

Collins smiled. "Well, one of them he never looked for, or at least not hard. She had had a very convincing death in the final days of the war, a flyer crash on Cenita, complete with death certificate and a grave."

A grave. "Elsa Watkins?"

He nodded. "Indeed, Mr. Fletcher. Elsa Watkins, or as she's been known for the last sixteen years, Jana Lewis, and as you've informed us, also known as Winged Lady."

"And the others?"

"All dead, though not all as convincingly as Miss Watkins. Johannes Richter supposedly died in a warehouse fire on Nasar, but there is no coroner's report. Stefan Carrillo supposedly drowned when his single-mast boat went down in a storm on Taschin, but the boat in question was never registered with any of the local ports. And finally, the man we believe was in command of the *Reilly*, Gunter Farlin, was reportedly on board the star liner *Lorista* when she went down into Callista's outer Jovian, but of course, no bodies were ever recovered from that disaster."

"The captain, huh? And you think he's still alive."

Collins shrugged. "Malcolm did. In fact, he thought... well, I'm sure you'll read his own files when you get back to the *Sophie's Grace*."

"What? He didn't think he was this Father Chessman, did he?"

Collins waved his hands dismissively. "We know very little about this Chessman figure. Truth be told, we're not even sure he exists. If he does, though, he's either a top strategist for the Yoshido pirate empire or perhaps even the true head of it, merely propping up the old Yoshido family as a shield. But if Gunter Farlin did live on after the *Lorista* crash, he has disappeared even more effectively than this Father Chessman."

"Ok, but what about Elsa Watkins? Lt. Commander Wheaton told me about the stolen Navy missiles. Surely you have her by now, right?"

Collins frowned. "We have the *Blue Jaguar*, to be certain, but not her captain."

284

"But I saw her run into the airlock not two minutes before it blew out."

"Yes, as did four other witnesses as well as the security footage. But when the marines boarded the *Jaguar*, she was not on board."

"Could she be hiding on it somewhere? I mean, look at the little spaces I found in three weeks."

"It's possible, but I doubt it. Certainly, we're going to have some fun dismantling the *Jaguar* at the Naval yard over the next few weeks, but my gut tells me that someone who evaded Malcolm's net for this long had an escape plan all set to go for circumstances like this."

Michael considered it, nodding. She had certainly sounded like a crafty woman. He could believe she had come up with something far better than Michael's cargo escape. "Then I guess I'll have to keep an eye out for her."

"Does that mean you're going to continue Malcolm's investigations?"

"I suppose," he replied. Certainly, if he did not find Elsa Watkins, she was likely to find him. "At the very least I want to get back to the *Sophie* and look over Malcolm's files."

"And I understand you're planning to take the captain's exam."

"Yeah, that was the plan."

"Well, if you can pass it and put together a crew, come see me. The *Sophie's Grace* is... well, she's a little special. If you're going to be running around with her, you should know. If not, tell me, and we'll take her off your hands for a generous price."

Michael stiffened. "You don't think I can do it?"

"I have no doubt in your abilities, but I'm not sure you'll want to." He glanced over to the door. "You have a family out there that loves you. They run good ships, and I'm sure you could do very well with them. Most people would consider that a very nice life."

He thought about it. Malcolm's cagey cooking vs. Maggie Nelson's pastries. Toilets that did not always seal right vs. a top notch environmental crew finding leaks before they happen. Ship shares earning tens of thousands per run vs. scraping by on marginal cargo. Collins had a point. Life with S&W would be a much nicer life.

But none of that mattered. Malcolm had been skilled enough to have gotten jobs like those. He could have had that life, but he chose not to. He was after something else, and it was much more important to him than pastries, toilets, or money.

"No," he said at last. "Malcolm started this, and I guess I'm going to finish it."

Collins stood, extending his hand. Michael took it.

"Malcolm was a good man," Collins said. "And from the looks of you, I'd say he kept his promise."

"His promise?"

"To your mother. It's a pleasure to make your acquaintance, Mr. Fletcher, and I hope we get to work together in the future."

His cousin and uncle were waiting outside, and Hans rose as soon as Michael emerged from the projection room.

Collins gave a short nod to them all and left them with the steward.

"Michael," Hans began. "I don't know what to say except that I was wrong, and you were right."

Michael shook his head. "You couldn't have known."

"No," he replied, "but I could have believed you about Malcolm. I should have, and I'm sorry that I didn't."

Michael shifted uncomfortably. "It's okay." He looked his uncle in the eye and tried to give a reassuring nod. "You never got to know him like I did."

"You're leaving then. Back to *Sophie's Grace?*"

"I think I have to. It's a long story."

Hans shook his head. "You don't have to explain. It's your decision, but know that there will always be a place for you at Schneider and Williams. Always."

Michael held out his hand. "I appreciate that, and I might take you up on it someday. I think Peter and Sophia would like that."

Hans took the offered hand. "Until then, Michael, good luck and safe travels." With that he walked away.

Michael watched him go, sensing Gabrielle at his side. "It's sad. He almost looks broken."

She wrapped an arm around for a gentle side hug. "I guess he is, in a way."

"What do you mean?"

"He promoted Ms. Corazon before we left. She finally made Captain and got the prize jewel of the fleet. Dad says he's going back to the corporate headquarters on Callista Prime. I hear Old Man Williams is stepping down, so I guess it's going to be Dad's turn to fly the desk."

"I'm sure he'll do well."

"And you? Have you been studying your navigation between escape attempts?"

"Yeah."

"Good."

"Look for me when you make ports, okay?"

"Sure thing, cousin," she replied, "but if you pass the exam, you're buying me a steak in the Guild hall."

"That's a date."

Chapter 27

"You know son, there are times when I am quite proud of you. Truly. Not that I'm saying this is one of those times, but they do exist." — Malcolm Fletcher

MICHAEL'S TRIP BACK TO Taschin was done in decreasing style. He had stayed for another three weeks at Arvin while they tore down the *Blue Jaguar*. It took some paperwork, but he was able to claim his few possessions, not that they mattered much. Then it was a trip aboard the CFS *Hidalgo* as she and her squadron of heavy cruisers made a run to Cenita. The *Hidalgo* was frequently used as a command ship for smaller task forces, and Michael was given the Admiral's suite, compliments of a grateful but unnamed patron in Naval ordinance.

The Naval facilities at Cenita were much smaller, but he was given a nice room for another week until the frigate CFS *Arroyo* departed for Ballison. He had a four-day layover there, and he made it a point to swing by the Hopping Hole at his earliest opportunity. The bouncer at the door took one look at him and waved him in, no questions asked.

The final leg of his journey was on a little courier, the CFS *CP-722*, which her crew had nicknamed the *Pretty Peg*. He celebrated his birthday on the second day of the run, not that it was much of a celebration. He was finishing up on the weight machine when the off-duty navigator came in to use the treadmill. "It's my birthday," he had said.

"Oh, congrats," was the reply. "I don't think we can muster up much of a party, but I saw a couple of cupcakes in the bottom of the freezer if you want one. Just don't tell skipper you took it."

So that was how he celebrated his long-awaited eighteenth birthday. At least it had sprinkles on the icing.

His return to Taschin seemed anti-climactic. No one there knew he was coming, and certainly none of them had heard of his adventures. He made it a point not to look up Annie or Josie. He would do so in time, but not quite yet.

The meetings with Hollings and the other lawyers had been perfunctory. After their first meeting — had it only been nine months ago? — Hollings knew better than to offer any unnecessary advice. This was a simple matter of processing paperwork. Some of it Hollings dealt with for him, but a few matters remained that Michael had to attend to personally.

So here he was, taking care of one final detail at the port registry, changing the ownership of *Sophie's Grace*. The clerk on the other side of the counter moved the papers with all the excitement of a rookie cleaning the sludge tank, but he did keep the forms coming.

They were almost done before the clerk finally took note of the names. "Say, it looks like the last registered owner was a Malcolm Fletcher. Any relation?"

"Yes," Michael replied, thumbing his signature on the last line. "He was my father."

ACKNOWLEDGEMENTS

There are so many people to thank for encouraging me to write. These include family, friends, teachers, and other authors. I could try to list them all, but who would read it? Still, I would never have gotten this far without their advice and encouragement.

For *Ships of My Fathers*, however, I can narrow it down. Julia and Rose showed tremendous patience and surprising support when I said, "Yep, it's time to write another novel." They also made excellent beta readers.

I must also thank Angela England, my copyeditor. She's the reason I'm doing the italics correctly. I also want to thank my fellow writers over on Google+ for their encouragement and their fine-tuning of my cover, especially John, Nathan, Jefferson, and Jennifer.

Lastly, I want to thank my father, because in a way, this book is about him. No, he wasn't a space captain, nor was he a privateer. He was not even one for boats, really. He was an electrical engineer who designed circuits to operate in the microwave part of the radio spectrum, a range most engineers liken to black magic. He did quite a few communication projects, from long distance towers to cell phones, and he did a number of defense projects as well, mostly ECM and other airborne defensive systems.

As technology advances, my father's work is being replaced piece by piece, but he did leave behind one enduring technological legacy. Neil Armstrong's "one small step" came to us through circuits my father designed. He died of cancer in 2005, and I miss him to this very day.

So how is this book about him? Quite simply, he was my father.

ABOUT THE AUTHOR

Dan Thompson started writing fiction at the age of ten. Luckily for the world, all copies of that early Star Wars rip-off have been lost to time and Sith retaliation. Moving on from that six-page handwritten epic, he wrote short stories through the 1980's and 1990's and sold a few of them to magazines that rarely lived past his stories' publication.

After three or four abandoned novels, he finally started finishing some and decided they should do more than collect dust and red scribbles. Because of the shakeup e-books have brought to publishing, he decided to pursue self-publishing for the time being. Thus Quantum Forge Press was born.

He lives near Austin with his wife and three children, drives old police cars, wears kilts when the weather permits, visits with friends as much as possible, and is generally considered to be the weirdo next door. Fortunately, the neighbors don't know how weird he really is.

OTHER BOOKS BY DAN THOMPSON

IN PRINT

BENEATH THE SKY, ISBN 978-0-9854146-0-3

COMING SOON

FALL 2013: *HELL BENT*
BOOK ONE OF THE PITTSBURGH HERALD

SPRING 2014: *DEBTS OF MY FATHERS*
BOOK TWO OF THE FATHER CHESSMAN SAGA